Praise for

DAVID

Winner of the CWA En~~~~~~~~~~~~~~~~~~~~~Dagger Award
Longlisted for the Theakston Old Peculier Crime Novel of
the Year Award
The Times Crime Book of the Month
Telegraph Pick of the Week

'Superb. A thrilling Cold War mystery that has the air time of
Robert Harris at his best'
MASON CROSS

'*A Darker State* is gripping, thrilling and very, very good – David
Young's Karin Müller series goes from strength to strength'
WILLIAM RYAN

'Deft, assured storytelling, a compelling new detective and a
fascinating setting – I was up late to finish it!'
GILLY MACMILLAN, AUTHOR OF *BURNT PAPER SKY*

'One of the best reads I've had in ages . . . this is a cracking debut'
DAVID JACKSON, BESTSELLING AUTHOR OF *CRY BABY*

'Deep and dark, this debut is utterly gripping . . . well observed
characters and a corker of an ending. Superb'
NIKKI OWEN, AUTHOR OF *THE SPIDER IN THE CORNER OF THE ROOM*

'Chilling'
DAILY TELEGRAPH

'Extremely engaging'
SUNDAY EXPRESS

'This fast-paced thriller hooks the readers from the start'
SUN

'A masterful evocation of the claustrophobic atmosphere of communist
era East Germany . . . an intricate, absorbing page-turner'
DAILY EXPRESS

A
DARKER
STATE

David Young was born near Hull and – after dropping out of a Bristol University science degree – studied Humanities at Bristol Polytechnic. Temporary jobs cleaning ferry toilets and driving a butcher's van were followed by a career in journalism with provincial newspapers, a London news agency, and international radio and TV newsrooms. He now writes in his garden shed and in his spare time supports Hull City AFC. You can follow him on Twitter @djy_writer.

Also by David Young

Stasi Child
Stasi Wolf

A
DARKER
STATE
DAVID YOUNG

ZAFFRE

First published in Great Britain in 2018 by

ZAFFRE PUBLISHING
80–81 Wimpole St, London W1G 9RE
www.zaffrebooks.co.uk

A CIP catalogue record for this book is
available from the British Library.

ISBN: 978–1–78576–070–9
Export Paperback ISBN: 978–1–78576–393–9

also available as an ebook

3 5 7 9 10 8 6 4 2

Typeset by IDSUK (Data Connection) Ltd
Printed and bound by Clays Ltd, St Ives Plc

Zaffre Publishing is an imprint of Bonnier Zaffre,
a Bonnier Publishing company
www.bonnierzaffre.co.uk
www.bonnierpublishing.co.uk

For Oliver Berlau

PROLOGUE

December 1976
Western Poland

The dog pulled him through the undergrowth of Wyspa Teatralna – the brittle, frozen branches snapping and crackling as the pair advanced. An early winter freeze. Already the river surrounding Theatre Island was thick with ice, from bank to bank, on every side. Kazimierz Wójcik wondered how strong it was. Strong enough to hold a man? A car? A tank? He'd seen it this way before, many times, but not usually until the depths of winter – late January, or early February.

'*Śnieżka! Śnieżka!*' he shouted, as he tried to hold the animal back on its lead. But in this bitter cold the dog was in its element. A Siberian sledding dog, its instinct for pulling things had kicked in, and Kazimierz, with his one good arm, didn't have the strength to fight. Instead he concentrated on holding on and not falling. He didn't want Śnieżka running down the bank and out onto the ice itself.

He didn't want to lose her.

He'd already lost too much in his life.

The Germans on the other bank had made sure of that; his withered left arm had been their souvenir gift. Our socialist *friends*.

But Kazimierz and other men and women of his age – those that were left – knew differently. They were no friends of Kazimierz or anyone of his generation. The German *Szkopy* – the castrated rams, as Poles of his vintage liked to call them – had much to answer for.

The dog stopped suddenly at the top of the riverbank, ears pricked, its white fur puffed out, matching the colour of Kazimierz's moustache and beard. The old man and his dog, for a moment, were as statuesque as the stone remains of the theatre that gave this area its name. The low hum of machinery from the wool factory on the German side of the river was all that punctured the silence – that and the sound of Kazimierz's own laboured breathing. Clouds of condensation immediately turned to ice as they hit the tips of his facial hair.

Śnieżka had seen something. Where the frozen river melded to the gravel shore.

Kazimierz's eyes followed the dog's gaze, past his own frost-coated moustache, to something that was dark, matted. His eyes weren't as good as they used to be, when he'd worked as a watchmaker in Leszno before the war, right on the old border. Before he'd been resettled here on the new border, more than a hundred kilometres further west. By that time, with his withered left arm, watchmaking was a thing of the past.

The object looked almost like a fur coat. *Perhaps I could dry it and sell it*, thought Kazimierz. But it was piled in a lump, and the man felt nausea sweep over him as it dawned on him what – in all probability – lay under the coat.

A body.

An unmoving, dead body.

Kazimierz tried to pull Śnieżka back. He didn't want any trouble. They'd just forget what they'd seen. It was safer that way.

Keep your head down; keep out of trouble. That's how Kazimierz had survived all these years, and he wasn't about to change.

But the dog had different ideas.

She started dragging her master down the bank, giving him no option but to follow, stumbling as he went, frantically trying to keep hold of the lead.

Kazimierz finally had to let go to avoid falling, and he started shouting the dog's name again.

But Śnieżka stopped dead as soon as she reached the bundle of fur.

Stopped dead and began howling.

A terrible keening wail of terror or lament. And Kazimierz knew his hopes of keeping this quiet had evaporated in an instant.

Finally, the old man's eyes and brain registered what the bundle was.

It wasn't a body, it was several bodies. Rats.

Contorted, fused together in a mass of brown hair, tipped with hoar frost. And what really made Kazimierz shudder were the tails.

Tens, scores of lifeless tails, each attached to its own bundle of fur.

1

September 1976
Strausberger Platz, East Berlin

The cool September breeze fanned People's Police *Oberleutnant* Karin Müller's lightly tanned face, and she had to fight to keep her blond hair from flying into her eyes as she looked down at her watch for the third time that minute. Already five past the hour and no sign of her boss, *Oberst* Reiniger, despite his exhortations that she should arrive on time.

She didn't feel much like an '*Oberleutnant*' at the moment. In fact, though it had been a few short months since the end of her last case, down in Halle-Neustadt rather than here in the Hauptstadt, she'd almost forgotten what it was like being a police officer, never mind the head of a murder squad. For several weeks now she'd been playing the part of a full-time, stay-at-home mother – something that was rare in their small republic, where babies were despatched to crèches almost as soon as they were born, with mothers quickly back in the workplace.

Now, standing here, at the northern exit to Strausberger Platz U-bahn station, she felt a terrible longing for the twin babies she'd left behind. An almost physical tugging at her heart. She had a horrible feeling, too, that whatever Reiniger wanted, it wasn't going to turn out well for her new-found family life. Her little miracles – Jannika and Johannes. The babies she'd been told – year after year, by doctor after doctor – that she'd never be able to have.

Swallowing, she held her hand up to her brow and peered eastwards along Karl-Marx-Allee, marvelling at its grandeur. Yes, the Republic wasn't perfect. The methods of the Ministry for State Security that she'd encountered in her previous investigation into the reform school teenagers, and then the search in Halle-Neustadt for the missing children, had left her feeling uneasy about being so aligned to the state. But this magnificent avenue – with its beautifully tiled, wedding-cake-style buildings lining each side – was testament to all that was good about the socialist system. In Paris, to live in apartments like these would cost a king's ransom. Here, those higher up in the Party might get priority, but there were ordinary workers too. The rubble women, for example. Those who had heroically cleared tonnes and tonnes of debris from the ruins of Berlin after the war to help build a new Hauptstadt, they had been given priority to get these apartments. Tenement palaces, they were called, and Müller could see why.

She swivelled on her heels to look the other way, back towards central Berlin and the TV tower, and beyond that the Anti-Fascist Protection Barrier. Past the glorious fountain in the centre of Strausberger Platz, the wind whipping up the water and dispersing it into a fine mist across the square. She breathed in the damp air and let the microscopic spray settle on her face. Where the sun hit the water you could see miniature rainbows forming. Never quite a complete arch, coming and going as the flow pulsed from the pumps.

Now, through one of the rainbows, she saw an overweight, middle-aged man approaching. Head down, walking a bit like a penguin. Every now and then brushing water droplets from his epaulettes, as much – no doubt – to draw attention to his rank as to actually wipe them. That was always her deputy Werner Tilsner's theory about Reiniger anyway. Unterleutnant Werner Tilsner found the People's Police colonel pompous and dull. Müller on the other hand rather liked him, and as he drew close her face widened into a broad smile.

'Karin, you're looking well,' he said, smiling equally broadly as he pumped her outstretched hand. 'Clearly motherhood suits you.'

'I'm not so sure about that, Comrade *Oberst*,' laughed Müller. 'You heard on the phone last night. It's a bit chaotic in the apartment at the moment.' Reiniger had rung her apartment police hotline in the midst of domestic chaos, a crying fit from both babies. The one-bedroom flat was overcrowded too: Müller, her hospital doctor boyfriend Emil Wollenburg, the twins themselves and, there to look after them, her newly discovered grandmother, Helga.

Reiniger waved his arm, as though by doing so it would magic her problems away. 'We'll have to see what we can do about your living conditions. I may have a possible solution. And sorry I was a little late. You know how it is. I had a meeting at the Café Moskau and thought I may as well walk after that. Actually, the person I was meeting asked after you.'

'Oh yes?' Müller was pleased she hadn't been totally forgotten by her People's Police colleagues during her maternity leave. 'Who was that?'

'Someone who – if you accept my little proposal – you may be seeing a lot more of again.'

There was something in Reiniger's smirking face that immediately made Müller wary. *Seeing a lot more of again.* The implication being it would happen, whether she wanted it to or not.

Müller was aware that her face must have fallen, even though she'd tried to keep a neutral expression. But the next words from Reiniger's mouth came as no surprise.

'It was your old Ministry for State Security contact, *Oberst* Jäger.'

Jäger. The Stasi colonel with the suave good looks of a West German TV presenter.

A manipulator. A string-puller. A man to fear.

Reiniger seemed in no hurry to get down to business. Instead, lunch – sitting outside the restaurant on the northern semi-circle of the Platz – was spent discussing the children, with Reiniger swapping tales about his first taste of fatherhood years earlier, and his recent reacquaintance after becoming a grandfather just the previous year.

In fact, the conversation was so convivial Müller had almost forgotten the sense of dread she'd felt earlier, when she heard Jäger's name again. Not that the Stasi officer was someone she hated. She was ambivalent. Some of his methods, and those of the agency he worked for, were ruthless, cruel, underhand. But it was Jäger who had traced her grandmother, Helga – allowing Müller to feel a sense of belonging, at last, after years of feeling like the odd one out in her adoptive family back in the forested, low mountains of Thuringia. And perhaps if Jäger were to re-enter her working life again, she might, this time, persuade him to try to find information about her natural father, who – as far as she knew – had been a victorious Soviet soldier who had got her teenage mother pregnant with her in the dying days of the war, or very shortly after.

Finally Reiniger belched, sending the fumes of his meal and accompanying smell of wheat beer across the table into Müller's face. She pretended not to notice. Then he wiped the linen napkin across his mouth, spat on it, and then repeated the action, examining the resulting red-brown sauce deposits with a curious look of satisfaction.

'So, I hope you enjoyed that as much as I did, Karin?'

'Certainly, Comrade *Oberst*. It's not often I get the chance to eat at a restaurant as fine as this.'

'Good. Good. On to the next part of our little outing, then. You don't have to rush back, do you?'

'Not at all.' Müller recalled Jannika and Johannes's whining from the previous night, and the way Helga had managed to calm them. Her grandmother was more than capable of looking after them on her own.

'All right, then. Let's get our coats. We're going to see something that I think you'll like.'

Reiniger used a key to enter the lobby of an apartment block just to the side of one of the four high towers that dominated each corner of Strausberger Platz. Everything was bright, white, clean – it had nothing in common with her crumbling block on Schönhauser Allee.

The lift accelerated them upwards in a smooth glide to the floor – the sixth – that Reiniger selected from the bank of brass buttons surrounded by glowing green neon. When they exited, the floor and architectural detailing had the same feeling of opulence. If it was polished concrete rather than actual marble or white stone, the designers had done an excellent job of camouflage. Müller suspected that at least *some* of this was the real thing, even though she knew the stone-effect exterior along the whole of the Allee was achieved by the clever use of ceramic tiles.

Reiniger's key ring jangled like a child's percussion triangle as he pulled it from his pocket and fitted one of the keys into a heavy oak door. He opened it and beckoned Müller to follow, still not revealing what the purpose of his little tour actually was.

Once inside, he gave another of his sweeping arm gestures around the expansive hallway – big enough, Müller noted, to have a dining table. The one here looked like it was antique. The apartment probably belonged to some high-up Party apparatchik. But if so, why was Müller being given a guided tour?

'What do you think? Impressive, isn't it?'

'It certainly is, Comrade *Oberst*.' Müller would usually have dropped the repetitive honorifics by now, even with a senior officer, but she knew Reiniger appreciated being reminded of his high rank as often as possible. She wasn't going to disappoint him.

'Take a look around. This is a three-bedroomed apartment. Highly unusual. And, of course, very much sought after. I think perhaps they knocked two together.'

Müller entered the lounge first. The furnishings here were ultra-modern: curved wooden table, an unusual all-white, leather-look sofa with a shiny chrome frame. Most impressive of all were the high windows, flooding light into every corner of the room. Müller ambled over to one of them. If you wanted to be picky, you could say that the view was only a side-on of Strausberger Platz – you couldn't see the whole square from here. But you could see enough: the fountain with its fine mist of blown spray, which a couple of children were running in and out of; the two imposing towers on the eastern side of the square; the start of the long, majestic Karl-Marx-Allee, leading past the U-bahn station entrance for kilometre after kilometre until it became the road that would take you to the very east of the Republic, and beyond that, to Poland.

She felt overwhelmed by all the luxury. Slightly guilty too, because it highlighted some of the inequalities of what was supposed to be an equal society. Had the *Trümmerfrauen* – the rubble women – really acquired the leases on apartments like these?

Müller made her way back to the hall, off which all the apartment's rooms led. She could see the corner of the kitchen, with its ultra-modern fitted cupboards. The bathroom, too, had its door open and looked to be of the highest specification.

At the dining table, Reiniger had sat down, and for once was in shirt sleeves, his jacket with its epaulettes of shiny stars hung over the back of his chair. In front of him, various papers were spread out on the table itself, with a pen alongside.

'Come,' he said, pointing to the chair opposite his. 'Sit yourself down, and I'll take you through everything.'

Müller frowned. 'Take me through everything?'

Reiniger was smiling broadly, his teeth unusually white for a man of his age. Müller knew that, like her, he didn't smoke, and was always casting disapproving glances towards Tilsner when he lit up. But as well as that, he must spend a lot of time polishing his teeth, just as he did the stars on his shoulders. That, or he'd found a very good dentist. He picked up the pen.

'Yes. The lease. There's a few things I need to explain.'

Müller felt the colour drain from her face, and a rapid trembling begin somewhere deep in her belly. 'I . . . well, even we . . . couldn't possibly afford something like this, Comrade *Oberst*. Not on the salary of a police first lieutenant nor a hospital doctor, and not even if we combined those with my grandmother's pension.'

'I think you'd be surprised, Karin. This is hardly more expensive than any other flat in the Republic. Cheaper than some, in fact. Less than one hundred marks a month. Surely you could manage that?'

Müller felt her heart racing. Of course they could afford that. It was virtually no more than the Schönhauser Allee apartment. *There has to be a catch. There's always a catch.* She started looking round the room furtively, up into each corner. Reiniger eyed her with suspicion.

'If you're doing what I think you're doing, Karin, don't worry. This is a police apartment. It's been thoroughly checked for surveillance devices. It's clean.'

Reiniger was turning one of the documents round, pushing it in front of her. She could see it had her name on the rental agreement, as yet unsigned. Immediately, however, she spotted a mistake in what had been typed, awaiting her signature. She traced the rank before her name.

'There's an error here, I'm afraid, Comrade *Oberst*. They've called me *Major*. I'm not a major. I'm a first lieutenant.'

'Hmm. Yes, that could be a problem. But have a look at the counter-signature.'

She recognised Reiniger's angled scrawl above his printed name.

'You don't think I would have signed a document and not noticed a mistake like that, Karin, do you? If so, you underestimate me.'

'I . . . I d-don't understand,' Müller said.

'There *is* a problem. Or rather there *was*. An apartment such as this can only be rented to a police officer of the rank of major and above.'

'So . . .'

'So usually, as a mere *Oberleutnant*, albeit a much-valued one, you would be disqualified. However, things have changed in your absence on maternity leave. A lot of talking's been going on. We realise it might be difficult for you to return to work and look after twins at the same time, although I gather from your personal circumstances that your grandmother should be able to help a great deal, and in effect be the twins' full-time carer?'

Müller nodded, but said nothing, too shocked to speak.

'At the same time, we in the People's Police want to use you to your full abilities, while realising you can't go gallivanting all over the place as the head of a murder squad.'

Müller had a sudden feeling of dread. Their answer would be pen-pushing. Not just pen-pushing, but pen-pushing as a major, in charge of a team of pen-pushers. If that was it she was going to say 'no', without question. But for now, she allowed Reiniger to continue without interruption.

'So there's been a bit of a reorganisation. Not solely to accommodate you, although that's part of it. We've been worried for some time about discrete murder squads in the various regions working in their own sweet, but perhaps idiosyncratic, ways. For the highest-profile cases we can't allow that to continue, so we're creating an overall Serious Crimes Department. Based in Keibelstrasse. Liaising at the highest levels with other agencies and ministries. I probably don't need to spell that out. You've done plenty of it in your last two cases.'

Liaising with the Stasi. That was what Reiniger meant. And that was where Jäger came into the equation.

Reiniger was still in mid-flow, though he now lowered his voice, despite what he'd said about the apartment being 'clean'.

'You'll be aware that the Ministry for State Security took a very close interest in your last two major cases. What you may not have been aware of at your previous rank is that, in some similar circumstances, inquiries have been taken away from the People's Police, by what are known as the *MfS*'s – the Stasi's – Special Commissions.'

Müller frowned. The conversation had taken an ominous turn. Reiniger's joviality had been replaced with an icy seriousness.

'It has tended to be cases with political overtones, or cases where the Ministry feels it is essential that ordinary citizens do not find out more than they need to. That has even included the families of the victims themselves.'

Reiniger glanced at each of his shoulders in turn, as though to admire his star-studded epaulettes – forgetting for a moment his uniform jacket was over the back of his chair. As though to check he really was a police colonel. That he really was in charge. Müller was starting to doubt it.

He cleared his throat. 'Now, you can imagine that if that continues, if it extends to more cases, the *Kripo*'s remit in tackling and solving serious crimes will be severely undermined.'

Müller watched Reiniger wringing his hands. Then he fixed her with a stare.

'So that is why we are creating this new department. To, if you like, get ahead of the game. So that we can make a case for our own specialist team to keep control of the most serious murders, rather than them being taken out of our hands and given straight to the Stasi.'

Müller felt tension taking over her body, constricting her throat. This all felt like she was being set up to fail again, that she would be in opposition to the Stasi from the word go. If that were the case, there would only be one winner.

'It will be a small team,' continued Reiniger, picking up the rental contract and turning it over. 'But you will have a roving brief across the whole country to oversee such murder investigations. Especially those that could, shall we say, prove embarrassing to the Republic. Werner Tilsner is being promoted to join this team, working as your deputy again. There is a catch, however. You probably knew there would be. You will have to start immediately and end your maternity leave.'

Müller was about to object. The twins were only six months old. She didn't feel ready, whatever carrots were being dangled in front of her. But before she could say anything, Reiniger was in full flow again.

'Don't say anything hasty. Hear me out. Both you and Tilsner will jump a couple of ranks. He's already working in his new role, although he doesn't know about yours, should you choose to accept. He will be your *Hauptmann* and you will be *Major* Karin Müller of the People's Police.' It was Reiniger's trump card, and with a flourish, he leant over and traced his finger under her rank on the rental agreement. 'Look around, Karin. Is it really fair to your family to deny them all this? You'll never get a chance like this again. It's not a desk job, if that's what you were afraid of. This will be real police work, real detective work. And you're being chosen because of your previous experience in dealing with the Stasi. But you will be the boss, able to ask for any assistance you require. That way, you can be certain, you can still look after your family in the way you want to.'

Reiniger lifted the pen and then stretched his arm out, offering it to Müller.

She lifted her hand as though to take it, then stopped the motion in mid-air.

Was it really what she wanted? Being separated from the children she'd yearned for, at such an early age?

To have the Stasi watching her every move again, as they surely would?

2

As he introduced himself, shaking the local *Kripo* captain's hand, Tilsner stumbled over his own rank.

'*Unt*— sorry . . . *Hauptmann* Werner Tilsner, Comrade.'

A *Hauptmann* now, not a mere *Unterleutnant*. Not that he really cared about the title, or the fact that *Oberst* Reiniger seemed to have secured him a double promotion. A jump up the ranks, missing out *Leutnant* and *Oberleutnant*. What Tilsner cared about was why. Why he'd once again been sent abruptly from his beloved Berlin to another godforsaken part of the Republic. This time, the banks of an artificial lake in the middle of the industrial Lausitz brown coal belt.

'Lovely spot, isn't it?' said his opposite number from the local force. The man had clearly mistaken Tilsner's gaze across the lake as one of admiration, rather than bewilderment. Tilsner, being Tilsner, had already forgotten the officer's name, so he just nodded to keep the peace. He could hear Karin's voice in his head admonishing him. *You wouldn't have forgotten the name if it was a woman, would you?*

Karin. Or, more correctly, *Oberleutnant* Karin Müller. He didn't expect her to be coming back to work at all, what with her new twins to look after.

Here, the wind whipping off the lake's surface made the canvas of the large tent erected by the local police slap rhythmically. To one side, the beached dinghies from the boating club joined in, their partly furled sails and lanyards snapping in Aeolian syncopation. Tilsner held his hand against his forehead for a moment, then moved it backwards through his hair. He could feel a migraine coming on.

He tried to focus. 'Sorry, Comrade *Hauptmann*? . . .' If he couldn't remember the other detective's name, he might at least give him his full honorifics.

'Schwarz. Helmut Schwarz,' the man replied. If Schwarz felt slighted at having to remind Tilsner of his name for a second time, he hid it well. Instead, a faint smile played across his face. 'Did you want to see the body, or did you come all the way down from Berlin just to stare into space?'

Now it was Tilsner's turn to grin. Schwarz didn't seem a bad sort. Better company than misery guts Jonas Schmidt. The forensic officer had accompanied Tilsner here in the Wartburg, but had hardly said a thing the whole journey. Usually Tilsner was grateful on the rare occasions Schmidt ended one of his tedious monologues. But the new silent Schmidt was even worse. Something was clearly troubling him, but the *Kriminaltechniker* didn't seem inclined to enlighten Tilsner as to what it was.

Schwarz pulled back the flap of the tent for his Berlin colleague to enter. Tilsner wondered how the man felt. This initiative from on high, delivered to him by Reiniger, had brought

Tilsner's team of two – himself and Schmidt – from Berlin to take charge of this investigation.

He swatted a fly away from his face, irritated by its buzzing.

All he could see of the body, almost completely encircled by policemen, police photographers and forensic experts, was the bottom portion of the young man's legs – pale and obscenely swollen from the time they'd been under the water.

Schwarz leant towards Tilsner's ear, as though about to impart some delicious piece of gossip. 'He was weighted down. We were never meant to find him. Someone didn't do a particularly good job, and the weight must have eventually come off. Perhaps whatever was binding it to the body rotted away. So the body floated to the surface.'

Tilsner knew all this already. He'd been fully briefed by Reiniger. But he wasn't about to play the clever fox with the locals. He'd need their help.

Having taken his place in the circle, Tilsner could see that Schmidt was at the head end of the body, talking and nodding away.

'So we don't know the cause of death yet?' the portly *Kriminaltechniker* asked, peering through his centimetre-thick spectacle lenses.

'I'm a pathologist, not a magician,' replied a fierce-looking middle-aged woman hunched down on the opposite side of the body.

'But do we know how long the body was in the water?' continued Schmidt.

'I refer you to my previous answer,' said the woman, gruffly, puffing out what Tilsner noted was a not inconsiderable chest.

'If you'd let me get on with my work, Comrade, I might have a chance of finding out. Though I won't be able to say anything with any certainty until the autopsy.'

Tilsner watched as the woman poked at the youth's face with an implement that looked a little like a speculum, occasionally brushing flies away as they hovered round her hair, which was such a lustreless, deep black that it was obviously dyed. The sooner the body was moved and put in the cooler, the better. At least they were planning to conduct the autopsy immediately – that afternoon, he'd been told. As soon as this initial external examination was over, the body would be moved to the nearby town of Hoyerswerda.

Schmidt's failure to elicit any useful information saw him cast an apologetic glance towards Tilsner, who beckoned him away from the pathologist with a slight jerk of his head.

'Just leave her to it for now, Jonas,' he whispered. 'She doesn't seem the friendliest of sorts.'

Tilsner turned back to Schwarz. 'Why don't you have a go?' he said quietly. 'Grumpy guts might respond better to questions from someone she knows.'

Schwarz smiled conspiratorially, and gave a slight nod.

'Come on, Gudrun, you could be a bit more welcoming to our visitors from Berlin. This must be an important case for them to have been sent here. A chance of a bit of glory for you.'

The pathologist lifted her head and shot Schwarz a withering look, then turned her attentions back to the body. 'Not more than two weeks,' she grunted.

'"*Not more than two weeks*", what?' asked Schwarz.

'That he was in the water for, of course.'

'And what makes you say that?' asked Tilsner.

This time it was the Berlin detective's turn to receive a glacial stare.

'Who is this one, Helmut? Another interloper?'

'He's Comrade *Hauptmann* Werner Tilsner. As I explained, he's come all the way from Berlin, Gudrun. So I'd be grateful if you could extend your usual helpfulness and cooperation to him too.'

'*Two* police captains on the same case? Isn't that overkill, even for you lot?'

Tilsner laughed. 'I agree,' he said. 'I'm sure Comrade Schwarz could have handled this perfectly well on his own, Comrade Gudrun . . .' Tilsner extended his hand. The pathologist peered at it for a few seconds, before putting down her implements. She wiped her gloved right hand on her white overalls, and took Tilsner's in a firm grip.

'Fenstermacher. Dr Gudrun Fenstermacher. Not Comrade, thank you.'

Tilsner was surprised that the woman was so ready to divorce herself from the greeting for a fellow Communist Party member. But there again, she didn't seem the type to be afraid of very much, rather someone content to plough her own furrow, whatever the consequences.

'*Citizen* if you must use these silly names, but certainly not Comrade.' The pathologist held the Berlin officer's gaze. 'The reason I can tell the body has not been in the water more than two weeks is the state of the hands and feet. There is wrinkling there, as you would expect.' She held up the dead youth's left arm to illustrate her point, turning it slightly so that Tilsner and the others could see the tiny ridges that had formed on the underside of the pale, waxy-looking hand. Then she pinched the index finger between her thumb and forefinger. 'But the skin is not yet fully detached,' she continued, maintaining her pincer grip. 'That usually happens between the first and second week of immersion, be it in seawater, or – as in this case – freshwater. So, not more than two weeks. When we do the full autopsy this afternoon, I'll be able to give you a better estimate. Now, I'd guess at about a week.'

'Impressive,' smiled Tilsner. 'Thank you.'

'It's not impressive. It's just science. It's simply doing my job. They only need one of me. Not two, as they seem to require of you, and your forensic scientists.' She threw a sarcastic grin towards Schmidt.

'Very useful anyway,' said Tilsner. 'I know it's a very early stage, but is there anything else – anything at all – that you can tell us?'

'Well, there is *something* slightly odd. There aren't the classic signs of drowning. Not all of them anyway.'

'So whoever it was, was killed *before* entering the water?'

'Possibly. See these marks round the stomach area?' The woman drew her finger backwards and forwards in mid-air, hovering a few millimetres above the body, where the skin, in two encircling stripes, was a slightly darker colour. 'They may have been caused by ropes or similar used to secure whatever weight was attached to make sure the body sank to the bottom of the lake. But at the moment that is speculation.'

'Cause of death, I would guess, is asphyxiation,' she continued. 'But not through drowning. No bruising round the neck, so at this stage I would say not through strangulation.'

'What then? Pillow across the face?' asked Tilsner.

The woman shrugged. 'I don't know . . . yet.' Then she lifted the left arm back up and gestured to the wrist. Then did the same to the body's right arm. 'See the marks here?'

'Weights again?' asked Schwarz.

The woman shook her head. 'Restraints. Cutting into the skin as this poor boy struggled against them.'

Tilsner furrowed his brow. 'So he was tortured?'

The woman held up her hand. 'I don't know, I don't know. And that's enough questions, thank you. I've told you all I know at this stage.'

'So we have no idea who this youth was, or indeed why the powers that be at Keibelstrasse have seen fit to send Schmidt and myself down here?' Tilsner wasn't entirely sure who he was directing this question to.

Schwarz shook his head. Then his face lit up. 'Ah, no. There is one other thing. On the other side. Can you show him, Gudrun?'

The pathologist lifted the body up by its left arm again, rotating it slightly to expose the underside of the left shoulder blade. A tattoo. Some sort of emblem permanently etched in black ink on the dead youth's skin.

'We've no idea what it is,' said Schwarz. 'It looks a bit like the Greek letter pi.'

Schmidt, who'd lapsed into a morose silence – similar to the one he'd maintained in the Wartburg – now spoke up. 'More likely to be Cyrillic, here in the Republic, surely? It looks a bit like a letter 'L'. But it's still not quite the right shape.'

Tilsner kept silent. He hadn't helped his children with their Russian lessons, and he certainly hadn't studied it at school. In fact, he hadn't done much of any worth at school at all, what with the war. But that didn't stop his brain working. There was something about the tattoo that was familiar.

'Of course,' said the pathologist, 'it's incomplete.'

'What do you mean, incomplete?' asked Schwarz, a note of annoyance in his voice. 'You didn't mention that before.'

'No, I had a better look. This is one area of the body where the skin *has* detached. Or where a fish has had a nibble. Or . . .'

'Or what?' asked Tilsner.

'Or where part of the design was deliberately cut off.'

'To make it look like something else?'

'Possibly,' replied Fenstermacher. 'I can't speculate as to motivation.'

'But how much of the design has disappeared?'

Fenstermacher was still partially holding up the body, but with her muscular arms it seemed to take little effort. 'Hard to say. Except if you look at the top and bottom of our Cyrillic "L" or Greek "pi" or whatever it is, you'll see the top, bottom and left-hand side are all smoothly curved.'

Schmidt looked excited, some of his old enthusiasm for the job temporarily overcoming whatever was weighing him down. 'On that basis, Comrades, I would say all that's left is the left-hand third of the design. It must, surely, be a circle, and the other two thirds are missing.'

For the first time in several hours, Tilsner felt a great love for his *Kriminaltechniker* colleague again. Because this was the key to his mental block. The image at the back of his mind suddenly became clear.

An image from a town at the east – the far east – of the Republic. Bordering the Oder river. Bordering Poland. As near to Lenin's mausoleum in Moscow as it was possible to get without actually leaving the borders of the *Deutsche Demokratische Republik*. So yes, perhaps the Cyrillic 'L' guess of Schmidt's had some significance.

But this wasn't an 'L'.

It wasn't 'pi'.

Instead, Tilsner knew the design showed two linked, cursive initials. Not one. And Roman – not Greek or Cyrillic.

And Tilsner knew the other letters in the puzzle too. But as the others scratched their heads and furrowed their brows, he wasn't going to let on that he knew the solution.

Some thirty minutes after leaving the lakeside, Tilsner and Schmidt watched rows and rows of *Plattenbauten* – concrete slab apartment blocks – rise up from the surrounding countryside of the Upper Lausitz. It was almost as though they'd gone back in time a few months to their previous case in Halle-Neustadt. Another new, model socialist town – although this one existed as a dormitory for lignite miners, rather than chemical workers.

Tilsner slapped his hand on the Wartburg's steering wheel. 'You see, Jonas, if we'd chosen to become brown coal miners, we could have had brand new flats like those ones.'

Schmidt didn't respond. *Still in his grumpy fug*, thought Tilsner.

Tilsner had been following Schwarz's car, until they'd lost him at a junction soon after Senftenberg. But the local police captain had given him detailed directions to the mortuary, and they found their way without trouble. Tilsner just hoped the prospect of seeing a dead body being sliced open might spark some life into his colleague. Forensic scientists seemed to revel in that sort of thing. And whatever was weighing Schmidt down, he shouldn't be letting it affect his work.

When they arrived at the mortuary in the local hospital, they found that Fenstermacher had wasted no time, and had already set to work. But that wasn't the only surprise. Tilsner recognised a familiar face. His old boss.

'What are you doing here?' Tilsner whispered, sidling up to Müller as she watched the pathologist making incisions in the youth's body. 'I thought you'd become a permanent childminder.'

'Don't you mean, "I thought you'd become a permanent childminder, Comrade *Major*."'

Tilsner rubbed his brow. '*Major*? Are they throwing around ranks and promotions like confetti?' He felt a momentary flash of annoyance – he'd thought that he might have been top dog in this new specialist crimes unit. Instead, he was still Karin's deputy – they just both had new ranks. And, he began to realise, that suited him just fine. Too much responsibility usually meant you ended up with too much of the blame when things went wrong.

'Careful, Comrade *Hauptmann*.' Müller grinned, then added quietly: 'I've the power to demote you if I wish, just like that.' She clicked her fingers to emphasise the point.

The sound attracted an angry glare from the pathologist. 'I do appreciate silence when I'm working, you know. It helps one to concentrate, especially if you're wielding one of these.' She nodded to the scalpel in her fist.

Fenstermacher then bent back over the body and began to make a cut through the upper section of the youth's neck. Once she considered the incision large enough, she plunged her hand into the cavity.

'Aha,' she exclaimed, with what Tilsner felt was an inappropriate amount of glee. 'Just as I thought.' She held out a piece of red material, covered in mucus and dried blood, then waved it from side to side. 'I couldn't understand how this young man had died through asphyxiation and yet the usual signs of death by drowning, or strangulation, were absent. Here, ladies and gentleman, is our answer.'

'And what exactly *is* the answer, Comrade Fenstermacher?' asked Müller.

'He couldn't breathe. And so he died. And he couldn't breathe because he'd had this sock stuffed down his windpipe.'

Tilsner fought the temptation to clutch at his own neck, and instead took several deep breaths. Normally he was unmoved by violent deaths – he'd seen much worse as a teenage boy in the war. But he could see Müller's face had gone pale too.

'Jesus,' he exclaimed. 'What a way to go.'

'Yes, unpleasant,' agreed the pathologist. 'And something that – due to the gag reflex – would be impossible to self-administer. So we have our answer and, perhaps, all of you many police officers haven't had a wasted journey. Because this boy was most definitely murdered. Murdered in a particularly sadistic way.'

3

Six months earlier (March 1976)
Pankow, East Berlin

'C'mon, speccy. Show us what you're going to do about it.'

I peer at what's being waved in front of my face.

My spectacles.

I know they're there, but I can't see them clearly. Just an unfocussed blob, like so many objects.

My spectacles with the centimetre-thick lenses.

They have to be that thick at the edges to allow sufficient concavity in the centre – sufficient concavity to finally give the world a hard-edged precision, rather than the blur it is without them.

I thrash my hands around trying to grasp them. But it's useless.

'Please give them back, Oskar,' I plead. Although I can't see my tormenter's face with any clarity, I know who it is from his voice.

'*Please give them back, Oskar,*' he repeats in a high-pitched whine. Then drops the glasses to the floor. The next thing I hear is the crunch of breaking plastic and glass as a foot stomps down on them.

'Whoops. Sorry, queer boy. That was a silly place to leave your specs, wasn't it?'

I can feel the tears start to sting my eyes. I get down on my knees and scrabble round to retrieve what I can of the broken pieces.

The second time it's happened this year.

Mutti and Vati will be furious.

But as I'm thinking about that, I feel the first blow to the side of my head, then another, then more to my back and bum. I roll into a ball with my hands clasped behind my skull, elbows protecting my face, willing them to stop. Then a shout.

'Oi! Krüge! Leave him alone. And you lot. Pick on someone your own size.'

'Ah shut up, Winkler. You're just another queer boy like him.'

I keep my elbows wrapped around my face till Jan Winkler prises them off. Oskar's friends laugh, but the laughter fades as they all move away, their sadistic urges temporarily sated.

'It's OK, Markus. They've gone now. Here, I'll help you clear up, though I'm afraid these are wrecked. Are *you* OK?'

I brush myself down. Feel my heart rate start to settle. Thankful that I have one friend here at Oberschule Pankow Ernst Thälmann. 'Bruised. Nothing broken, I don't think.' I flex my arms. There'll be swelling by the morning. A black eye. But what hurts most – as usual – is my pride, or what's left of it.

'They're just bullies,' says Jan. 'It's best to try to ignore them.'

I try to focus on his face, but can't. I know what he looks like anyway. A pretty-boy face. All the girls fancy him, but Jan Winkler just ignores them. And that makes them fancy him even more.

'Here. Take my arm,' he says. 'I'll help you home.'

I'm grateful for the help. Grateful, too, in an odd way, to Oskar Krüge in that he waited till the end of the school day – the end of the school week – to pick me out for his sadistic games. At least I don't have to go back into class and invent some stupid excuse.

I know I could walk unaided, but I rather like having Jan holding me. He seems to pull me along effortlessly. Most things are effortless to Jan Winkler. Top of the class. Destined for university. Unlike me. I know I'm a disappointment to my People's Police forensic scientist father. Jan's as clever as my father expected *me* to be. Each week, when *Kriminaltechniker* Jonas Schmidt quizzes me over Sunday lunch, I can feel the disappointment radiating from him as I recount how well I'm doing – or rather how well I'm *not* doing – in various subjects. How he would love to have a son like Jan Winkler.

Jan bundles me onto the tram, so we get home quicker.

'Isn't this out of your way?' I ask him.

'Don't worry. What are friends for if they can't help out in times of need? I'm sure you'd do the same for me.'

Yes, yes, of course I would, Jan, I think. *The difference is you'd never get in a situation like that.* I think all this but say nothing.

'Cheer up, Markus. Oskar will have forgotten all about it by Monday. I'll look out for you.'

The disapproval on my mother's face as she opens the apartment door couldn't be clearer.

'Don't be too harsh on him, Frau Schmidt,' says Jan. 'I challenged him to a run and there's a bit of rough ground on the way back. Markus caught his foot and fell over. I think he's all right, but I'm afraid his specs aren't.' He hands the broken pieces of glass and plastic to Mutti even though all three of us know they aren't repairable. But I'm thankful. Thankful he didn't tell the truth about the bullying. If Mutti went to the school, if Oskar was hauled in front of the head teacher, it would only make things ten times worse and mean the next beating probably *would* result in broken bones, not just wounded pride and a smashed pair of glasses.

'Hmm,' sighs my mother. 'Well, thank you for helping him back at least, Jan. I bet your mother doesn't have to put up with this sort of thing.'

'Oh, I've got into my fair share of scrapes during my time, Frau Schmidt, don't you worry about that.'

I've already stumbled ahead into the flat, eager to get into the bathroom to check the damage, when Jan shouts to me before my mother has a chance to shut the door in his face.

'What are you doing this weekend, Markus? Do you fancy hanging out together tomorrow? I'm expecting the delivery of my new scooter.'

My mother's ears prick up at that. 'I don't want you riding on the back of a motor scooter, Markus. And certainly not without your glasses.'

'Mum,' I sigh.

'It's OK, Frau Schmidt. I'll make sure I look after him. He can hang on tightly to me. And it's not very powerful. We won't go far.'

My mother's resistance crumbles in the face of Jan's pretty-boy charm. It's the same for all women and girls. He just has a way with them. I wish I could learn a few tricks from him.

'Oh all right, then. As you say, I suppose it's not his fault he's broken his glasses, again. And he has got a spare pair, although they're old ones and not as strong.'

'Great. That's a deal, then. I'll make sure he doesn't come to any harm. You can rely on me, Frau Schmidt.'

'I hope I can, Jan.'

'So, Markus. Ten o'clock sharp tomorrow morning at mine, OK? Don't be late.'

'Wow.' That one word of exclamation is enough. Jan beams with pride.

'It's great, isn't it?' he says.

Even though with my old pair of glasses things aren't quite as sharp as they should be, I can tell this is an impressive machine. I run my hand over the gleaming, mustard-painted metal of the teardrop-shaped fuel tank.

'Isn't there a huge waiting list for these, like for Trabis?' I ask. 'My dad had to wait years for his car, even though he works for the police.'

'There is, yes, but my dad managed to swing it.'

I'm never very sure what Jan's father does for a living, other than that he's a fairly high-up official. Not police, not government, but something like that. Jan will never say. I always feel myself reddening in his father's presence. He has the same personal magnetism as Jan, and it's from him – rather than his mother – that Jan gets his striking good looks.

'What's it called?' I ask, aware of the naive note of wonder in my voice.

'It's a Simson S-50. The latest model. They only started producing them last year.'

'Are you going to give me a ride?'

'Soon. Some friends are coming round first and then we're all heading off together.'

Jan thinks I'll be excited by this news, but I'm not. It makes me slightly apprehensive. I'm never good with new people. I break out in a cold sweat at the slightest embarrassment, and especially hate being asked questions about myself. My life's so boring. They'll all be cool, no doubt with the latest motorcycles. I'll just be the hanger-on.

'I thought we were just going for a short trip in the Hauptstadt?'

'Nah. Live a little, Markus. It's a lovely day. I'm taking you abroad.'

'Abroad?' I have ridiculous visions of a group of us getting together and jumping the Anti-Fascist Protection Barrier on the bikes. Motorised *Republikflüchtlingen*. I don't want anything like that. I don't want to embarrass my father any further. He's angry enough about my school results as it is. 'My mum won't like that, Jan. Maybe I'd better not come. Couldn't you just give me a quick ride round the block before the others arrive?'

He ruffles the hair on the top of my head. It feels strangely intimate. 'Nonsense, young master Schmidt. You're riding with me. Guest of honour, no less. And don't worry. It's not far.'

'But you said abroad!'

'Ach, I was only joking. How would we go abroad from here? We're not about to scale the Wall, are we?'

When the others arrive with their gleaming machines, I feel strangely relaxed. They gather round Jan's bike, admiring and stroking it, just as I had minutes earlier. And instead of mocking me, as Oskar Krüge would have done, I seem to be the object of their envy, because I'm the one being allowed to ride pillion on the new Simson S-50.

Jan has a smart set of figure-hugging black leathers to go with the new bike. I climb aboard behind him as he revs the engine, not knowing where to put my hands. He grabs them from behind and folds them round his middle. It feels strange, almost as though it should be his girlfriend doing something like this. Not his speccy, bullied, teenage male friend.

'Hold on tight and don't let go,' he shouts, trying to make himself heard above the roar of the engine and through the helmet he's lent me. That's what my mother had insisted on when I set off that morning. That I wear a helmet, even though most of Jan's mates haven't bothered. 'The only other thing you need to remember is to make sure you lean with me as I corner,' Jan says. 'I'll be leaning into the corner. Sometimes, if it's your first time, it seems unnatural, and you might feel as though you want to lean the other way. Don't. Just lean the same way I do. Remember that, hold on tight and we can't go wrong. I promise.'

We travel south towards the *Fernsehturm* in the centre of the Hauptstadt. Seeing it always lifts my spirits, reminds me of better times, queuing up with Mutti and Vati soon after it opened. A wide-eyed boy of ten, proud that his father – an important scientist with the People's Police – could get the family priority tickets. And then whooshing upwards in the space-age lifts, looking up through the glass ceiling, marvelling at the wonders of modern technology as we accelerated towards the two-hundred-metre-high viewing platform. Looking out over Berlin for the first time: Karl-Marx-Allee heading east towards our friends in the Soviet Union; the Spree winding its way through the city; the jagged outline of the Wall. From up there you could see mysterious *Westberlin*, somewhere I wondered if I'd ever be allowed to visit.

I remember the security of holding my father's hand, of feeling important doing so. I feel much the same now, riding on Jan's brand new motorbike, the most coveted spot in our little convoy. The line of bikes turns now onto Karl-Marx-Allee itself, heading east – although Jan hasn't revealed our destination. I squeeze my arms ever tighter round his waist, hunch in towards him, feeling at last as though I belong. He takes one hand off the handlebars and squeezes my arm – just for a moment – as the motor hums between our thighs. A gesture of friendship, from someone I'm proud to call a friend.

4

Another side benefit of their promotions and working for the new Serious Crimes Department was that Müller and Tilsner had been billeted in the most luxurious hotel in the area, the Interhotel am See. Tilsner was all for trying out the swimming pool and sauna before their evening meal, but Müller wanted to go over what they knew about the case so far – and in any event wasn't in any hurry to show her messy caesarean scars to her deputy. They'd healed, of course, but the fact that her babies had been delivered by an amateur – albeit a trained amateur, in the shape of her former childhood friend, Johannes Traugott – had left its mark. She wouldn't be hurrying to show herself off naked in the spa area.

The scars were almost a form of branding that the previous case had left on her body. Next year, if she managed to get a suntan on holiday, they might start to fade. With the higher salary that went with her promotion, she, Emil, the twins and Helga could afford a holiday by the coast – perhaps the Black Sea in Bulgaria.

Freshly washed and scrubbed after their day of looking at a dead body being chopped into pieces, Tilsner sat down next to her at a table in the hotel's bar area.

'What are you drinking?' asked Tilsner.

'A Vita Cola, maybe? With ice.'

'Do you want anything more exciting in it?'

She shook her head. Since her unexpected pregnancy, the taste of alcohol had left her feeling slightly queasy.

Tilsner went up to the bar and returned with a beer for himself, Müller's Cola, and two smaller glasses filled with a colourless liquid.

'I need something stronger after seeing all that blood and guts today. If you don't want yours, I'm sure I can manage both.'

'What is it?'

Tilsner smiled. 'Blue Strangler. Your favourite, remember?'

Müller made a retching gesture.

'I remember you doing that for real in that graveyard.'

'No, you're mistaken, Werner. I had a very bad cold. I was simply coughing up phlegm.'

Tilsner laughed, then downed the shot in one, banging the glass back down on the table, provoking looks of disapproval from neighbouring drinkers in the rather upmarket bar.

Müller examined the drink in front of her for a moment, then picked it up and followed suit. As the fiery liquid hit the back of her throat, she fought the urge to cough. 'I thought we weren't supposed to slam down the glasses. That's a fascist thing, isn't it?'

Tilsner just shrugged and took a swig of beer. 'Where's Jonas?'

'In his room. I tried to get him to come and join us, but he says he has to make a phone call home. He says he'll be down for dinner, but may be late.'

Tilsner emitted a long sigh. 'He's no fun any more. Not that he ever was much fun. But he used to be able to talk a hole in anyone's belly. Now he's as silent as the Mona Lisa. It all seemed to start back in Halle-Neustadt, didn't it?'

Müller nodded. 'Family trouble. Well, teenage boy trouble, I think.'

'He's never shown him enough discipline. That's the problem. Now if it were my son, Marius—'

'You're suddenly a paragon of family virtue, are you, Werner? That's not the way I've always seen you.'

The jibe seemed to hit home. Tilsner reddened slightly and shrugged. 'Anyway, I don't think he knows anything we don't know. And he's wrong about his Cyrillic theory on the tattoo as well.'

'And you know that for sure, do you?'

'I do, Comrade *Major*.' The tone was sarcastic, but Müller let it slip by. They knew each other too well to bother with Comrade this, Comrade that, except when they were being light-hearted.

'And were you ever going to enlighten me, or was this a choice bit of information you were saving for someone else?' Müller glanced openly at the sparkling western watch on Tilsner's wrist. The one that had become a standing joke. 'The organisation that provided you with that luxury timepiece, for example.' The timepiece that, to Müller, had always been an overt signal that Tilsner's police pay was being augmented from somewhere, perhaps the Ministry for State Security.

Tilsner sighed again and held his forehead with his hand. 'Jesus, not that again. Change the record, please. Of course I was going to tell you.' He reached into his jacket and pulled out a Polaroid-style photograph. 'One useful thing *Kriminaltechniker* Schmidt did do for me before he went off to sulk in his hotel room was take this photo of the tattoo.' He handed it to Müller.

She examined the strange symbol. It did indeed look something like a letter from the Greek or Cyrillic alphabets, not that Müller was an expert in the former. But her schoolgirl Russian lessons told her it wasn't really close enough to the Russian 'L' – capital or lower case.

'And while you were prettying yourself up before dinner, I was actually working. They've got all the latest technology in the office here, including a photocopier, and in the children's library I found a book I was looking for.'

'The *children's* library?'

Tilsner nodded. 'An *Oberliga* football annual. Last year's. With details of all the members of the top league, their club crests, etc. Although it's a good thing it *was* last year's issue.'

Müller had little interest in football. Winter sports were more her thing. She just wanted Tilsner to get to the point, quickly. This was becoming like one of Schmidt's elongated explanations. 'And?' she prompted, impatiently.

From his other jacket pocket Tilsner pulled out a photocopied design, which he'd cut into a circle about two centimetres in diameter. Then he laid it out next to the photo of the tattoo.

Müller immediately saw that the tattoo's symbol exactly matched the first part of the photocopied football logo. The only two letters that were obvious to her in the rest of the logo were an 'A' and an 'H', but eventually her eyes saw the word that was being spelt out.

'S-T-A-H-L? So, steel? What's that got to do with football?'

'They're Eisenhüttendstadt's *Oberliga* team, BSG Stahl – or rather they *were* the town's *Oberliga* team.'

Eisenhüttenstadt. The Ironworks City. On the banks of the Oder river, just before the border with Poland on the very eastern edge of the Republic. 'Were? What do you mean by that?'

'Relegated last season due to an illegal payments scandal. Not just one division, but kicked right down to the regional third division. It'll take them years to recover, if they ever do.' Tilsner rocked back on two legs of his chair, his hands clasped behind his head, looking very pleased with himself. 'Allegedly they were guilty of giving illegal cash backhanders to some of their imported Yugoslav stars. Although the word on the street is it was more to do with the patrons of my team, Dynamo Berlin, getting jealous about their success.'

Despite her lack of knowledge of, or interest in, a sport involving grown men kicking a leather ball amid a sea of mud, Müller did at least know that Dynamo were known as the Stasi team – the pet project of its head, Erich Mielke. There'd been rumours of various underhand things going on to undermine rival teams when they became too successful and threatened Dynamo's dominance.

'That's all fascinating, but hardly relevant.'

Tilsner held his arms out wide. 'Who knows, at this stage? It *may* prove very relevant. In any case, what we do know from this,' he pointed at the photo of the tattoo, 'is that the victim had some connection to Eisenhüttenstadt and its football team. So in the absence of anything else, till we see if the dental records or fingerprints give us a match, this at least gives us a starting point.'

Müller nodded slowly. 'Well done, Werner. So how quickly can you go there?'

'Well, I could go tonight and take Schmidt with me. But grumpy guts will no doubt have some sort of excuse lined up. How about first thing tomorrow morning?'

'That would be good. Unfortunately, I have to go back to the Hauptstadt first. We're starting to move into our new flat tomorrow.'

'Already?'

'It's vacant and we're getting under each other's feet at my place. It's chaotic. So there's no point in delaying.'

'And where exactly is your new flat?'

'Ah, didn't I tell you? Strausberger Platz.'

'What, one of those fancy apartments right on the square? I thought they were reserved just for high-ups?'

'It's on the side. So only a partial view of the square. Still lovely though. So while I was in two minds about accepting this promotion, it does have some benefits.'

'And how did your hospital doctor boyfriend react to the news you were going back to work?'

Müller shrugged. 'Men in this Republic expect their women to work. Women expect to work. The trouble is, men expect their wives or partners to be good little housewives too.'

She wasn't going to give Tilsner a blow-by-blow account of Emil's actual reaction. When she'd phoned him after her meeting with Reiniger and Jäger, to say he'd been less than enthusiastic was an understatement. Despite the impressive new Strausberger Platz apartment, their tetchy words had escalated into a full-blown row – and ended up with him slamming down the phone.

Müller gathered up the documents and handed them back to Tilsner. 'Anyway, we're not here to chat about my living arrangements. What I suggest you do is go to the local People's Police HQ and check all the missing persons files as a first step. Then perhaps go to this football club, although if he's simply a fan he'll be one of thousands, I suppose, so they may not be able to help. If I can, I'll drive across from Berlin tomorrow night. You can make the decision whether we base our incident room in Eisenhüttenstadt itself, or where the main regional police HQ is.'

'And where is it, do you know?'

'Presumably Frankfurt.'

'Frankfurt?' exclaimed Tilsner.

'*An der Oder*, idiot. *Frankfurt an der Oder*. Not the one in the West, obviously.' Then she saw his wink. He'd been pulling her leg. Müller threw him a sarcastic smile. 'As far as I know, Eisenhüttenstadt is in *Bezirk* Frankfurt.'

5

Another perk of her new job was that they actually had removal men helping Müller and Emil to move into the new apartment. So, while Emil was orchestrating proceedings, she decided to escape and join Helga on a walk with the twins – one of the many her grandmother was having to take them on to keep them from under everyone's feet.

'You don't mind, do you, *Liebling*?'

Emil smiled, and gave her a brief peck on the lips. 'We'll be fine. Maybe you should pop back before too long to check we're putting everything in the right place. But until we're sorted out, it's not really any place for the twins.'

As she wheeled the double buggy along Karl-Marx-Allee, she fretted about her babies staring back at her. Children that she'd been told for years she was physically unable to conceive, because of what had gone on at that police college all those years before. Children born in shocking circumstances that could easily have led to their deaths – and hers. Yet now she had chosen to leave them and go back to work.

In the apartment in Strausberger Platz she'd almost said no to Reiniger. Almost. But the lure of a bigger home for her family, the attraction of the double promotion and the challenge of a fresh start had found her signing the documents under the police colonel's watchful eye.

She hadn't been surprised when – even before the ink was dry – Reiniger made a telephone call urging someone to come and join them for a celebration schnapps. That someone had, of course, been Jäger, and as they'd downed their shots, Müller couldn't help feeling that she was drinking with the Devil. The way Jäger had surveyed her home with an almost proprietorial air had made her shiver.

And when the three of them had finally exited the apartment block, her sense of disquiet turned to dread. A Barkas B1000 camper van was parked directly outside, and the occupants' lazy attempts to hide their surveillance camera behind partly closed curtains almost seemed like a deliberate provocation. But that was how it was going to be. When she'd signed on the dotted line she'd known what it would entail.

'I'd give anything to know what you're thinking,' Müller's grandmother said as they walked along.

Müller didn't want to share her misgivings. 'I was just reflecting on how lucky I am, I suppose, Helga.' She turned and smiled at the older woman, who most people here in Berlin had taken for her mother, rather than grandmother. That had been the only dark cloud about discovering her true past: her natural mother was dead – she had died heartbroken a few short years after giving birth to Müller as a young teenager. Her child had been taken away to be placed with another family just days after being born. Müller still hadn't managed to trace her real father – perhaps she never would.

'Are you happy about the new flat?' asked Helga. 'I got the impression that Emil felt I was getting under his feet in the old apartment.'

Müller stopped for a moment and looked her grandmother in the eye. 'I don't think that was the case. But we've plenty of room now anyway. You being with us is a godsend – don't ever think otherwise.'

Helga smiled and nodded, reaching down to adjust the blanket covering the twins. Müller started pushing the buggy again, heading for a café with outside tables and a view towards the centre of the Hauptstadt. Towards the *Fernsehturm* – and the West.

'How has he reacted to you going back to work?'

'It was always what we expected. Nothing's changed really. But I'm so grateful you're here, Helga. We couldn't manage without you.'

Helga reached down, pinching Johannes and Jannika each on the cheek. 'It's a privilege for me, Karin. You know it is. After all that's happened, for us to find each other . . . for you to have these two little darlings . . . well, it's nothing short of a miracle. So I will do all I can to help, don't you worry. But I do wonder if things might be more settled for you and Emil if you were married.'

For Müller, it was too soon to contemplate that. 'A good thing always needs to take a while,' she replied, taking sanctuary in an old German proverb. The wounds of the break-up of her marriage to Gottfried still weren't fully healed. As far as she knew, he was safe in the West, building a new life. But she had still only ever received that one, typewritten, signed letter. Perhaps any other letters he had sent had been intercepted by the Stasi? The reason he'd been allowed to go to the West, after all, was that he was considered an enemy of the Republic and someone to whom Müller, as a servant of the state with the People's Police, should not be married.

Helga's question about Emil, though, was a fair one. Was he her future, or had their relationship started on the rebound?

They'd lapsed into silence, and had now reached the Ampelmann crossing near the café. As they waited, Helga cleared her throat.

'I know it's not my place to say it, Karin, but sometimes – to throw a proverb back to you – no answer is also an answer.'

Müller felt a momentary flash of anger, and knew it was evident in her reply. 'Meaning what, exactly?'

Helga held up her palms. 'As I said, I know it's not my place. And I'm not trying to interfere. I only want the best for you and these little darlings. All I meant was that in this case you could perhaps say "no *question* is also an answer". If he doesn't ask you, perhaps that tells you all you need to know.'

Müller didn't give her grandmother the satisfaction of a reply, even though she knew the woman meant well – and was probably correct in her warning.

Instead, she changed the subject. 'Look. There's one table free outside. Let's hurry and get it.'

The thorny subject of Müller's relationship with Emil was avoided for the rest of the family's short outing. But her worries around her new position were reawakened as they returned to Strausberger Platz and approached the apartment block's entrance. A telltale twitch of the curtains of the camper van parked outside. Even an innocent stroll with her children and their great-grandmother was being watched. Watched and, no doubt, recorded.

Later that day, after the removal men had finally gone, she, Emil and Helga were having a late lunch surrounded by crates of unpacked items from the old flat.

Müller had put Jannika and Johannes in their cots – but neither would settle. Emil, too, now seemed to be in a foul mood.

When Müller rose from the dining table for a third time, Helga got up instead and waved Müller to stay where she was.

'You two enjoy your meal. I'll go to them.'

Müller and Emil resumed eating, but in silence, other than the sound of Emil chewing his food, something that had recently begun grating on Müller. She was still attracted to him – he was a handsome man, of that there was no doubt. But she was starting to discover things about him that almost annoyed her more than Gottfried at his most infuriating. And the rhythmic sound of his mastication was just one in a growing list. His attitude to her grandmother, and what he saw as her constant interfering, was another.

He finally swallowed his mouthful.

'Should we discuss things?' ventured Müller.

'Discuss what? You seem to have made your decisions, and here we are.'

'I thought this was what you wanted, a bigger flat. You were always complaining the old one was too cramped. You always knew I was going to go back to work too. It's just happened a little more suddenly than expected.'

Emil pursed his lips, as though he was going to say more, but had then thought better of it.

'I'm going to need your support, Emil,' she pleaded. 'This new job . . . I have to give it my full attention, at least to begin with. And it's going to take me away from the Hauptstadt.'

'Not overnight, I hope.'

'No. Well . . . I hope not. But I've got to go and meet the rest of the team to follow up leads in Frankfurt and Eisenhüttenstadt this evening.' Müller became aware she was twisting her hair around a finger, something she often did when she was anxious.

'This evening? The first night in our new home? Well . . . *your* new home, as you like to point out.'

Müller put down her knife and fork. First the twins. Now Emil. She clearly wasn't going to get much more of her meal eaten.

Emil lapsed into a morose silence, interrupted by the harsh ringing of the telephone. As Müller moved to pick up the receiver, she saw him look at the telephone with disdain.

'Karin.' It was Tilsner. 'Have you got a moment?'

Just then, Johannes started screaming again. She saw Emil putting his hands to his ears.

'What is it, Werner?'

Before Tilsner had the chance to reply, she noticed from the corner of her eye Emil rising from his seat and putting on his coat. 'Hang on a second, Werner.' She placed her hand over the mouthpiece.

'Where are you going, Emil?' she whispered urgently.

'Back to the hospital. Someone covered for me this morning; in return I've got to do the late shift.'

'Hang on, we were going to—'

But he had gone, slamming the apartment door behind him. Müller took a couple of deep breaths to try to compose herself.

'Sorry, Werner. A bit of trouble with one of the children again.' A lie, but not far from the truth. These days she often felt Emil *was* acting like a spoilt child.

6

That evening
Frankfurt an der Oder

Another bar, another town in the Republic, this time at its eastern most limits. Across the river, linked to Frankfurt by a bridge, was Polish territory, and the town of Słubice.

Schmidt and Tilsner were already sitting at a table. Müller spotted them, walked across and sat down, folding her red rain coat across the seat back behind her.

'Did you settle in all right?' asked Tilsner.

'Yes and no,' replied Müller. Tilsner raised his eyebrows, prompting her to elucidate, but she didn't feel like it with Schmidt present. Instead, she shrugged. 'It's all fine,' she lied. In fact, she'd rung Emil at the hospital after his display of petulance, hoping to get to the bottom of why he seemed so moody. But the phone conversation had quickly deteriorated into another row. The fallout had been that he wasn't going to move in for the time being after all. Müller, Helga and the twins would be staying in the new Strausberger Platz apartment, Müller was adamant about that. But – for the moment at least – Emil was going to base himself in his own one-bed hospital apartment.

'What about you?' she asked, turning back to the case. 'Any progress in identifying our lake boy?'

'We think so, don't we, Jonas?'

Schmidt nodded. He still wasn't saying very much, but did at least seem to be in a better mood tonight. 'We think we've found your man, Comrade *Major*.' Her new rank seemed to roll easily off her *Kriminaltechniker*'s tongue, even though to her it still sounded strange – as though he was addressing someone else entirely.

'So have you tried to contact the parents yet?'

'Not as yet, no,' said Tilsner. 'We only found the relevant missing persons file late in the day. But the age, physical appearance and Eisenhüttenstadt link all seem to fit – although there was no mention of the tattoo. The file seems to have been put to one side, almost as though they didn't *want* us to find it. And there was a note attached to it, implying it was no longer a police matter.'

'What? Referred to another ministry?'

'Exactly. And I'm sure you can guess which one.'

Müller nodded, then frowned. 'But why?'

'I'm sure we'll find out in the fullness of time, *if* they want us to find out. Perhaps it's to do with the illegal payments scandal I was talking to you about. And –' Tilsner lowered his voice to a conspiratorial whisper – 'don't look now, and when you do, make sure it's not obvious, but directly behind you is a guy who I'm sure followed us all the way from the People's Police HQ, and still seems to be keeping his beady eyes on us. He's certainly not here to drink, because he's not touched a drop of his beer.'

'What's he look like?'

'Blond hair, fresh-faced. Handsome square jaw like me.' He rubbed his stubbled chin as Schmidt rolled his eyes. 'A bit like your Emil, actually.' Tilsner grinned. 'Though I don't think it is him. Unless you make a habit of fucking Stasi agents.'

Müller shook her head, but decided against giving Tilsner a dressing down, even though she didn't like him undermining her authority in front of Schmidt. In any case, there was no point. Tilsner would simply laugh it off. She'd have a good look at the man in question when she got up to go to the toilet.

'Anyway,' continued Tilsner, 'we've made you an appointment with the parents for tomorrow morning. As we thought, they live in Eisenhüttenstadt itself. The lad was an apprentice at the steelworks, so that's another lead. Although almost everyone in the town works at the steelworks, or has something to do with it. It's another new town – like Hoyerswerda and Ha-Neu, although here it's iron and steel that keeps the city's heart beating, not lignite or chemicals as with the other two. And we thought a woman's touch would help in breaking the news to them, didn't we, Jonas?'

'Well, I'm sure Comrade *Ober*— sorry, Comrade *Major* Müller will be more tactful than you would be, Comrade *Unter*— sorry, I'll get the hang of this eventually, will be more tactful than yourself, Comrade *Hauptmann*.'

'Hmph,' snorted Tilsner. 'Telling parents their child is dead is something I never want to excel at, Jonas, I can assure you.'

Müller took the opportunity provided by her two colleagues' verbal sparring to excuse herself and head to the toilets, making sure she took a good look at the alleged Stasi agent on the way. As she went past, she couldn't help catching the man's eye. A look passed between them and Müller found her heart rate quickening.

The next day the weather continued much in the same vein for Müller's drive back towards the Polish border from Berlin. Windy but bright. She parked her new Lada next to Tilsner's on Eisenhüttenstadt's main street as they tried to get their bearings to find the Nadels' apartment. Because the body they'd come to refer to as 'lake boy' now had a name. Eighteen-year-old Dominik Nadel.

Despite its industrial heritage, and the smoke billowing from the chimneys of the steelworks, the new town had a fresh, clean feel. At least at this time of year, the smogs that blighted the Hauptstadt and similarly Ha-Neu seemed to be absent. Perhaps that had something to do with the blustery September weather. The eye of everyone in the town was drawn to its industrial heart, however. The main street ran in a straight line right to the steel plant. It sat there, imperiously, on the horizon, reminding all the citizens why they were fortunate enough to have their own flat in the city. To work. To work for the Republic of Workers and Peasants.

Tilsner smoothed out his street map on top of the Wartburg, while Schmidt helped to hold down the corners as they flapped in the breeze.

'They live in *Wohnkomplex I* – so in the new town, but the oldest bit of the new town. Dates from the fifties, whereas these blocks round here –' Tilsner waved his arm in a sweeping gesture – 'these are much more recent. Look, they're still building over there.'

Müller could see the cranes moving, lifting into place the concrete slabs to make the walls of the newest blocks. The clatter and clangs of concrete and metal reverberated above the traffic noise.

'Where they live used to be the original Stalinstadt,' added Schmidt, pointing to the map. 'The first of our new towns, reputed to be the best.'

The construction of the original Stalinstadt sounded as though it was from the same era as her new home off Karl-Marx-Allee, thought Müller. And, like Karl-Marx-Allee, originally Stalin-Allee, it had been renamed once the moustachioed Comrade Stalin fell out of favour at the beginning of the sixties.

'Well, if you two know where you're going, lead the way and I'll follow behind.'

Müller decided a delegation of all three of them visiting the parents might be too much. So once they were there, she sent Schmidt off to liaise with the local forensic science team at the town's People's Police office, to see if they'd uncovered anything that might be of use to the investigation.

Outside the apartment entrance, Müller put on her red raincoat, ignoring Tilsner's raised eyebrows. Wearing it helped steel her for the unpleasant task ahead.

Whether Herr and Frau Nadel had any real idea of the information the police now possessed was hard to tell from their expressions. They seemed a timid couple, unwilling to make eye contact, both of them rubbing their hands together as they sat side by side on the apartment's dark-brown corduroy sofa.

'So, as you know, Herr and Frau Nadel, we've made this appointment because we're a new team looking into the disappearance of your son.' Müller was tempted to go straight in with the terrible news that Dominik had been found dead – murdered even – although she was going to spare them the details about a sock being stuffed down his throat. To come straight out with it was often the kindest way. But her aim was to find out information as much as to impart it. Sympathising with their loss would have to wait. If she told them immediately he was dead, they might clam up, or their grief might render the rest of the interview worthless. So, however heartless it might be, she was going to delay the news as long as possible.

'What can you tell us about Dominik? Anything would be helpful. His interests, his friends – any enemies he has – what sort of a boy he is.' Müller was careful to refer to their son in the present tense. 'That kind of thing. Has he ever done anything like this before?'

There was – initially – silence, as though both parents were too stunned to speak, or too weary from recounting the same story to a succession of police officers, of whom Müller and Tilsner were only the latest, and two who had yet to build up any sense of trust.

Eventually, Frau Nadel began to speak in a soft voice while her husband sat, eyes still downcast, still wringing his hands. 'He did go away for a while last year. But he said it was part of his apprenticeship.'

'Apprenticeship?' prodded Tilsner. He and Müller knew perfectly well where the boy was apprenticed, but the more they could get from the Nadels' own mouths, the more useful it was likely to be. And the more likely the parents would be to tell them something they *didn't* already know.

'At the steelworks. He was doing well, apparently. At least, that's what he told us.'

'What about girlfriends?' asked Müller. 'Was he going out with anyone?'

'He's a bit young for that.' The intervention came from Herr Nadel, and sounded defensive to Müller. Wrong too. Why was eighteen too young to be having a relationship? She saw Tilsner give her a look out of the corner of his eye. Evidently he thought the same.

'What about interests, hobbies? There must have been something in his life apart from work,' continued Müller.

'His motorbike. He's obsessed with that,' said the mother.

'Hmm. We should never have let him get one,' added the father, attracting a glare from his wife. 'There's no need to look at me like that. I'm going to tell them what I think. We need to be honest to help them find him.'

Müller ignored the pointed look Tilsner gave her. She wasn't yet ready to tell them about the body washed up on the banks of an artificial lake, some hundred kilometres or so to the south.

'When you say "obsessed", what do you mean?' probed Müller.

'Well, he's always toying with it. Taking it apart, putting it back together again, buying little bits to soup it up, that sort of thing. His hands were always filthy dirty . . .' Frau Nadel started to laugh at the memory, then the laughter died in her mouth and transformed itself into a strangled sob as the horrific reality of the present reasserted itself. 'Sorry, *are. Are* . . . always filthy.' She brought one hand up to wipe her eye, as her husband clasped the other and squeezed it. 'And then there were the club meetings.'

'Club meetings?' prompted Tilsner.

'Well, I think it was a club. He never really talked about the details to us. But he stopped going to the Free German Youth meetings to go to this motorbike club thing.'

'We tried to talk him out of it,' added Herr Nadel. 'Didn't we, *Liebling*? But he's always been a bit of a loner. Always wanted to do his own thing. He's a good socialist though.' His wife nodded at this.

Such a good little socialist he stopped going to communist youth meetings, thought Müller.

'So motorbikes were his only interest?' asked Tilsner. Müller knew what he was thinking. If that was the case, why the Stahl Eisenhüttenstadt tattoo? 'He wasn't the sporty type, nothing like that?'

'Well . . .' Frau Nadel hesitated.

'You might as well tell us everything, Frau Nadel,' said Müller. 'We need as much information as possible to help our inquiry.' The exact nature of the investigation – the fact that it had transformed from one involving a missing person to one of murder, and a particularly brutal and sadistic murder at that – was still something Müller wasn't prepared to divulge.

Dominik's mother sighed. 'He used to be very into football. He wanted to become a professional. Until he got involved with the motorbikes. We were sad he gave it up.'

'So he played for a team?' asked Tilsner.

Herr Nadel nodded. 'The youth team of the local club, BSG Stahl.'

'Stahl Eisenhüttenstadt?' said Tilsner, feigning surprise. 'They're a good team, aren't they? Used to be in the *Oberliga*.'

'Used to be,' confirmed Herr Nadel. Then seemed disinclined to say anything further.

'So he just gave up a promising career in football to mess around on his motorbike at weekends?' asked Müller. 'That seems strange.'

The Nadels both nodded in unison. 'We tried to dissuade him,' said the mother. 'But he wouldn't talk about it. Said he'd had it with football. I got the feeling he was being teased or bullied about something, but we never found out what.'

'He used to be a big Stahl fan, as well as one of their youth players,' said the father. 'He even had a tattoo of the team's emblem on his shoulder.'

'Which shoulder?' asked Müller, even though she and Tilsner knew very well what the answer was.

'His left,' said the mother. 'But he was so fed up with it, he was getting it removed. Stupid things, tattoos. I don't know why anyone would want to defile their body in that way. We were really angry about it. But at least he tried to get it off.'

'Tried?' asked Tilsner.

'It was such a big design, removing it was very painful. He managed to get about two-thirds of it off, and then I think the pain got too much for him and he stopped. Then it went septic, and the skin didn't heal properly . . .'

'It was a stupid thing to do,' said the father, shaking his head. 'But he's our son. Wherever he is, whatever he's been up to. We want him back.'

Müller realised she couldn't delay imparting the dreadful news any longer. She sighed heavily, and then inhaled just as deeply, to prepare herself for the moment.

'Herr and Frau Nadel . . .' Müller watched the faces of the two parents become quizzical, than fearful. 'We had to ask you this series of questions to establish the facts, but I'm afraid what you've just said about Dominik's tattoo has left no doubts.'

'W-w-what d-d-do you mean?' asked the mother, her voice querulous, as her husband moved his hand from hers to grip her in a hug.

Try as she might, Müller found she couldn't meet the woman's gaze, or that of her husband. Instead, she spotted a piece of fluff on the linoleum floor and spoke to that. 'We've found the body of a young male . . .'

'Oh my God!' shrieked the woman, burying her head in her husband's chest.

'. . . in Senftenberg, by the new lake there. We believe it's Dominik. I'm truly sorry . . .'

Out of the corner of her eye, Müller saw the husband's face suddenly erupt in fury. 'You knew all along, didn't you?' he shouted. 'Why didn't you just tell us, put us out of our misery?'

Müller met the eyes of each parent in turn. 'I am so sorry, but what you say about the partially removed tattoo leaves little doubt that this body is that of your son.'

'No! No! No!' cried the woman, beating her hands on her husband's abdomen.

Müller allowed the Nadels a few moments to comfort each other. 'I'm sorry, Frau and Herr Nadel. Truly, I am. But I am afraid we will need you to go to the mortuary in Hoyerswerda tomorrow to formally identify him. An officer of the People's Police will accompany you.'

7

'That didn't go so well,' said Tilsner. 'Maybe we should have strung them out a bit longer.'

'I didn't have the heart to, Werner, to be honest.'

The interview had pretty much come to an end as soon as Müller had revealed that the police were certain Dominik was dead. Müller hadn't gone into the sickening details of the cause of death, but even so, the two detectives could tell that the Nadels weren't going to say much more. Before they finally left the apartment, Müller had managed to get some contact details for Dominik's friends, few though they were: a couple of mates from his footballing days, and the names of fellow apprentices at the steelworks. They hadn't managed to find out any more about the mysterious motorbike club. When the initial shock of the news about their son had sunk in, they could try the parents again. Even if they had no further information, Tilsner assured Müller that by talking to motorbike dealerships the club – or gang – ought to be easy to track down.

Darkness had fallen as Tilsner drove out towards the steel-works along Lenin-Allee. Müller watched the queues outside the theatre, with its classical façade, and wished her own evening's entertainment were something a little lighter than a murder inquiry. She chastised herself too that she hadn't yet phoned home to check that Helga was coping with the twins. Neither had she phoned Emil. She looked across at Tilsner, his square jaw even more be-stubbled than usual, highlighted in a flashing yellow glow as they drove past each street light into semi-darkness. It felt easy, comfortable, slipping back into the old routine. She and Tilsner working together.

Directly ahead, the glow of the steelworks illuminated an ever-present plume of pollution. With the wind having finally dropped, it looked like a stairway of white cloud connecting to the heavens.

The steelworks of Ironworks City – known to the locals as *EKO*.

She and Tilsner hadn't understood the reference to start with, as the Nadels – through their grief – reluctantly gave them a list of Dominik's contacts, most of whom they already knew from liaising with the local police team. It turned out it was an acronym for the plant that was the beating heart of this town, and one of the beating hearts of the Republic. *EKO*. Also known as *Eisenhüttenkombinat Ost* – the former workplace of Dominik Nadel, deceased.

After showing their *Kripo* IDs at the reception, Müller and Tilsner were kitted out with hard hats, protective overalls, and steel-toed boots before being allowed to venture further into the complex. And even then they were accompanied every step of the way by a senior worker.

Müller found herself working up a sweat under the heavy overalls. Although the night-time air had cooled, here in the complex it felt like high summer. The two detectives had established that Dominik had been – until recently – an apprentice in the blast furnace area, one of the most unforgiving jobs according to the stocky, ruddy-faced worker who was showing them round.

'I managed to get out of it,' he said, gruffly. 'It's a hard job. You go home at the end of each shift feeling like *you've* been baked in the oven, rather than the iron. I don't think it was the most popular of apprenticeships. But once you're skilled in doing it, it's a job for life – if that's what you want.'

Müller bit her tongue. Every job in the Republic was a job for life, if that was what the worker wanted.

They came to another changing area, with lockers and hooks covered in overalls similar to the ones they were wearing.

'You'll have to change again here, I'm afraid, if you insist on actually seeing where Nadel worked.'

Müller watched Tilsner nod at the man with a resigned expression. On the way, he'd argued that all they needed to do was find out if any of Dominik's old colleagues were on shift, and then call them away to a side room to interview them, rather than actually going into the work area itself. Müller had demurred. The best policing, in her view, was policing that actually reconstructed the life of victims and possible perpetrators.

That's how you got under their skin. Discovered what was really driving them.

You entered and understood their lives.

You actually lived it.

So this must be how a Cosmonaut feels, thought Müller. *Except they have the advantage of weightlessness in outer space*. Instead, she and Tilsner were horribly weighed down by heat-resistant white suits and overboots. Worst of all, though, was the face mask, with its heat-proof shield. Tilsner looked like something out of a western science fiction movie, and although there was no mirror for Müller to examine herself in, she was sure she looked equally ridiculous.

Heat-proof was in any case a bit of a misnomer. Inside, Müller felt her temperature rising as she struggled to put even one foot in front of the other. Their escort had given up trying to communicate verbally and was simply using basic hand signals to direct them. Her earlier decision to overrule Tilsner's idea of conducting the interviews away from the work area was now looking misguided, if not downright stupid.

Their escort – who, inside his oversized suit, looked more like an inflatable figure, one that would surely explode in this heat – had now changed his arm gestures to a kind of all-encompassing circular wave. Müller surmised that it meant they'd finally reached the exact site of Dominik Nadel's former workplace. They'd been told that one of the workers currently on shift had been a fellow apprentice with their victim. Now their companion was pointing towards a figure wielding some sort of long-handled shovel, who was using it to feed material into a white-hot ball of fire. Even with the protective shield on her face mask closed, Müller found herself having to clumsily lift her forearm to protect her eyes from the glare. One thing was obvious – Tilsner had been correct. There was no way, no way at all, that they would be able to interview the worker here.

Once they'd retreated to a side office, away from the stifling heat of the blast furnace, Müller loosened the protective clothes as quickly as possible. Their escort opened a floor-to-ceiling cupboard and threw Tilsner and her a towel and fresh set of overalls each.

'I'll go and get someone to relieve him at the furnace, and I'll bring him here,' he said.

Müller waited for the man to exit the room before she took her outer layer of clothing off completely and started to wipe down her body. Both her knickers and T-shirt were soaked with sweat. She was grateful she was wearing a bra. Before having the twins she hadn't always bothered. Even now, Tilsner was showing an unhealthy interest.

'It's sweat, Werner. That's all it is. Perfectly natural.'

Tilsner said nothing, but unpeeled his own shirt and started rubbing himself down. She, in turn, found herself staring at him. *I've never seen him do any exercise. How the hell does he keep so toned?* Tilsner suddenly looked up and caught her gaze, even though she quickly dropped it.

'It's sweat, Karin,' he mimicked her. 'That's all it is. Perfectly natural.'

Müller's face burned with embarrassment – even more than it had earlier from the heat of the steel mill.

Before they'd had a chance to get into the overalls, there was a knock on the door.

'Just wait a minute, please,' shouted Müller.

She hurriedly dressed, then checked her hair and make-up with her compact mirror. Her face was flushed and her eyeliner had smudged. She tried to effect some running repairs with the end of the towel, and then smoothed down her blond hair, trying to get it back to its usual sleek straightness, even though it looked like she'd been out in a force eight gale in driving rain.

'Come in,' she shouted.

The youth, little more than a boy, really, thought Müller, stopped as soon as he was through the doorway, struggling to meet their eyes and shifting from foot to foot as though he needed to use the toilet.

'Citizen Schneider said you wanted to talk to me about something,' he finally said.

'That's right,' said Tilsner. 'I gather you used to work with Dominik Nadel.'

'For a few months,' shrugged the youth. 'I don't know him very well.'

'OK,' said Müller. 'Well, this is *Hauptmann* Tilsner, and I'm *Major* Müller. We work for the People's Police. And you are?'

'Robrecht. Robrecht Manshalle. I was an apprentice with Nadel for a short time. But we were never friends.'

'OK. We understand that, Robrecht,' said Müller. 'But anything you can tell us will be very useful.'

The youth was silent and continued to shuffle from one foot to the other.

'Well?' bellowed Tilsner. 'You heard the Comrade *Major*. Start talking. Now.'

'I didn't like him. Not many people in Hütte do. We didn't get on.'

For an instant, Müller was confused by the use of 'Hütte'. Then she realised it was probably the nickname locals used for Eisenhüttenstadt.

'Not liking him isn't particularly useful for us,' said Tilsner. 'You'll need to try a bit harder than that. Failing to pass on relevant information to the police is a crime. If we arrest you, that's your safe little steelworks job out the window in no time.'

The youth sighed and brought his hands up to cover his face.

'OK. Well . . . I don't know this first-hand, you understand. I'm not like that. I won't have anything to do with guys like that.'

'Guys like what?' asked Müller.

'You know, *that* sort.'

'*What* sort?' shouted Tilsner. 'Spit it out. Don't talk in riddles.'

But Müller had guessed what the youth meant even before he'd vocalised it.

'Queers,' Manshalle finally said. 'Dominik Nadel was a queer.'

8

Six months earlier (March 1976)
The road to Frankfurt an der Oder

We seem to be going further this week. Last week we took the turning to Stienitzsee lake and hung out at the Strandbad. But this time, Jan, who's leading the motorbike convoy, with me riding pillion, just carries straight on, on *Fernverkehrsstrasse* 1. I don't know where we're going. I hope we won't be late again. Mutti and Vati were angry enough last week.

I move my head forward and to the side, trying to get as close to Jan's ear as possible. 'Where are we heading?' I shout.

He says something back, but it's lost in the onrushing air.

'What?'

He turns his head slightly towards me, while trying to keep half an eye on the road.

'You'll see. It's a surprise.'

I've never been one for surprises, really. I like a bit of certainty in my life. But to be with Jan, to be part of their gang, I'm happy to go along with it. I hug my arms round his midriff again, tightly. And just as he did last week, he takes one hand from the handlebars and presses it against mine. There's a slight downward pressure. My hands slip down his leathers a couple of centimetres. I feel a little embarrassed, but there's also a warm feeling in the pit of my stomach.

I feel wanted. Needed.

We stop on the outskirts of Frankfurt, in what looks like an old, disused industrial area. Everyone dismounts and heads towards one of the low buildings. I can hear the boom of loud rock music through the walls even before anyone opens the doors. When they do, the noise is overwhelming. It looks like everyone else has been here before. The man on the door lets them all in.

But then he stops me, with a heavy hand against my chest. When he realises what's happened, Jan, who'd gone on ahead inside, turns back and grabs my hand to pull me in.

'He's with me,' he tells the doorman. It sounds proprietorial – as though he owns me.

I rather like it.

Inside all is in semi-darkness, even though it's still daylight outside, except for the flashing coloured lights that seem to pulse to the same beat as the music. I'm not even sure what music is being played. Jan is still holding one of my hands. With the other, I try to waft away the smoke. So many people are smoking in here and the smell is pungent, sickly sweet, like nothing I've ever smelt before.

Suddenly I know what it is, and I'm frightened.

Weed, pot.

Jesus, these people would be jailed if this place were raided by the police. I also feel disloyal. My father is a policeman – well, he's a forensic scientist – and he's warned me about places like this.

But Jan seems unconcerned. He pulls out a sheaf of cigarette papers and a packet of rolling tobacco. He pinches some of the tobacco between his thumb and forefinger, then spreads it over one of the unwrapped papers. Then he fishes in his pocket for something else. A small block of something wrapped in a twisted paper wrapper. He opens the package, breaks off a small piece and starts crumbling it into the tobacco, spreading it out. He rolls the cigarette up. Someone offers him a light from their own joint. He bends over and I see each of the tips glow orange in the darkness – two tiny spots of fire.

He turns to me.

'Do you want to try some, little Markus?'

I don't like it when he says that. '*Little Markus.*' It's like he's making fun of me, like I'm his plaything. I'm nervous, but I don't want to let him down. Don't want to be the spoilsport, the teacher's pet of a policeman's son.

I hold out my hand, expecting him to pass me the joint.

But instead, he grips my hand and pulls me towards him so we're face to face in the gloom. 'Like this,' he whispers. I watch him take a long drag as I breathe in the aroma of sharp sweetness.

Then he leans forward, and we're not just face to face but mouth to mouth. I open my mouth and breathe in the pungent fumes. He pulls his face away slightly, but keeps staring right into my eyes. As though he can suck the soul from my body.

'Hold it, breathe it right down into your lungs, then just let it out slowly.' I do as he says, conscious all the time that his arm has stayed round my waist, pulling me tightly into him. I let the smoke trail languidly from my mouth and nose, feeling the hit from the drug almost instantly. I feel light, giggly, happy, as though I've finally found myself.

Jan leans in again and I assume he's about to feed me another hit, mouth to mouth like before. I don't realise until his lips are on mine and both our mouths are open that there is no smoke in his lungs this time. He's not feeding me cannabis fumes. Instead, his tongue is in my mouth and I don't resist it. I don't resist either as his hand drops down from my back, pulling my buttocks forward, pressing me into him.

9

Two months later (May 1976)
A forest in East Germany

'It's a motion sensor. As soon as anyone gets in the car, it triggers.'

The Stasi officer nodded, peering down at the device. 'And how reliable is it?'

'As long as it's placed correctly, then virtually one hundred per cent reliable.'

'Virtually?' He looked sharply at the other man. He was a scientist. A disgraced scientist. Some sort of sexual impropriety. Doing this work was his ticket out of jail. The Stasi officer wasn't sure exactly what, and furthermore didn't care. All he needed was a compliant expert.

'They use them all the time in Ireland. If the IRA use them, you can be sure they're as reliable as you can get.'

'Let's see. It's always safest to taste something before deciding to eat it.'

The man asked for help fixing the explosives to the underside of the vehicle. The officer declined. They couldn't afford any of this to be traced back; he didn't want to leave any forensic traces. There would be a record – on some card index, in some office somewhere. The Ministry liked its records. But no names of those involved would be mentioned.

The problem was finding something of a similar weight to the target. Something that moved in a similar way. The officer had had to call in some favours at the Tierpark. No one refused to offer the Ministry for State Security a favour, not if they knew what was good for them.

They'd trained the animal over a number of weeks. It wasn't an unintelligent beast, but it was larger than many of its species. Hungrier. It soon learnt how to open the driver's door of the Mercedes, much in the same way a human would. It learnt to put the ignition key in the slot the correct way, and to turn it to the start position. Unless it did exactly that, the animal didn't get its reward of a piece of fruit. And as – during its training period – its usual meals had been restricted, that piece of fruit tasted particularly sweet and delicious.

From their hideout, deep in the trees, the two men watched through binoculars. The animal had been released from the back of a truck by another Ministry agent, who was under strict instructions to drive off immediately and not look back. He had no idea what the purpose of his task was.

At first, the beast didn't seem to spot the car.

When it did, it sauntered over furtively, its head swivelling all the while, checking it had no rivals for the prize.

Knowing what it had to do, it approached the unlocked driver's door.

The Stasi officer could feel the tension in the other man crouched by his side. If anything went wrong, he knew he would be locked back up in Hohenschönhausen. Perhaps, even worse, sent to Bautzen II.

They saw the sunlight hit the metal of the key as the animal lifted it and placed it in the ignition slot.

There were a couple of seconds when even the Stasi officer felt some of the tension. He knew the man next to him would be virtually unable to breathe.

And then the explosion came. The flash of light first, orange and white.

Then microseconds later, the boom, and the pressure wave hitting their faces. The forest was now in near silence, the only sound the pitter-patter of shrapnel and ash as it fell like rain.

After perhaps a minute, the birdsong started again. Nature starting to reassert itself.

He heard the man next to him exhale in relief: a job well done. But the Stasi officer himself experienced a fleeting moment of regret. Regret at the destruction. Not for the life of the overweight chimpanzee that had no doubt been blown into thousands of pieces of sinew and bone, its soft tissue destroyed, its last meal – that tantalising piece of fruit – never eaten.

No. His regret was for the Mercedes. A symbol of western decadence – of western capitalism, perhaps. But they were damn fine motors.

10

Four months later (September 1976)
Eisenhüttenstadt

'Where's Schmidt?' asked Tilsner. 'I thought he was supposed to be liaising with the local forensic team to see if there's anything more they can tell us? It's not like him to say no to a free meal.'

All three had arranged to meet in a nice-looking restaurant Müller had spotted on the Strasse des Komsomol – an attractive street that bisected *Wohnkomplex II* – but the *Kriminaltechniker* was missing.

'I gave him leave to return to the Hauptstadt,' said Müller, while perusing the menu.

'Why the hell did you do that? I'd like to return to the bloody Hauptstadt, but this is the first inquiry to be handed to our new specialist team. If we mess this up, it won't take long for them to decide it's all a stupid idea. And then bang goes our promotions, the extra cash that goes with them, and we'll no doubt be sent out on the beat again. Or, worse than that, sent to traffic to give out speeding and parking tickets for the rest of our miserable little lives.'

Müller let her head slump forward onto her hands. 'Give it a rest, Werner. He said there were urgent family problems to deal with.'

'He pulled that one in Halle-Neustadt too. What precisely *are* these urgent family problems? Presumably you found out before allowing him to go swanning off?'

Müller ignored the question. 'What do you fancy? I think I'm going to be boring and go for the *Goldbroiler* and chips.'

Tilsner slapped the table. 'Karin! Answer the question.'

'Shush,' she hissed, glancing round the restaurant, worried in case other diners started to take an interest in the tetchy exchange. She lowered her voice. 'Whether or not I asked him exactly what these serious family issues were before I gave him leave is none of your business. And even if he *had* told me, with the mood you're in, I'm not about to share his secrets with you.' She put the menu down in a slow, deliberate movement. 'Now, what are you going to eat? Or shall we just forget about this and go straight back to the hotel?'

Tilsner pursed his lips and began to leaf through the menu.

The truth was, Müller hadn't asked Schmidt exactly what the problems were. Something to do with his son Markus, just as it had been in Ha-Neu. But this time there was more urgency, more fear in the request to his superior. Müller had simply decided that his mind wouldn't be on the job if he were to stay. They would be better off availing themselves of the forensic scientists in Hütte or Frankfurt for the time being, should they need to.

The comments from Robrecht Manshalle, back at the steelworks, disturbed her too. Homosexuality – male or female – was something that held little interest for her. She knew her own tastes were strictly heterosexual, but homosexuality wasn't a crime in the Republic, even if there were some who wished it still were. It was another area in which their small country was more open-minded, more fair-minded, than parts of the West. The way Manshalle had talked about Dominik Nadel, however, spoke of insularity and prejudice. Müller found it unsettling.

She was chewing this over in her mind, and waiting for Tilsner to finally choose his meal, when her deputy kicked her under the table.

Müller was about to tear him off a strip, when he interrupted her. 'Don't look now. But Frankfurt Fred – the blond boy from the bar the other night – is about to pay us a visit again. They're certainly active here.'

Instead of turning round, Müller reached into her handbag and pulled out her make-up compact. She flipped up the lid and angled it so the mirror showed her the reflection of the doorway. At that very moment, in walked the Stasi officer – or at least the man they'd assumed was a Stasi officer – who'd kept an eye on them in the Frankfurt bar.

Why the close interest? Was he part of one of these Stasi Special Commissions that Reiniger had warned her about? As she continued to study him surreptitiously, Tilsner kicked her gently again.

'He's not that good-looking, you know,' he whispered. 'And I'm ready to order.'

11

The next day
Eisenhüttenstadt

'You wouldn't believe this was once an *Oberliga* ground, and that even Dynamo Berlin were scared of coming here,' said Tilsner.

'Why wouldn't I believe that?' They were sitting in the front seats of Müller's Lada, although Tilsner was on the driver's side. They'd left Tilsner's car in the Frankfurt People's Police compound. He'd fancied a bit of Soviet luxury – or semi-luxury – for a change, over the East German practicality of a Wartburg. 'Not that I care, of course. I have no interest in football at all. But why wouldn't I believe that?'

'Look around. Crappy little ground, tin sheds for stands – and only two of them at that. It looks more like a village club.'

Müller shrugged and climbed out of the car. Through a gap in the fencing surrounding the ground she could see a training session under way. Shouts pierced the air as the players were thrown ball after ball by one of the coaches, and one by one set off weaving their way in and out of what looked like plastic traffic cones.

When Tilsner caught up with her, Müller realised they'd been too busy theorising about the case in the short journey from Frankfurt to have discussed their tactics for the morning. Whether to interview the players and staff individually or as a group. It made sense to do it individually, in case anyone was hiding anything.

'I want us both to conduct each interview,' said Müller. 'If I'm asking the questions, you concentrate on the body language, and vice versa.'

Their main interest was in those who'd played with or coached Dominik Nadel. During the time Nadel had been in the youth team, as Tilsner had pointed out, the first team were in the Republic's *Oberliga*, the highest division. At least a couple of Nadel's contemporaries had now moved on to bigger and better things. They went through the printed list provided for them by the local People's Police, who'd been in charge of the missing persons inquiry until it had turned into a murder hunt. One was currently playing for Tilsner's team, Dynamo Berlin, in the Hauptstadt.

'I need to go back to Berlin tomorrow, in any case, to see the kids and Helga,' said Müller.

'They're OK, I hope?' said Tilsner.

'They're fine. She's fine. But I'm their mother. I've already been away for two nights on the trot. I don't want them to forget me.'

'Who could forget *you*, Karin?'

Müller matched her deputy's sarcasm with an insincere smile. 'You're such a charmer. Anyway, what about the others?'

'One's a promising striker, snapped up by Dynamo Dresden. So unless we want another trip down south we'll have to leave him – or do him by phone.'

'I don't want to do a telephone interview. It's too easy to lie over the phone. One or both of us will have to go back to Hoyerswerda at some stage I'm sure. Dresden's not too far from there. What about the others who are still here?'

Tilsner looked down at the list again. 'We could start with number one.'

'What's that mean?'

'The keeper. Used to be the youth team keeper, but he's graduated to the first team now.'

'OK. Let's call him in.'

Karlheinz Pohl was a gangling young man who towered over both Müller and Tilsner. Müller gestured to the chair on the other side of the table they'd set up for interviews in the club bar, and the rangy goalkeeper sat down awkwardly into it.

'How's it going?' asked Tilsner, to break the ice. 'Do you have a match this weekend?'

'Yes,' replied Pohl. 'Away to BSG Chemie Wilhelm-Pieck-Stadt.'

Müller was surprised how high his voice sounded. Almost like that of a young boy. Yet he was at least late teens, possibly even twenty. The voice contrasted oddly with his masculinity too. Although he was tall, Müller had noticed he was muscular, and the menthol-like smell of liniment that had no doubt been applied to those aching muscles sat heavy in the air, alongside the more obvious musk of a sweaty male body.

'So, Guben?' asked Tilsner. Wilhelm Pieck – East Germany's first president – was from Guben, although that part of the town was now Polish territory. Müller knew Pieck's name had been appended to Guben's in the early sixties. The full name for the town was now the slightly unfeasible Wilhelm-Pieck-Stadt Guben. Only those nicknamed 'one-hundred-and-fifty per centers' – who spouted every Party diktat at every opportunity – bothered with its full title.

'That's right. They're top of the league. Although there's a few murmurs of discontent because they draw their players from the other side of the river too.'

'The Oder?' Müller asked.

'No, the Neisse. But it flows into the Oder within a few kilometres.'

'So they have Polish players on their team?' asked Tilsner. 'Doesn't seem fair, does it?'

'No,' laughed Pohl. 'We'll have our work cut out.'

'Anyway, as you can probably guess, it's not really football we want to talk about, at least not directly,' said Müller. 'What we *are* interested in is anything you can tell us about Dominik Nadel, who I think you used to play with in the youth team here.'

Pohl nodded. He seemed untroubled. 'I've already told the local police everything I know. Which isn't very much. I liked Dom. But not everyone here did. He had a bit of a falling out.'

'Over what?' asked Tilsner.

Pohl hesitated before answering. Then he frowned. 'It's not really my place to say.'

'It certainly is your place to say because that question is being posed by the police. And we're not just any old police. We're the criminal police. The *K*.'

'It was the *Kripo* that I talked to before.'

'We know that,' said Müller. 'But the nature of the inquiry has changed now. Dominik's been found.'

The relief was obvious on the young goalkeeper's face. 'Found? Well that's great news.'

'Hmm,' said Tilsner. 'Not so great for Dominik, or his parents. He *has* been found. Found murdered.'

Pohl's complexion immediately went white. 'Jesus.'

A name it is sometimes unwise to utter in the Republic, thought Müller. She gave the young man a few seconds to let the news sink in. 'So, Karlheinz. As you can imagine, this inquiry takes on a totally different tone. Therefore we need to know everything you told the local police. And anything more you can think of.'

The picture that emerged was one of a keen young footballer who, although shy, was initially popular. According to Pohl, Dominik Nadel was a talented midfielder – although still a little lightweight. The club's hope had been that he would bulk up as he grew. But something had happened to sour the relationship between Nadel and the club. Pohl seemed unsure – or unwilling to divulge – what that was.

'So suddenly, almost overnight, Dominik Nadel went from being a popular member of the youth squad to being an outcast?

And you've no idea why that was. Is that what you're saying?' asked Tilsner.

'That's right.'

Müller noticed the goalkeeper's eyes dart to the left as he said this. It was a classic sign of deceit.

'About the same time, or soon after, something went wrong at the club too, didn't it?' asked Müller.

'You could say that. In fact that would be an understatement.'

'You dropped down two divisions due to financial irregularities,' said Tilsner.

Pohl nodded.

'Were the two things connected?' asked Müller.

'What two things?'

Tilsner sighed slowly. 'Don't try to play us for fools, Karlheinz. Dominik's fall from grace and the payments scandal. The Comrade *Major* here asked if they were connected.'

'Not as far as I know.' Eyes left again, noted Müller. She was fairly certain Pohl knew more than he was letting on. But for the moment, it didn't look like they were going to be able to force him to reveal what that was.

'OK. Let's leave that for now,' she said. 'What about Dominik as a person? Did he have a girlfriend as far as you know?'

The young man blushed slightly. 'No.'

'Don't you find that strange?' asked Tilsner. 'He was a good-looking lad by all accounts.'

Pohl shrugged.

'I think you know why he didn't have a girlfriend, don't you, Karlheinz?' asked Müller.

The young goalkeeper gave a resigned sigh. 'OK. Look, I know why you're asking the question. But it's not something I knew about or suspected while he was here. It's just something I've heard rumoured since he's gone missing.'

'He's no longer missing. As we told you, he's been found. Murdered.'

Frustrated, Pohl breathed in and out slowly through his nose, with his mouth pursed shut. 'I know. Anyway, I know what you're driving at. That he was a homo. But as I say, I've only heard that second-hand. And there were no whispers of that sort while he was here. Certainly not as far as I knew.'

The story was the same with all the other players and coaches on their list. All seemed, to Müller, to be holding something back. None would admit to knowing why Dominik Nadel had fallen out with the club, or why anyone would want to kill him.

Their final interviewee was the youth team coach. He kept up the party line. But at the end of the interview, as they left the room, Müller felt something brush her side, almost as if someone were trying to pick her jacket pocket. Tilsner was ahead of her, already marching down the corridor, so it clearly hadn't been him. She turned towards the coach and he gave an almost imperceptible shake of his head.

Müller surreptitiously ran her hand over the jacket pocket. Something – a piece of paper or an envelope – had been placed into it. Why – and why so secretively? Perhaps he suspected Tilsner of being a Stasi agent. If that were the case, he was probably correct, although Tilsner was more complicated than that, and Müller was never too sure where his loyalties lay. What she did know was that he had never let her down.

Müller wondered if the man knew the room where they had been conducting the interview was bugged. By video surveillance, audio surveillance, or both. With the ever-present Stasi agent following them, the Stasi's interest in her – and their latest investigation – had heightened. Clearly they had an interest in the local football team too.

12

Müller wasn't sure this was going to work. The sense of disapproval from Helga hung heavily in the apartment. Even the twins didn't seem to want to smile for their mama.

'I'm sorry, Helga. I hadn't expected to be away for two nights. I know that wasn't really part of the deal.'

'You've a difficult job. I understand it can't be regular hours.'

But despite what her grandmother said, she felt guilty, and felt as though Helga *wanted* her to feel guilty, to make sure the same thing wouldn't happen again. She knew Jannika and Johannes at six months old were too young to be apart from their mother overnight. In any case, their base at Frankfurt was only around a hundred kilometres from Berlin. She would just have to drive there and back each day – unless there was a really dramatic development.

Perhaps the football coach might provide that.

All his note had said was that he was willing to meet, and talk, but that it would have to be in three days' time, after their crunch match with Guben, and that it would need to be at a bar in Neuzelle, a village just to the south of Hütte.

Her body felt like it needed to rest in the new apartment – she'd hardly had a chance to enjoy the surroundings – but Emil had taken advantage of her return to Berlin to arrange to meet for coffee. She had a sense of dread about what he might be about to say.

Müller could see that Helga was tired. The thrill of quasi motherhood for someone who was actually the twins' great-grandmother had kept her adrenalin pumping, but now Müller was back she could see the older woman wilting before her eyes. Müller would take the twins with her for the short walk to the Kino International – Emil had suggested meeting in the bar there.

Despite their difficulties, which in many ways echoed those she'd had with Gottfried, there was genuine warmth in Emil's greeting, and some of her feelings of apprehension dissipated.

'How have they been?' he asked, glancing towards the twins as they slept in the pushchair Müller had brought up in the lift. 'They both look well.'

'They are. We're all settling in, although this new case is over in Eisenhüttenstadt, which means I've been away more than I'd like. And *you've* been away more than I'd like. I want you to be part of their lives . . . to be part of my life. There's so much more space in the new flat. I wish you'd move back in with us. Now

Helga has her own room it's so much better. I've even bought her a second-hand television . . . she doesn't need to be in the lounge all the time any more.'

Emil smiled. *When he does that, his face lights up. He looks like the man I first fell for last year in Ha-Neu. I'd be mad to lose him*, thought Müller.

'I've been thinking too. I'd like to give it another try, if you would.'

Müller felt her heart pound. *Of course I would give it another try*. She leant towards him, pulled his face towards hers, and kissed him full on the lips. She saw the barman smirking at them. She didn't care.

Müller was perfectly content in her near ignorance of football. But she was aware that Tilsner's team – Dynamo Berlin – was the subject of allegations that its patron, Stasi head Erick Mielke, had intervened to try to weaken its main rival – Dresden. Supposedly, he'd forced the transfer of Dresden players to the Berlin side.

For her meeting with Florian Voigt, the young full back who played with Dominik Nadel on Eisenhüttenstadt's youth team, and who was now starring in Dynamo Berlin's attempt to finally beat Dresden to the title, she knew she'd be forced to travel out to Hohenschönhausen again, the scene of Gottfried's incarceration in the Stasi jail. Thankfully, Dynamo's home stadium, at the Sportforum Berlin, wasn't actually within the closed Stasi area, otherwise she doubted she'd have got permission to interview Voigt.

But she had. And she hoped this might finally give her and Tilsner their breakthrough.

What immediately struck her about Voigt was that he was small. Small and wiry, with wiry hair to match. Diminutive was probably the way the sports reporters would describe him. He was also – Müller quickly realised – extremely nervous. Perhaps it was just his age. He *did* look like a teenager. But he must be used to playing in front of big crowds every week. Surely that would make him immune to nerves?

Unless he had something to hide.

And she was sure *someone* involved with the former youth team at BSG Stahl *did* have something to hide.

Voigt refused her offer of a seat in the changing room she'd been assigned to talk to him in. Instead, he suggested going for a stroll around the perimeter of the pitch.

'I won't feel as nervous there,' he explained.

Once they were out on the pitch he immediately apologised.

'Sorry. I hope you didn't think I was being uncooperative in there. It's just . . . well, there is more privacy here. In an open space. If you know what I mean.'

'You mean someone could have been listening to our conversation in there?'

The youth stopped in his tracks and looked her straight in the eyes. 'You do *know* who in effect runs this team, don't you?'

Müller nodded.

'Well, that answers your question, then. One more thing, if you want me to talk, this has to be off the record.'

Müller frowned. '*Off the record?* I'm a police officer, Florian. Not a journalist. I don't do off the record.'

'Well, those are my conditions.'

This time it was Müller's turn to stop in her tracks. 'Look, I don't know what American detective shows you've been watching on western TV. But that's not the way we do things in the Republic.' She watched his mouth turn down. 'However . . .' She held her hands up. 'I can't easily take notes as we're walking along. And I don't have a tape recorder with me, not that I'm going to let you frisk me to check.' She smiled at him. 'That's about as off the record as it's going to get.'

'OK. But what I'm about to tell you can't be made public. And can't be used against me.'

Müller frowned. 'Not being made public? Fine, I give you my word. As for using it against you, as long as you haven't committed a crime, then you have nothing to fear on that score. *Have* you committed a crime?'

The young footballer didn't answer for a few seconds, and instead resumed his walk around the perimeter of the ground, beckoning Müller to follow. At one end of the pitch, one of the team's goalkeepers was throwing himself from side to side as a coach fired in ball after ball towards the goal. But they were both out of earshot, and no one else was within sight. Nevertheless, Voigt gave a furtive glance around every corner of the ground before he started speaking again.

'Do you know Dominik was homosexual?'

'Yes,' nodded Müller.

The young footballer raised his eyebrows. 'Ah. Then there might not be much I can tell you that you don't already know.'

'Is that why he was ostracised from BSG?'

Voigt shook his head vigorously. 'No, no. As far as I know, no one there knew. It's not something you advertise at a football club, believe me.'

'So how did you know?' asked Müller.

Again, Voigt checked there was no one in earshot or in sight before answering. 'How do you think I knew?'

Realisation suddenly dawned for Müller.

'Exactly. That's why I didn't want to talk to you in the changing room.'

'So you were lovers?'

'No, no. Don't be daft. Dominik could get anyone he wanted. He wouldn't be interested in someone like me. He was a pretty boy, and he preferred pretty boys.'

'So how did you find out?'

They'd reached the end of the ground where the goalkeeper was saving shots. Voigt lowered his voice further when he answered, to ensure neither the keeper nor his coach could hear.

'You know Dom was a keen motorcyclist?'

Müller nodded.

'Well, let's just say the group he was involved with wasn't just about motorbikes. It was bikes . . . and a bit of fun too. Man-to-man fun. If you understand what I mean.'

'How do you know that?'

Voigt sighed. 'OK, well this is another tricky bit. An off-the-record bit.' He paused, waiting for some sort of sign from Müller.

She gave a long sigh. 'OK, OK. Off the record.'

'Well, when I said I hadn't committed a crime, that wasn't entirely true.'

'Careful, Florian,' warned Müller. 'I made it quite clear our agreement only holds if there is no crime involved.'

'It's only a little crime.'

'What?'

'Smoking dope. Pot.'

'OK.'

'OK, what?'

'OK, I'm not interested in low-level dope smoking. That's not to say some of my other colleagues wouldn't be. Just make sure we don't find you with any. Now, how does this relate to Dominik Nadel? And does it have any relevance to his murder?'

The young footballer stopped in his tracks and turned to the detective. 'Murder? Oh my God! I'd heard he was missing, but that's awful. I'm so sorry. I liked Dom. I had a lot of time for him.'

Müller breathed in slowly. They'd almost completed a full lap of the pitch by now, but she got the feeling Voigt still hadn't got round to the key thing he wanted to tell her.

'So come on, then, Florian. I've said it's off the record. Where does this all fit in?'

'Their bike group met at a club on the outskirts of Frankfurt.'

Müller was of course well aware of this already. But she wanted to keep Voigt talking to see if he had any new information to reveal. 'And why were you there?'

'I think I've made that clear, haven't I? But I wasn't part of the motorbike gang. I just saw them there. And saw Dominik there.'

'Do you know the motorbike group's name?'

The footballer shook his head. 'No. But I can tell you the names of some of the members . . . as long as you keep my name out of it, and as long as you forget what I told you about the dope. And I can tell you the address of the club. They're there virtually every Sunday afternoon.'

13

Six months earlier
Pankow, East Berlin

It's late by the time we get back to Pankow and my family apartment. My head is still buzzing from the dope. And that kiss. It hurts me, though, that Jan seemed stand-offish the rest of the time at the club. Flirting with some of the others. I realise that's not what I want. I want him for myself.

My mood lifts on the journey back though. I was worried he might choose someone else to ride pillion. After all, not everyone there had a bike. Some were like me and had just hitched along for the ride. I hold him tightly all the way back, though I notice this time his hand isn't over mine.

When we get back to mine, I get off the bike. It looks like he's about to drive straight off, but instead he gets off too, kicks the side stand on, and then takes his helmet off.

'Are you coming in?' I ask, slightly alarmed. I don't think my parents will appreciate it.

'No, don't worry, little Markus.' He moves over towards me, gently undoes the helmet chin clasp, and lifts the protective headgear away. 'We were quite naughty today, weren't we?'

I nod, wary of his playful tone. Wary, too, that he's standing so close to me outside our apartment block. Someone might see.

'Do you enjoy being naughty, little Markus?' He grabs me round my lower back and pulls me towards him, our groins crushing together again. Just like at the club. And then he's leaning in for a kiss. But at the last moment, he lets me go and laughs.

'You thought I was going to kiss you, didn't you? I was just checking your breath to make sure you don't still smell of dope.' He thrusts something into my hand and then curls my fingers round it. I look down. It's a packet of mints.

'Put some in your pretty little mouth now, Markus. Before your policeman daddy finds out what you've been up to.' As he says this, he looks up pointedly at the windows of our flat. To my horror I see the curtain has, until that instant, been held open, and someone has just let it fall back into place.

Someone who's been watching us.

Jan knows too.

'I hope they enjoyed the show,' he laughs.

I use my key to let myself in, hoping against hope that I was imagining the curtain moving. As I get into the hall I see my father there waiting, glowering at me through his thick-glassed spectacles – the ones that match mine.

'Get ... in ... there ... now.' He whispers the words as he points to my bedroom, enunciating each one with menace. I go into my room. He follows, and slams the door behind us.

'I saw that,' he says, in the same vicious voice.

'What do you mean?' I've got to try to brazen it out, to convince him he was mistaken.

'Kissing . . . that other . . .' He can't bring himself to say it.

'I don't know what you think you saw. But you're mistaken, Father. Jan was simply taking off my helmet.'

I see the look of doubt enter his eyes. Maybe, just maybe, all isn't lost yet.

'I don't want you to see him again.'

'What?! He's my friend. We've done nothing wrong. You're putting two and two together and making five.'

My father holds his hand up, palm outwards. 'No more, Markus. No son of mine is going to turn out like that. I forbid you to see him. That's an end to it. I mean it.' His voice quivers with rage. I've never seen him like this before. I can feel the tears welling in my eyes.

After standing there a moment, looking at me like I'm a piece of dog shit, he turns on his heels and exits, slamming the door behind him.

I flop down on the bed face first. I bury my head in the pillow. I don't want to fall out with my father. But I won't bend to his wishes. I will see Jan again if I want to . . . and I know I want to.

I move the pillow round so that it's under me, lengthways. And then I pretend it's Jan, that he's comforting me, and press myself into it.

14

Six months later (September 1976)
Strausberger Platz, East Berlin

Emil was back in her bed. Müller had hugged him to her on the sofa, but had no need to try to excite him. He seemed to be on fire. As soon as they were in the bedroom, alone at last, he tore at her clothes, literally ripping her underwear off. She was already aroused, but the sound of the material tearing – the expensive, western material, the last pair she'd secreted away from her and Tilsner's trip over the Wall some eighteen months earlier – well, that made her even more ready.

Suddenly the doorbell began to ring. Urgently, one press after another. Emil – lost in the moment – seemed to want to ignore it. Müller knew she couldn't. She wriggled out of his grip, got up and put on her dressing gown.

Helga was already up, answering the entryphone.

She passed the handset to Müller.

Müller cupped her hand over the mouthpiece. 'Sorry, Helga,' she whispered. 'I'll deal with it. You go back to sleep.'

'I couldn't sleep anyway,' her grandmother said, trudging back to her bedroom. There was an accusatory tone to her voice.

Müller turned her attention back to the entryphone.

'Comrade *Major*! Is that you?' The voice sounded familiar, but with her mind elsewhere she couldn't immediately place it.

'Who is this, please?'

'Comrade *Major*! Thank God. It's Jonas. *Kriminaltechniker* Jonas Schmidt. You've got to help me. Please.'

'Calm down, Jonas. What's so urgent at this time of night?' She glanced down at her watch. It was already the morning – nearly 1 a.m.

'It's Markus, my son. He's disappeared.'

Schmidt – even in the half-light of the street lamps – looked a complete mess. His shirt half-unbuttoned, his hair greasy and uncombed, and a wild look in his eyes behind the thick spectacles.

'I don't know what to do,' he sobbed. 'I just don't know what to do.'

Müller placed her hand lightly on his shoulder. 'Are you all right to drive?'

'Yes, I think so. I drove here. Why? Where are we going?'

'Let's go back to your apartment. Get all the facts straight, and then proceed in a logical way.'

'But he's not there. I know he's not there.'

'I know, Jonas. But Markus isn't a young child. He's nearly a man. He's eighteen, isn't he?'

Schmidt nodded, his head slumping forwards.

'Well, then. In my experience with boys of that age, they haven't really gone missing at all. They'll just be staying at a friend's . . . or a girlfriend's.'

Schmidt shook his head violently. 'No, no. You don't understand. You see, we had an argument. A really bad argument. He said he never wanted to see me again.'

Müller placed both her hands on Schmidt's shoulders.

'A lot of things said in the heat of the moment are forgotten about the next day. Let's get over to your place, talk to your wife, and go through all of Markus's movements. I'm sure we'll be able to work out where he is, and then you two can make it up.'

'So when was the last time you saw him?'

Müller had insisted that Schmidt and his wife sit down in the kitchen while she made them both a coffee. The forensic officer was clearly at the end of his tether, and in that state the information he provided was likely to be less than helpful.

'Two days ago.'

'Two days?'

Schmidt nodded. 'That's why I had to come back from Eisenhüttenstadt. We'd had another row.'

'Another?'

'It all started last year when we were involved in the missing baby case in Halle-Neustadt. That's why I was quite glad the team was slimmed down at one point and I was allowed to return to Berlin.'

Frau Schmidt, her nightgown pulled tightly up to her chin, nodded in assent. 'He was getting bullied and teased at school.

He would regularly come home with his glasses broken after some fight or other.'

'Are you sure it was bullying, and that he wasn't the one starting the fights?'

Schmidt shook his head. 'Markus isn't the sort to start a fight, I can assure you, Comrade *Major*.'

'OK, so he was getting bullied, but that was several months ago,' said Müller. 'Did something change, or did it just get worse?'

'Well,' Frau Schmidt answered, 'at first I was pleased. He found this new friend who he used to hang around with at weekends. He suddenly seemed happier, more alive.'

'But that didn't continue?' prompted Müller.

'Jonas, do you want to explain?' There was a hard edge to the woman's voice, as though she blamed her husband for something.

Jonas Schmidt pressed his hands against his face then lowered them slowly. This was clearly painful for him. 'Markus and I have always been close,' he sighed. 'I'd hoped he might follow me into a scientific career with the police.'

'You put too much pressure on him at school,' said his wife.

'Maybe,' shrugged Schmidt. 'If so, I'm sorry. I only wanted what's best for him. I'd do anything for him – you know that, Hanne.'

Hanne Schmidt just sat there glowering at her husband.

'So you had an argument about his school results?' asked Müller.

'No ... well, yes, but that's not what this is all about. That was before. I'd come to accept it all – all the school stuff. I don't think he doesn't try. He's intelligent, I know that, just not academic, if you know what I mean?' There was a pleading look in Schmidt's eyes. His wife nudged the cup of coffee Müller had made in front of him, and encouraged him to drink it.

'I understand,' said Müller. 'But this latest argument, these latest arguments weren't about that?'

'No . . . it was . . . it was something more personal.'

Müller sighed. 'Jonas, I will do what I can to help to find your son, although in my experience with teenage boys they tend to turn up eventually anyway. But I can only do that if you're fully open with me, if you tell me everything. Do you understand?'

Schmidt took a long gulp of coffee. 'This friendship he developed with the boy who protected him from the bullying. Jan. Jan Winkler. I wasn't happy about it.'

'Why?' Müller asked. She was starting to get slightly nervous about what Schmidt was about to tell her.

'I felt it was unhealthy. Two boys like that.' Schmidt looked at her. His expression full of meaning. He wasn't prepared to say the word, he wasn't prepared to label his son as one of them, but Müller knew full well what he was talking about. It was Dominik Nadel all over again.

'And this led to the arguments?'

Schmidt rotated the cup of coffee in his hands, again and again. Müller inhaled the aroma, and wished she'd made a mug for herself too. 'We had a big showdown. The first time was about six months ago. This Jan boy had just dropped him off outside. I thought I saw them kissing.'

Hanne Schmidt tutted. 'How could you accuse him without being sure?'

Schmidt hung his head. 'I just wanted to do my best for him. To protect him. That's all. Anyway, he denied it all. Said the boy was just helping him with something, that's why they were so close together. I thought it would blow over.'

'Did you apologise?' asked Müller.

'What?'

'Did you say sorry?'

'No, as I said, I just thought it would blow over.'

His wife sighed again.

'But it didn't. The next day was the first time he ran away.'

Müller threw her hands up in the air in exasperation. 'Jonas! So he's done it before. He's come back before. Why didn't you tell me that earlier? Why do you think this time is any different?'

Schmidt shook his head. 'I just know. That's all. Something's happened. He's never been away this long before. He's in trouble. I know he is.'

'That's all very well, Jonas,' said his wife. 'But Comrade *Oberleutnant* Müller—'

'*Major*,' said Schmidt. 'Comrade Müller here has been promoted now, I told you, *Liebling*.'

'Oh, I'm sorry Com—'

'It doesn't matter, Frau Schmidt. Honestly. Karin is fine. Just call me Karin.'

'What I was going to say to my husband, Karin, is that you need hard information. Facts to try to help to find Markus.'

Müller nodded.

'I think you need to look at that club they used to go to.'

'Hanne!' warned Schmidt.

'What? She needs to know. It's the only way we're going to find him. They used to go to this club on Sunday afternoons. I found a ticket in Markus's pocket when I was cleaning his clothes one day. He clammed up when I tried to talk to him about it. And sometimes, when they came back, I could smell—'

'Hanne, no! This is just tittle-tattle. I don't want you mentioning—'

'Marijuana,' his wife said, with grim determination.

Schmidt sighed angrily.

'I'm sure that's what it was,' Hanne continued.

'And where exactly was this club?' asked Müller. But in her mind she was already making the link – to Dominik Nadel. Her blood ran cold. It was a big leap, a huge coincidence, but she was sure – somehow – it was the same club.

'In Frankfurt. Frankfurt Oder, of course.'

Müller tried to keep her expression neutral. Then she thought back to something Schmidt had said a little earlier. *This Jan boy had just dropped him off outside.* A car, Müller had assumed. Now she knew differently.

Once again, her next question was redundant. But she asked it to make sure. 'And how did they get to and from Frankfurt O?'

'Winkler had a motorbike. Probably acquired for him by his father,' spat Schmidt. 'Then Markus saved up and got one too. Although I don't know how he did that with the amount of pocket money we gave him, or how he jumped the waiting list. Maybe Winkler could tell you. Although I'd tread carefully there.'

Müller furrowed her brow. 'Why do you say that?'

'His father. He's a high-up,' said Frau Schmidt, scarcely disguising her contempt.

'A high-up where?' asked Müller.

Schmidt took over from his wife. 'We never got to the bottom of that. But either the government, or the Party, or . . .'

The forensic officer didn't complete the sentence. He didn't have to. Müller understood his meaning.

The government.

The Party.

Or the Stasi.

15

Müller was tempted simply to haul Winkler in for questioning, despite the Schmidts' veiled warning. Not in relation to Markus Schmidt, whom she was still confident would turn up unharmed – but to find out if he really did have any connection to Dominik Nadel. That was, after all, her and Tilsner's main inquiry. But perhaps a more subtle approach might get better results, and be less likely to prompt his influential father to interfere in the investigation. Meanwhile she convinced Jonas and his wife that their cause would be best served if they tried to get some sleep. Müller did the same, although she didn't get back to Strausberger Platz till 3 a.m. after diverting to Keibelstrasse to put out an all-bulletins alert for Markus.

She tried to be as quiet as possible re-entering the apartment, hoping she wouldn't disturb the twins, her grandmother, or Emil. But her partner emerged bleary-eyed from the bedroom.

'Sorry. I didn't mean to wake you.'

Emil raised a smile. 'It's fine, *Liebling*.' He kissed her lightly on the lips, and Müller felt such a rush of emotion she had to fight back tears. He was a lovely man. He was the father of her wonderful children. And she wanted it to work. 'Do you want me to make you a coffee or something?'

'No, but that's sweet of you. You go back to bed. I'll be there in a moment.'

She'd thought Emil would be annoyed about the disruption to their first weekend together in the new flat. But he seemed genuinely delighted to be spending time with the twins and putting his own stamp on the apartment, moving stuff across gradually from his hospital flat.

They wouldn't be spending Sunday together either, because she had a job to do that afternoon. And, to that end, she summoned Tilsner on the police radio and told him to put what he was doing in Eisenhüttenstadt on hold, and to return to the Hauptstadt immediately.

'You look quite fetching in that.' Müller was admiring Tilsner's new uniform of black motorbike leathers, and a helmet not unlike the ones they'd both had to wear when visiting the blast furnace in Hütte.

'Hmm. I hope the People's Police have sorted the proper insurance for me. I'm happy enough riding a motorbike, but four wheels are always safer than two – and I don't like the look of that weather.'

Dark clouds had gathered over the Hauptstadt. October was fast approaching, along with the changeable autumn weather it always brought, but despite the cloud cover, Müller knew that rain wasn't forecast. Or, at worst, light rain or drizzle in scattered bursts. It wouldn't be bad enough to prevent Jan Winkler and his friends from making their regular excursion to the eastern edge of the Republic.

Tilsner revved the machine, which responded with a throaty roar. Müller – using the privileges her new position brought – had managed to secure a powerful bike for him from the police pool. She'd insisted on an unmarked one, used for surveillance and tracking activities. Although it was unmarked, it still had a police radio hidden in the helmet. It was an MZ ETS Trophy Sport – its 250cc engine enough to take it up to a top speed of over 130 kilometres per hour – and in demand in the capitalist West as well as friendly socialist countries, helping to bring in much-needed hard currency for the Republic.

Tilsner saw her staring at the speedometer. 'I know what you're thinking. But I won't be going that fast, I can assure you. From what Jonas says, all these teenagers have much less powerful machines – little more than mopeds or small scooters.' He looked up at the sky once again, and then dropped his helmet visor. His next sentence came out muffled from behind the plastic screen, but she just about made out what he was saying. 'As long as it doesn't rain. If it does, you'll probably be picking little pieces of me, and this,' he slapped the fuel tank to emphasise the point, 'off the surface of the road.'

They knew approximately the route the bikers, led by Winkler, planned to take. They weren't expecting Markus Schmidt to be there – apparently he and Winkler had fallen out and he no longer joined the group on their weekly jaunts, or at least that's what his parents claimed.

Müller was surprised how smart Winkler's home was. But given what the Schmidts had said about his father, perhaps not that surprised. An attractive detached house in a tree-lined road. Unusual in the more central parts of Berlin, where apartments – either historic ones like Müller's old one in Schönhauser Allee, or the new *Plattenbauten* planned for suburbs like Marzahn – were the order of the day.

The teens on their motorbikes gathered and circled outside the Winkler home. They looked almost like the racehorses Gottfried had enjoyed watching on western TV, herded by the starter into an approximate straight line before the tape was raised. Here the starter was Winkler himself, and he was joining in the race.

Müller and Tilsner had discussed tactics. She would follow first in the Lada, to try to avoid any suspicion. Tilsner would in turn follow her, but once they hit traffic – as they knew they would – Tilsner would take up the chase. Although Voigt had given them the address of the club, Müller wanted to check whether other riders joined the convoy en route. Other riders who could lead them to Markus Schmidt and, more importantly, the killer of Dominik Nadel.

Müller soon found she was lagging behind. Although the Lada was faster than any of the bikes in the convoy, and could even give Tilsner's supercharged machine a run for his money, it couldn't weave through the traffic in the same way. Once she'd lost them, she decided she might as well take the motorway route to Frankfurt, rather than *Fernverkehrsstrassen* 1 and 5 – the main non-motorway roads. The motorway swung south of Frankfurt. It was further. But at the Lada's maximum speed, she might still get there first. Going the other way, she would never catch up.

The old industrial building housing the club was in a run-down area just off Route 112 – the main road between Frankfurt and Eisenhüttenstadt – on the banks of the Oder–Spree canal, the waterway that linked the Oder river to Berlin.

Müller parked in the shadow of a building, where she had a clear view of the club entrance.

She'd clearly made up time with the motorway detour, as it was some ten minutes before Winkler and his gang arrived in a cacophony of tinny noise. Some of the bikers started circling the cinder yard, deliberately making their machines skid to a halt, a bit like speedway riders taking a corner.

Out of the corner of her eye, a few seconds after the convoy arrived, she saw Tilsner's machine passing the entrance. He would double back and join her once they were all safely inside.

'What are we actually hoping to achieve by this?' he asked once he was with her in their lookout – a disused shed to the side of the complex, with a broken window, and piles of dirt and empty sacks over the floor. To Tilsner's obvious distaste, Müller had partially concealed herself under some of the sacks, and was gesturing to her deputy to do the same.

'What choice did we have?'

'Plenty. I'd have taken this Winkler fellow in and given him a bit of a frightener. See if he's prepared to cough.'

'I don't want to do that yet. I want to give him as much rope as he needs for as long as we can.' Müller also wanted to fully clarify Winkler's father's position before she did anything to rile either him – or his son. If they gathered evidence of any wrongdoing on the part of the son first, it might put them in a stronger position. 'Did you find out anything on the journey?'

'Other than that riding more than a hundred kilometres on a motorbike is bloody uncomfortable? No.' Tilsner shook his head. 'Not a sausage. You?'

Müller sighed and shook her head. Perhaps her deputy was right. Perhaps this was a waste of time.

'Maybe we should just raid the whole place?' suggested Tilsner. 'We know there's drug taking going on.'

'It's only cannabis.'

'It's illegal though, isn't it?'

Tilsner's moaning that they were wasting their time was interrupted when Winkler and another youth came out of the club's front door.

'What are they up to?' he whispered.

There seemed to be some sort of exchange between the two. Winkler gave the shorter teen something, and then in return received some sort of package, which he slipped into the pocket of his motorcycle jacket. The two then shook hands. The shorter teen, instead of going back into the club, got onto his bike, and roared off towards Frankfurt.

'Do we follow?' asked Tilsner.

'We don't know who he is or what he's doing. It might just be another wild-goose chase. It's Winkler I'm more interested in.'

Winkler had now gone over to a wall at the side of the building and removed what looked like a brick. Müller couldn't see clearly enough. He either placed something in the wall, or took something from it. She wasn't sure.

'*Scheisse*, he's doing a runner too,' Tilsner hissed. 'Look, he's putting his helmet on. Shall I follow?'

Müller had wondered if they should get uniform or the local *Kripo* involved in their stake-out. She'd discounted it – this was just a fishing expedition, and she hadn't wanted to waste more manpower. Now she had a choice. Let Tilsner chase Winkler alone, with all the dangers involved in that. She wasn't sure if, once he caught up with him, he wouldn't just beat the teen to a pulp to get information out of him. Or she went too. She also wanted to check what Winkler had been placing – or taking from – behind the brick. But that would have to wait.

'OK, *we'll* follow,' she said.

'There's no point, Karin. You can't keep pace in a car.'

'I'm not going in the car. I'm coming on the back of the bike with you.'

If she'd thought for a moment longer she'd have realised it was an utterly stupid idea. Almost as bad as when she'd insisted they go it alone in the Harz in the graveyard girl case – nearly getting them both killed in the process. Tilsner had been seriously injured then. It was testament to his recovery that these days she didn't think about that incident. In the missing baby case, his injuries had still troubled him. Now he seemed fully fit.

She hunched into his back, holding tightly just under his chest.

'I bet you're enjoying this,' she shouted, hoping to be heard above the roar of the engine and the rush of air as they sped along behind Winkler. He'd turned left out of the club yard, which had surprised them, and seemed to be heading towards Hütte – or perhaps further south. *As far as Senftenberg, perhaps? If there really was a connection there, and it wasn't just a conveni-ent dumping ground for Dominik Nadel's body.*

Tilsner had been concentrating on the road ahead and their quarry speeding along it, so it took a few seconds before he replied to her question. He had to turn his head to the side, and shouted towards her helmet – or rather *his* helmet. They only had the one, and he'd insisted she wear it.

'I'd enjoy it a heck of a lot more if I were able to sit at the back. With my arms wrapped round *your* chest.'

She punched him in the back.

'Oi! Watch it.' The bike wobbled alarmingly, but Tilsner man-aged to get it back under control. Under her helmet, Müller felt her face burn. It had been a stupid thing to do.

Then Tilsner was trying to shout at her again, at the same time as jabbing his gloved finger towards the left-hand wing mirror. 'Look. We've got company.'

Müller could see two motorbikes on their tail in the reflective glass. She turned her head to look over her shoulder for a better look. Both riders had black helmets and reflective visors. But it didn't appear to be any of the teens from the club – even with her limited knowledge of motorbikes, Müller could tell these were much more powerful machines.

One of the bikes moved up alongside them, accelerating easily, confirming Müller's estimate of its power. The rider started to gesture with his arm, indicating they should pull over. He accelerated further forward, and then the second rider was parallel with them, just a couple of metres behind his colleague.

Again, the same hand signals from the second rider.

Müller could see the bridge ahead, which took them over the canal. Tilsner had been forced towards the road edge, the wheels spraying road dust and dirt up into his face. Müller could see – and feel – him trying to shield his eyes with one hand, with no visor to protect them.

The bridge was fast approaching.

The road narrowed as it crossed. They were heading straight for the iron railings at its side.

She could feel Tilsner trying to force the machine back onto the road.

'Hang on!' he shouted.

It looked like he'd managed to force the MZ far enough over; they might just squeeze through the gap and over the bridge.

The rider alongside raised his right hand. Müller was convinced he was about to push her and Tilsner to their deaths. She braced herself, ready to jump clear.

Instead he just waved, adjusted his helmet and accelerated away.

Tilsner successfully rejoined the asphalt road a split second before they reached the bridge.

Once across, he slowed to a halt, and Müller felt her heart rate begin to return to normal once more.

'What was all that about?' she shouted to her deputy, as the motorbike's engine idled beneath them.

Tilsner shrugged. 'I've no idea. And I've no idea who they were either.'

But Müller could make a very good guess who they might be.

16

Five months earlier (April 1976)
Outskirts of Frankfurt an der Oder

Something's changed between Jan and me. He still lets me ride pillion to the club this week, but once we get inside he seems to be avoiding me. In fact, everyone seems to be avoiding me.

The new thing is pills. I don't trust them. Jan says they make the world a faster place, a more exciting place. For me, fast isn't good. I prefer the mellowness of dope, the giggliness, the fun. The fact you don't have a hangover the next day. About the only friendly thing Jan did today, as we set off from Pankow, was thrust a handful of pills into my hand.

'Take one now,' he said. 'They feel fantastic when you're on the bike. The world just whizzes by. It feels like you're starring in a feature film. And all the colours seem so bright. You should try it.'

I don't take his advice, and instead put the pills in my pocket. When he's not looking, I'll throw them away.

I look furtively up at the apartment windows. I wonder if my father's watching again. We've made our peace – but the atmosphere between us is still awkward. I think my running away from home before made him think. Perhaps he won't be so hard on me in future.

The music booms out as usual, but nothing seems as much fun. I sit in the corner, leaning back, just smoking dope. Far too much, probably. It's a fine line between feeling *nicely* happy, then *too* happy, and finally, starting to worry. I'm worrying now. I'm not sure what about. But one thing that worries me is seeing Jan dancing with another guy. I'm sure he's just trying to make me jealous. But then, if he does go off with him, how will I get back to the Hauptstadt, to Pankow? The world starts to spin. I think I'm going to throw up.

I run outside and lean over, my eyes closed as the pressure bursts in my head and I empty my guts. I feel so awful. I don't think I can face going back to Berlin sitting on the back of a motorbike. I don't think I'll be able to cling on. As it is, I can hardly even stand.

I crouch down on my haunches. Holding my head as though it's going to explode into tiny pieces. My eyes closed. Trying to breathe slowly, deeply.

Eyes closed.

So I don't see them coming.

The first I realise is when my breath is being knocked out of me, wanting to be sick again as one of them hits me hard in my stomach. They're pinning me back against the wall. Leather jackets. Sunglasses. But they're not bikers.

I feel my arms being yanked up behind my back, wrists shackled, metal cutting into my skin as I try to wriggle free.

'Markus Schmidt.' *How do they know my name? How do they know my name?!*

'You're under arrest.' *Arrest! Scheisse! What will happen to my father now? My mother? He'll lose his job. We'll be thrown out of our apartment. He'll hate me even more.*

One of them is waving something in front of my face. I try to focus. My eyes won't let me. But I see an emblem. A shield. A muscular arm. Holding up an automatic rifle – I've seen it before somewhere. But I can't place it.

Then I read the words. The Ministry for State Security. The Stasi.

Now there are camera flashes going off.

I finally find my voice.

'Arrest?' I slur. 'But I haven't done anything.' Even as I speak the words, I know my breath – and the sickly-sweet smell wafting on it – will give me away. I've been smoking dope all afternoon. That's enough for them.

But it's not the dope they're interested in.

The cameras are still flashing as one of them reaches into my pocket. I suddenly remember. *The pills.* And it's not every pocket they're searching – just that one. *The one where I put the pills. The pills I meant to throw away. The pills given to me by . . .*

And then all of a sudden, my mind clears.

I know who's done this. I know why they aren't searching every one of my pockets. Only one person knew what I'd put into that pocket.

The person who gave me the pills.

The boy I thought was my only friend. Perhaps more than that.

The boy who protected me from the bullies.

Jan Winkler.

17

Five months later (September 1976)
The banks of the Oder–Spree canal

Within an hour they were back at the club. Loud rock music was still pounding away inside.

'Shall we keep watch again?' asked Müller.

Tilsner shook his head. 'We need to go somewhere and talk everything through. We need a better plan, Karin. I don't want to go haring off on daft motorcycle chases again. Can we do some real detective work, please?'

Before they left – while making sure no one was watching them – Müller checked behind the loose brick that Winkler had moved. There was nothing there. Whatever it had been, the youth had taken it with him.

In the event, Tilsner's plea for a meeting to thrash out where they went next went unheeded. Not because Müller disagreed with him. What he said made sense. The news of Markus Schmidt's disappearance had distracted Müller. At first she'd been sure it was just another teenage row – and that Markus would be home before they'd managed to get any search into gear. The news about the links to the Frankfurt club – the possible connection to Dominik Nadel, the fact that Jan Winkler had been behaving so suspiciously – it all left her with a deep sense of unease about the fate of her forensic officer's son.

No, the reason Tilsner's idea didn't get off the ground was that, as soon as they reached the Frankfurt People's Police offices where they'd planned to find a room for their meeting, Müller was handed a note by the receptionist. She tore open the envelope and began to read.

'Who's it from?' asked Tilsner.

'Your opposite number in Senftenberg. Helmut Schwarz. That pathologist has some new information, he says.'

'What information?'

'She's not prepared to discuss it over the phone or in writing.'

'Well, that's not very helpful. What then?'

'She wants to meet us in Hoyerswerda.'

'When?'

'As soon as possible. And there's no time like the present.'

'Oh God. Not another drive. Can't we have the evening off? Go to a bar? Discuss the case?'

Müller shook her head. 'If I'm going to be away from the twins another night, I don't want to waste it. We might as well go now. It's only a couple of hours' drive.'

In fact, the journey was slightly shorter. When she rang Schwarz, he suggested meeting in the bar of the same Interhotel at Senftenberger See lakeside that the two Berlin detectives had stayed in before.

It didn't seem as though Dr Gudrun Fenstermacher approved.

'Not my idea, this,' she said. 'I'd have been happy with a café. But you police officers obviously have healthy expense accounts.'

'Still, it's very good of you to make yourself available on a Sunday, Comrade Fenstermacher,' said Müller.

The older woman glowered. 'She prefers *Citizen*,' interjected Tilsner. This brought a nod and a smile from the pathologist.

'So, *Citizen* Fenstermacher,' continued Müller. 'What is it you've found?'

Fenstermacher lowered her voice conspiratorially. 'It's a bit strange. I've not seen anything like it before.'

Müller wondered why – if the woman thought it necessary to lower her voice in order not to be heard – they were meeting in an Interhotel bar. With the number of western businessmen visiting Interhotels, they were likely to be the most spied-upon places in the Republic. But that decision must have been Schwarz's. And perhaps *Hauptmann* Schwarz – like his fellow police captain, Werner Tilsner – wasn't averse to serving two masters at the same time.

'Strange in what way?' asked Tilsner.

'Unusual chemical compounds in the body. I've only just got the test results through. Well, they came on Friday, but initially I wanted to check on them and work out what they meant.'

'And what exactly were these chemicals?'

'A surfeit of testosterone and metabolites from the break-down of testosterone – testosterone glucuronide, testosterone sulphate. That sort of thing. So, odd hormone levels. I can give you a full list if that's helpful, but all you need to know, really, is that they're all linked to testosterone. Too much of it.'

'Couldn't that happen naturally?' asked Müller

'Not at these sorts of levels it couldn't. And there was some-thing else that made me suspicious.'

'What?' asked Tilsner.

'Well, perhaps it's my own fault. It was something I noticed at the autopsy but dismissed. I put it down to pitting of the skin due to extended contact with water. But there were injection marks, all in a similar place. At first I thought perhaps it was simply a vaccination scar.'

'Where?' asked Müller.

'On the victim's upper left arm just below the shoulder.'

'Which is the usual place for a vaccination scar, isn't it?' asked Tilsner. 'So why do you now think it wasn't one?'

'It's not quite the right pattern. The test results prompted me to have another look at the photos I took of the body.'

'And your conclusion?' asked Müller.

'My conclusion is that the victim was repeatedly injected into the upper arm.'

Müller frowned. 'With testosterone? Why would anyone do that?'

'Possibly with testosterone. Or possibly with some other drug that's already washed out of his system that would have prompted an overproduction of testosterone. As to why, well, then we'd be entering the realms of speculation and, as I've already told you, I don't like to speculate if I can help it.'

'But if I were to twist your arm?' smiled Tilsner with his most winning smile.

'If you were to twist my arm, dear *Hauptmann*, I would probably use the other one to punch you in the face. Or use my leg to knee you in the groin.' Tilsner laughed. Müller just wished the woman would get on with it. 'However, as it's you, and as the People's Police – as usual – seem to have sent so many officers to talk to me about this particularly nasty killing, I will indulge you for once. My best guess is that this young man was restrained in some way, and forcibly injected. Several times. That's why there are also marks on his wrists.'

'Who would do something like that, though?' asked Müller.

'Ah. Well that, you see, *Major*, isn't my problem. And I have to say I'm rather glad it isn't. Germany has a bit of a history of this sort of thing, much as I love my homeland. There was a lot of it before the war, and during it.'

'But that was the Nazis,' said Müller.

'They were still Germans, dear. But perhaps I'm wrong. Perhaps my conclusions are incorrect. If I am correct, however, you might find this is a can of worms you'll come to wish you'd never opened.'

18

Five months earlier (April 1976)
Frankfurt an der Oder Stasi office

The light is blinding and my head is pounding. I want to be sick again, but I know there is nothing left in my body except bile. And the ever-repeating thought in my head is, *I wish I'd listened to my father. I wish I'd listened to my father.*

'So, Markus,' said the officer sitting behind the desk. 'You still deny knowing anything about these pills. Your *story* – and I have to be honest, I think it's exactly that, a *story* – is that the drugs must have been planted. Is that correct?'

I know he doesn't believe me, but equally I know I cannot implicate Jan. In any case, now I've planted the lie, I have to see it through.

'OK. Let's assume you're telling the truth.' He reaches into a folder on the desk, which otherwise simply has a single typewriter, a single light, and a telephone. 'How, then, do you account for this?'

It's a black-and-white photo of me outside the club. Clearly being handed something by another youth of about my age.

I can't remember his name. Oh yes, Florian. That was it. On what was it, my second visit there? Jan had told me Florian could give me a packet of mints. They'd been brought over from Poland, just across the bridge from Frankfurt. I'd handed him a five-mark note and he'd given me change and the unbranded mints.

'I was buying some sweets.'

The Stasi officer rocked back on his chair, laughing from deep within his stomach. 'Of course, sweets. Not drugs, sweets.'

'They were mints.'

'Unusual sweets to be buying outside an illegal club, don't you think?'

I shrug.

The office raises his eyebrows. 'Of course, you don't have to answer my questions. Could you also take a look at this photograph?'

It's the same scene. Only this time, the unbranded packet of mints in my hand has been enlarged.

'What brand of mints are they?'

'They don't have a brand marked.'

'Why not?'

'They were imported from Poland.'

'*Polish* mints. Aha. Why, then, don't they have Polish writing on? Why don't they have a Polish brand name? There's nothing wrong with buying sweets in Poland and selling them in the Republic. It's not a crime.'

'I thought—'

'Hmm, no, I think that's where you're wrong. You didn't think. You didn't think ahead. To the consequences of your

actions. Your actions in buying a quantity of amphetamines –
an illegal drug – and then using them, and having them in your
possession. Of course, this photograph isn't necessarily of you
buying them. Here, have a look.'

He shows me similar photographs, obviously taken a few
seconds apart, when I bought the mints. He places them on the
table facing me. One – on the left – shows the note, or notes,
in my hand. The second – on the right – shows the unbranded
packet of mints in my hand.

'So you're saying the left comes before the right? That this
transaction shows you buying a packet of –' he pauses, and
coughs sarcastically – 'a packet of *unbranded* mints, not that I've
seen a packet of unbranded mints before.'

He pauses again, and switches the photos. So that the one
with me holding the mints is on the left, the one with the money
on the right.

'What if the story is this way round? What if there's a time
stamp that proves that?' I feel a mounting sense of dread. There
are date and time stamps. I look at them. Even I can see that the
photo now on the left is – allegedly – from five seconds before
the one on the right.

'That's not right!' I shout. 'I was buying them, not selling
them.'

'Calm down, Markus. Calm down. I've already said that
it's not a crime to sell Polish mints in the Republic.' I see him
frown. It's a false frown. A play-acting frown. 'Aha,' he says,
this time with false surprise. 'I see the problem now. You're
worried that they're *not* mints, and that we're right, and they're

amphetamines. It wouldn't really matter, then, if they're Polish or not, would it?'

I know I look defeated. I know they've defeated me. I know I've let my father down. I let him down with my school results, and now this. And this is far, far worse.

'It wouldn't matter, because we have evidence of you possessing amphetamines. You were caught red-handed by our agents outside the club. But we also,' he pointed to the doctored photos, each in turn, 'have evidence of you *selling* amphetamines. Dealing in drugs. And that, Markus, is a very different ball game.'

19

Five months later (September 1976)
Neuzelle, Bezirk Frankfurt

The choice of bar of Günther Klug, the youth team coach from BSG Stahl Eisenhüttenstadt, evidently met with Tilsner's approval.

'This is more like it,' he said.

For Müller, Neuzelle itself – a historic Prussian village full of lovely old buildings – was totally different to Hütte, a few kilometres north. But both were dominated by an institution – a building or series of buildings – that had come to define the locality. In the latter's case it was the steel complex of Eisenhüttenkombinat Ost, and its iconic address of Number 1, Work Street. For the former, it was the beautiful abbey that rose on a slight hill above the Oder valley. Each making sure the citizens worshipped their particular gods – the god of work and communism in Hütte, and the god of religion in Neuzelle.

They spotted Klug in the far corner of the bar, already nursing a small beer.

'Thanks for agreeing to this meeting, Günther.'

'My pleasure,' replied the football coach, in little more than a whisper. 'But I'd appreciate it if we could keep our voices as low as possible. You never know who's listening, and what I have to say is . . . well, a little controversial. It might be seen as disloyal to the club.'

'And how did the club get on?' asked Tilsner.

Klug frowned. 'How do you mean?'

'In the game at the weekend. I thought you had a big match against Guben?'

'Ah yes. We won 3–0. But as you know, we shouldn't really be in this league.'

'Does that have something to do with what you want to tell us, Günther?' asked Müller. 'Was Dominik Nadel somehow involved in all that?'

'Involved? I don't know if he was directly involved. You mean in the whistle-blowing? The uncovering of the scandal?'

Müller and Tilsner both nodded.

'That I can't say. Sorry to disappoint you. What I *can* tell you is that Dominik was the one *blamed* for it.'

'So why don't you think he did it?' asked Tilsner.

'How would he know the details? He played for the youth team, remember? Not the first team. The scandal was in the first team – if, indeed, it was a scandal. The club was paying some of its players illegally. It was found guilty of damaging the principles of a socialist society. Why would one of the youth team know the ins and outs of secret payments to members of the first team squad? He wouldn't. I always felt he was innocent. He was a scapegoat. But – having been made the scapegoat – he would have had enemies. Plenty of enemies.'

'Why do you say that?' asked Müller.

'People lost their jobs, their livelihoods. At least initially. Most of the foreign players involved – the ones receiving the alleged illegal payments – were Yugoslavs. They'd brought their entire families here, to Eisenhüttenstadt. Some would have found new clubs here in the Republic. But even that would have meant uprooting families again. We were the only *Oberliga* club around here. Although Frankfurt played in the top league a couple of years ago. But consider those who'd come to Eisenhüttenstadt towards the end of their careers, thinking it was their last decent payday. And then suddenly – uh-oh! – in effect there's no club any more. You'd be pretty cut up about it, wouldn't you? And if someone was named as responsible, even if they didn't actually blow the whistle, well . . .' The man leant back in his chair and opened his arms wide.

Tilsner raised his eyebrows. Müller could tell he was sceptical. It was all too easy just to blame the foreigner. It had echoes of their investigation in Ha-Neu, when locals had been all too ready to point the finger at Vietnamese guest workers for the baby abductions. 'So,' said Tilsner, wearily, after a few seconds of silence. 'You're saying we should be looking for a disgruntled Yugoslav player who was thrown out of work by Stahl's enforced relegation?'

'Well, the whisper is that Dominik was murdered, isn't it?'

Tilsner shrugged.

'And that the method was stuffing a sock down his windpipe, yes?'

Müller frowned. 'Who told you that?'

'It's true, then.' The man smiled. 'If I were you, and I don't want to tell you how to do your job, but I'd get that sock checked and tested. It's rumoured to be a method of murder favoured in the Balkans.'

Tilsner snorted. Müller threw him an angry glance. But she was also angry with herself. She didn't believe for one second that 'death by sock' was a favoured Balkan murder method. That was just the Hütte bar-talk rumour mill going into overdrive. Now it had been raised though, she'd have to check it out. Schmidt wouldn't be around to do it, so it would have to be his opposite number in either Hütte itself, or in Frankfurt. But what she *had* asked Schmidt to do was forensic tests on the sock. To try to identify its origin and whether there was anything that pointed to its owner.

The two detectives left Krug to his beer and exited the bar. A colder wind outside signalled that autumn was just around the corner. They had a short autumn in these eastern parts, followed by a bitter, long winter. Müller pulled the collar of her raincoat up under her chin.

'Well, that was slightly underwhelming,' said Tilsner, before they got into the Lada.

'Agreed. Tittle-tattle, rumour. Nothing much of substance. I thought he actually had something useful for us when he passed that note at the football ground.'

'I suppose his assertion that Dominik wouldn't have been in a position to whistle-blow about the illegal payments is of some use.'

Müller nodded. 'But it's still only that. An assertion.'

They'd already opened their respective car doors and were about to duck inside when Tilsner hissed at her. 'Look out. Here comes trouble. He's been watching us again.'

Walking across the main road from his own car, parked directly opposite the bar – which Müller and Tilsner should have noticed earlier – was the young, blond-haired man they both assumed was a Stasi officer. This time he didn't seem content with just observing and making his presence known. He approached Müller with a piece of paper in one hand, his other outstretched in greeting.

'Comrade *Major* Müller,' he said, shaking the hand that Müller had felt obliged to extend in return. 'I'm *Hauptmann* Walter Diederich, of the local Ministry for State Security here in *Bezirk* Frankfurt. We haven't yet had the pleasure of meeting, although I think I've seen you out and about. I hope your inquiry is proving productive. Did Krug give you anything helpful? I wouldn't believe everything he says.'

'It was a useful meeting,' said Müller, giving the man a thin smile.

'Good, good. Well, look.' He passed her the piece of paper, which she now saw was an envelope. 'Here's an invitation to come and meet us at our offices in Frankfurt this afternoon, if it's convenient for you. And do bring Comrade *Hauptmann* Tilsner with you. He'll be very welcome too.' He gestured to the envelope. 'All the directions are in there, but it's easy enough to find. Two o'clock, if that suits you both.'

20

They parked the Lada in a side street outside the fenced-off Stasi compound and then approached the entry gate. The guard examined their *Kripo* IDs and then showed them to a side room attached to the gatehouse. Through the internal window they saw him pick up the phone.

A couple of minutes later, an unsmiling plain-clothes officer walked into the room and asked them to follow him.

'You've probably been here before, haven't you, Werner?'

Tilsner gave her a mock snarl. 'Give it a rest, Karin. I'm not in the mood. What do you think this is about?'

Müller didn't bother lowering her voice. 'They probably want to give us some "assistance". That's the usual story.' She wondered if this would be the moment one of the Stasi's Special Commissions – the ones Reiniger had originally talked about – would try to take over the case. *Perhaps that's who Diederich really works for?*

'To be honest,' said Tilsner, 'any help we could get would be welcome. I feel as though we're still just scratching the surface of this one.'

They were shown into a small, brightly lit office, with a window overlooking the courtyard on one side of the room, and a mirror covering much of the opposite wall. It made the room look bigger – which was presumably what it was meant to do – but Müller found it slightly unnerving.

Sitting behind a desk against the far wall was Diederich, wearing the same plain clothes he'd been in that morning at Neuzelle. Next to him was another, more senior, officer. A major, it looked like from the epaulettes, which were similar to those of both the People's Police and the People's Army, although the uniforms of the former were a darker green.

Diederich immediately leapt to his feet and moved round to the front of the desk.

'Excellent, excellent. We're so pleased you could take time out from your inquiry to come and meet us. We really believe in cooperation between the Ministry and the police. This is Comrade *Major* Jörg Baum.' The bald-headed, round-faced man behind the desk was smiling equally broadly, and extended his hand, first to Müller then Tilsner, as Diederich made the formal introductions.

'Please sit down anyway. Make yourselves comfortable. We think this new initiative of the Serious Crimes Department is an excellent idea, don't we, *Major* Baum?'

The older man nodded. His smile was almost a smirk; he knew that Müller was aware all of this was just shadow-boxing. Diederich's words were meaningless. The true purpose of their summons had yet to emerge.

'Thanks for all that, Walter,' said Baum, jovially. 'First names OK for you two as well? I hate all that formal crap. Although given I'm wearing this,' he ran his hands down the front of his uniform, 'it probably doesn't look like it. Anyway, although this is partly a "get to know you" visit, let's not beat around the bush. I'm sure you're busy, as are we, but we have some information that may be useful for you.' He took the top two files from a pile on his desk and then handed one each to Müller and Tilsner. 'They're both the same. They concern this so-called club for queers just outside Frankfurt. We've been thinking of closing it down for a while, but . . . Well, as you can imagine, it's a bit of a honey trap. And it's amazing what kind of flies get trapped in it. So for the moment we're under instructions to leave things be, up to a point.'

'Instructions?' queried Müller.

'From above. Normannenstrasse.' *The Stasi headquarters in the Hauptstadt*, thought Müller. *Why are they taking such an interest?* 'I'm sure you understand. That said, the key phrase there is "up to a point". If anything gets seriously out of hand we have to step in. And as part of that, we've also got a little apology to make. Walter?'

'Yes, thanks, Jörg.' Müller did a double take. Their dispensing of formalities wasn't just for show, then. They actually seemed to be on first-name terms. Diederich smiled at Müller, then continued. 'We're glad, actually, that neither of you look any the worse for wear. I'm afraid it was our agents who gave you a little fright on your motorbike yesterday.'

'You'd better have a good explanation,' snarled Tilsner.

Baum held up his hand. Müller wasn't sure if it was an admission of liability, or just an indication that Tilsner should tone his rhetoric down. But Müller felt equally affronted.

'I fully understand your anger. But no bones were broken. Just let Walter finish, if you would.'

'Yes,' said Diederich. 'When we heard what had happened we were equally alarmed. They shouldn't have done that near the canal bridge. The thing is, we didn't know who you were. To our agents, you were two people on a motorcycle chasing one of our contacts.'

'You could have checked the registration plate for the bike,' insisted Tilsner. 'A quick radio call would have established it belongs to Keibelstrasse special ops.'

'Fair enough,' said Diederich. 'As I say, we're delighted you're both all right. We thought you were part of a drugs gang target- ing our contact, Jan Winkler.'

'When you say "contact", do you mean he works directly for you?' asked Müller. It was a worrying development, worrying for the well-being of Markus Schmidt.

'No, he simply provides us with some information. In return, we provide him with protection. Our agents were only meant to intercept you, so that you didn't find out where he was going. By doing so near the canal bridge, I gather you nearly came off the bike. It was a misjudgement on their part.'

Müller exhaled slowly. This wasn't going the way she expected. In her recent cases, there had been high-level Stasi involvement. This seemed altogether different. And disturbing. Not only did it look like Winkler's father worked for the Stasi – Winkler did too.

'Thanks, Walter,' said Baum. 'Now, why don't we look at these files? If you turn to page one, you'll see a summary. Basically, we've known for some time that illegal drugs are openly traded at this club. But, until fairly recently, it was just cannabis. We were happy to go along with that as part of our honey trap.'

'To trap what, or who?' asked Müller.

'Ah,' said Baum. 'I thought you might ask me that. I'm afraid I'm not allowed to say.' Müller heard Tilsner snort with derision. 'Anyway,' continued Baum, 'recently we discovered some of them had moved on to harder drugs. Amphetamines.'

'*Speed*, I think it's known as in the West,' added Diederich. 'You might have seen mention of it on some of the West German news reports. Of course I *know* none of us watch western TV for pleasure. But sometimes we need to for the job, don't we?'

'And if you look at exhibit A,' said Baum, 'the first set of photographs, you'll see a sting operation we recently carried out at the club. It was a few months back now. The suspect's identity has been disguised.'

Müller peered at the photo. The guilty youth's face had been completely obscured. 'Why do that? And given you have, what's the relevance for us?'

'We're protecting the suspect's identity for security reasons,' replied Baum. 'As to the second part of your question, we simply need to demonstrate that there is an ongoing operation involving our agents surrounding this club. Therefore we need to make sure your team doesn't – how shall we put it? – trample on our flower bed. Does that make sense?'

Müller nodded. *It makes sense. But it doesn't necessarily mean we're going to do their bidding*, she thought.

'There are also some sensitive links to the case you're investigating,' said Diederich.

'How so?' asked Tilsner.

'If you turn to page five of your folder, please,' said Baum. 'Exhibit B.'

Müller drew her head back in shock. 'Exhibit B', as Baum termed it, was an autopsy photograph – of *their* murder victim, Dominik Nadel, concentrating on the injection mark on his arm identified by the pathologist, Dr Fenstermacher. She quickly skim-read it: *Heroin . . . addict . . . needles . . . dealer*. She heard Tilsner next to her sigh in exasperation. She turned and saw him shaking his head, looking at her.

'So you're saying you've solved our murder?'

'Not necessarily, Karin. My problem with that last sentence of yours is the word *murder*. What we're saying – what our investigation department has discovered – is that there was no murder. Some of the conclusions passed to you by . . . who was it? . . .' Baum picked up another file from his desk, one he hadn't shared with the Berlin officers, and flicked through it. 'Ah yes, Dr Fenstermacher. Well, I wouldn't believe all that she tells you. She's a bit of a loose cannon, to be honest, according to our colleagues in *Bezirk* Cottbus. So yes, some of her conclusions are, I'm afraid, mistaken. Dominik Nadel's death was not a murder.' Baum closed both files with an air of finality.

'I think my team will be the judge of that,' said Müller.

'Quite so,' said Baum. 'But your team isn't some private little organisation, Karin. You answer to your People's Police bosses at Keibelstrasse, just as we answer to ours at Normannenstrasse. And ultimately, of course, to Comrade Minister Mielke. So, just to summarise, Dominik Nadel was not murdered. He was a drug addict, a heroin addict, and his death was self-inflicted. And I'm sure you'll be hearing from Keibelstrasse before too long confirming that you're to return to the Hauptstadt and drop this inquiry.'

Watching Müller and Tilsner from the other side of the mirror – through the one-way reflective glass – the Stasi colonel frowned.

'Do you think they will drop it, even if they're told to by Reiniger?' his colleague asked.

'Probably not. They're not always the most sensible pair. They're not always the best detectives either.'

'You've worked with them before then, Klaus?'

The colonel nodded. 'Most notably on the case involving Ackermann.'

'Ah yes. That was a convenient one for your boss, wasn't it?'

'My boss?'

'Markus Wolf. Cleared his way to succeed Mielke – got his main rival out of the picture.'

'I'm not sure what you mean. Colonel General Horst Ackermann died tragically in a car accident. Surely you read about it in Neues Deutschland? As far as I'm aware Ackermann and Wolf were friends.'

The other man let out a huge guffaw. 'Pull the other one. So our two Berlin detectives helped you with that, did they?'

'After a fashion. Although, as I was saying, they weren't recruited for their abilities or experience. The opposite, in fact. She was the youngest head of a murder squad in the Republic. The only woman too. Over-promoted, out of her depth.'

'I thought she'd just been promoted again, to head this new Serious Crimes Department?'

'Exactly. As I was saying, over-promoted, out of her depth. Only now even more so. It makes her more . . . open to suggestion, shall we say.'

'And isn't he one of ours?'

'To some extent. I get some information from him. We worked together a long time ago.'

'Doing what?'

'That's hardly your business, is it?' said the colonel. He ran his fingers through his sandy-coloured, shoulder-length hair. The style that he knew people said made him look like a West German newsreader. 'Anyway, I'm not sure our problem is really those two. If they do go ahead and defy orders, someone will put a stop to it pretty quickly. What's more problematic is the mess those other two goons in there have made – Baum and Diederich.'

'This isn't their fault. It was all approved at a higher level.'

'You may be right. But we need to make sure it gets disapproved at a higher level, and quickly. Otherwise it's going to blow up in all our faces. And you probably have bigger fish to fry – I know I certainly do.'

'What? The Red Army Faction thing?'

The colonel became silent. How did he know about that? It was supposed to be secret. The trouble was, the Firm was starting to get leaky.

'As I say,' the colonel finally replied, although not to the question posed. 'We need to get Baum and Diederich's operation closed down – quickly.'

21

Müller didn't have long to wait for the phone call from Reiniger at Keibelstrasse. She'd returned immediately to the Hauptstadt to see the twins and Emil, and relieve Helga from her nanny duties – at least temporarily. The same night, last night, Reiniger had rung.

'We've a bit of problem, Karin,' he said. 'I think you may have got wind of it from the Ministry for State Security in Frankfurt.'

Müller started to object. 'Surely you're not—'

Reiniger cut her short. 'Let's not argue on an open line, Karin. Come in and see me at Keibelstrasse tomorrow morning. Is 8 a.m. too early?'

Was it fair to foist the twins onto Helga once more, when she'd only been back a few hours? Well, that was the agreement they'd made, when her grandmother had come up from Leipzig and given up her own apartment there to live with them in Berlin. 'Eight is fine. I'll see you then, Comrade *Oberst*.'

Müller had half-expected Reiniger to be joined by Stasi bigwigs, given their apparent close involvement with the case. In the event, they *were* joined by another officer – someone she hadn't been expecting. Her deputy Werner Tilsner, who appeared to have been summoned back from Eisenhüttenstadt.

Reiniger seemed to be in a perfectly affable mood, holding the meeting in his side lounge, rather than his office, and ushering them to sit on his comfortable armchairs – normally solely reserved for high-ups. 'Coffee?' he asked.

The two detectives both nodded, and Reiniger rang down to get the coffee delivered to the room. 'A plate of biscuits, too, please, Truda.'

Tilsner started to speak. 'I don't think we should let the Stasi in Frankfurt—'

Reiniger held his finger to his mouth. 'Stop, please, Comrade *Hauptmann*. Don't jump the gun. Please listen to what I have to say first.'

'Of course, Comrade *Oberst*,' said Müller. Tilsner threw her an angry look.

'Now it's going to be very difficult going against the express instructions of the Ministry for State Security. The whole reason your new unit was set up was to secure a greater level of cooperation on sensitive murder inquiries. Unless we do what they say, then they'll just have their own investigation department – or indeed one of their own Special Commissions – take over all inquiries like this. We'll find that the *Kriminalpolizei* no longer have a role. That won't be good for any of us.'

Tilsner interrupted again. 'So you are going to—'

'Shut up for a moment, Werner,' said Müller. She could tell Reiniger, from his tone of voice, was on their side. And that he had some sort of plan worked out.

'Thank you, Karin.' The colonel sent a withering look in Tilsner's direction.

'So,' he continued, 'we are going to accept – *for the time being* – their account of Dominik Nadel's death. Our investigation into that – *for the time being* – is closed. However—'

Reiniger was interrupted by a knock on the door. Their coffee had arrived. A trolley – replete with biscuits, little cakes, and the coffee and cups – was wheeled in. 'Thank you, Truda,' Reiniger said, then got up to close the door after her, making sure it was securely shut. He then turned the catch to lock it. He moved to the side door which led to his office, checked that was securely fastened, and again turned the lock.

'We won't be disturbed again. Karin, could you perhaps serve?'

Müller could have taken umbrage at this. But she knew Reiniger was a traditionalist, a chauvinist even. There was no point arguing, despite the fact that she had to put up with Tilsner's smirking as she played the good little waitress, asking each of them how many sugars, which cakes and biscuits they wanted. It was demeaning to her position, but she wanted something out of Reiniger, something she felt she was going to be successful in getting, so she let it pass.

'I suppose now you're a major I shouldn't be asking you to do such things,' laughed Reiniger.

'Oh, Karin doesn't mind, Comrade *Oberst*. She's used to it at home.'

Müller, facing away from the colonel, mouthed '*Arschloch*' silently at Tilsner, then made sure as she passed him his cup that she spilt some of the boiling liquid over his trousers.

'Ouch!' he exclaimed.

'Apologies, Comrade *Hauptmann*,' she said, the sarcasm dripping from her words in the same way the coffee was now dripping from Tilsner's saucer.

The exchange seemed to be missed by Reiniger, who simply continued with his interrupted monologue.

'So, as I was saying, we *do* unfortunately have to accede to the Stasi's version of events, for now, in respect of Dominik Nadel. However, I've looked at their files – just as I'm sure you have – and there is no way, in my view, that this boy died from a self-administered heroin overdose. There's clearly something fishy going on. And also, I have absolute faith in Gudrun Fenstermacher. I've come across her before, when I was climbing the greasy pole, as it were, and she tells it how it is – and is usually absolutely correct in her findings.'

Müller wondered for a moment if the pathologist and Reiniger had been closer than he admitted, and had to stifle a giggle. She quickly took a sip of coffee. Reiniger gave her a quizzical look.

'However, the son of one of our trusted forensic scientists is also missing, and as you know, we like to look after our own. And I gather from you two that there is almost certainly a connection with this "club" the Stasi have been investigating.'

'That's right,' said Müller. 'And to the motorcycle gang that congregate there. And possibly –' she hesitated when she said this, and hoped it wasn't true – 'to the drugs they were taking.'

'Exactly,' tutted Reiniger. 'Well, as you can imagine, it's of the utmost importance to the People's Police that young Markus

Schmidt is found safe and well. So important that I've decided the task of finding him has to be handled by our new Serious Crimes Department. In other words, the two of you.'

'So . . .?' Reiniger's scheme had finally become clear to Müller.

'So, in effect, it's as you were. You're expressly forbidden to investigate the death of Dominik Nadel itself, as the Stasi assure us their investigations team have solved that matter. However, you may now turn your full attentions to finding Markus – and, of course, the case of Nadel may be an important part of that, so I'm not suggesting you ignore it.'

'So we just carry on as before?' said Müller. She tried to keep the relief out of her voice, although she was heartened by the mischievous look in Reiniger's eyes. He was enjoying this.

'In effect, yes. I'll get all the paperwork signed off, switching your attentions to Markus. There will be one change, however.'

'What's that?' asked Tilsner.

'I'm taking a bit of a risk with this one, and breaking procedure. But despite his intimate link to the case, I'm asking Jonas Schmidt to come back to work. It's no good him moping at home. I've explained everything to him, and while his head will be in a complete mess – that's understandable, whose wouldn't be in similar circumstances? – he's going to be newly energised by all this. Perhaps he can find the forensic evidence that will help us to track down his son.'

Before they left the People's Police headquarters, Reiniger gave Müller a letter. She was unsurprised to see it looked like it had been steamed open and clumsily resealed.

Once Tilsner had left her to collect the Wartburg from the car park – with the aim of getting straight back to Frankfurt and Hütte to continue their inquiries – Müller tore it open.

The letterhead surprised her. She recognised the emblem of the Federal Republic immediately – the strange-looking eagle, with its wings stretched in such a way it looked like it was at a bodybuilding class. Encircling it, the logo of a factory. It was from the West German Ministry for Economic Cooperation, dated just three days earlier.

Dear Major Müller

I understand you are making inquiries into the death of a teenage boy from Eisenhüttenstadt.

I am a junior minister of the Ministry for Economic Cooperation in the Federal Republic. As part of my work, I've spent a lot of time in Eisenhüttenstadt negotiating contracts for the supply of steel from the EKO plant there.

I may have some information that might help your inquiries, and I would therefore ask you to contact me at your earliest convenience. If you're in Hütte, you can try to reach me via the steelworks. Otherwise, for the next few days, I'm actually staying in East Berlin on official business.

I can be contacted at the Hotel Berolina, just behind Kino International on Karl-Marx-Alee. I'm sure you know it. Room 2024.

If for any reason you don't receive this until after I've left Berlin, then my Bonn number is at the top of this letter.

I appreciate you must get plenty of people contacting you, saying they have information. All I would say is that – clearly – given my position, I'm not seeking any reward for information given. I simply have concerns about something, and information to pass on that I think may help you.

It may be advisable to meet somewhere discreet where we can talk freely, rather than at the People's Police headquarters.

With friendly greetings,

Georg Metzger

The name meant nothing to Müller. But the letter intrigued her. How did this West German politician even know she was the officer in charge? Nadel's death hadn't been widely reported in the newspapers. There may have been a paragraph in the local paper near Senftenberg, whatever that was called, but as far as she knew there had been nothing nationally, and nothing in Hütte or Frankfurt, where Metzger seemed to have his connections.

Müller went into her old office at headquarters, the one where she'd been kicking her heels between murder investigations after the end of the graveyard girl case. A few fellow officers nodded cursory greetings, but she hadn't liked it here, and hadn't made friends. All she wanted was to use a telephone.

She spotted an empty desk and dialled the hotel's number, asking to be put through to Metzger's room. It rang for a few seconds, then the receptionist came back on the line.

'No one appears to be in that room at present. Can I take a message for you, Comrade?'

Müller gave the girl her own private number at the Strausberger Platz flat, and a message asking Metzger to ring her as soon as he was back.

On the short U-bahn journey from Alexanderplatz, Müller considered where best to meet if – as she hoped – Metzger returned her call. His request was for 'somewhere discreet'. Müller thought back to all her clandestine meetings with Jäger when they were investigating the deaths of the *Jugendwerkhof* teens. Perhaps she should adopt one of his favourite meeting spots.

22

Metzger was a slender, slightly nervous-looking man. Not how she'd imagined a West German politician at all. She would, of course, ask for all the intelligence the Republic had about him – it would be a thorough briefing, she was sure – but she hadn't wanted to do that before meeting the man. She didn't want to prejudge him.

Much in the same way Jäger had done more than eighteen months earlier, Müller rowed slowly to the centre of the lake, with Metzger looking round anxiously, presumably checking if anyone was following them. It was possible that they *were* being observed, Müller knew. She hadn't taken the same precautions as Jäger. He'd always arranged their rendezvous by sealed telegrams, presumably delivered by a trusted messenger. Müller couldn't be bothered with all that. If the Stasi wanted to follow her, they would follow her. There was nothing she could do about it. She knew the likelihood was that both her phones at the Strausberger Platz apartment – the private one and the police hotline – were tapped. But surely they couldn't have agents listening to every conversation at every hour of the day? It would need a huge amount of manpower. It would be a huge *waste* of manpower.

Müller glanced up at the sky. Dark clouds, although the rain had held off so far. She had her raincoat on anyway, which would offer some protection, and Metzger at the opposite end of the little boat was hunched down into an anorak. Not the typical coat for a government minister, but at least it would be practical if the heavens opened.

She'd worried about doing the actual rowing. Jäger had been the one to take the oars when they met here. But Metzger didn't offer, so it was left to Müller to propel the tiny craft to the centre of the lake – where they could be certain no one would eavesdrop.

Once she was satisfied they were as close to the centre of the lake as possible, she rested the oars in the rowlocks and waited for Metzger to tell her whatever it was he had to say. Initially, though, he was silent. The only sound was of water dripping from the resting oars back into the lake, and a gentle slapping of small waves against the side of the wooden boat.

Eventually, Metzger spoke up. 'Thank you for agreeing to meet me, Comrade *Major*.' Müller was impressed at the attempt at the official greeting between Party members in the East, but assured the politician there was no need.

'Karin is fine, Herr Metzger.'

'You're probably wondering why I asked to meet somewhere private.'

Müller shrugged. She suspected he wasn't here simply to talk about steel contracts.

'I'd like to know, though, if I can trust you.'

'Ha!' exclaimed Müller. 'I don't know if I can give you any assurances there. I'm a police officer, but I work for the People's Police of the *Deutsche Demokratische Republik*. I'm therefore also a servant of the state. What I will say, though, is that I have no agenda against you. I don't even know you. So I don't see why you would have anything to fear. If it helps ease your mind, I am known as an honest officer. Perhaps, sometimes, too honest for my own good.'

Müller could feel the man appraising her. But not in the way a Tilsner, or possibly even a Jäger would. If Müller's suspicions were correct, Metzger's links to this case had come about precisely because of his lack of interest in the female sex.

'All right,' he said slowly, drawing out the words. 'I suppose I can't ask for any more than that, and it was I who asked for this meeting, not you.'

Müller nodded.

'This is difficult to admit to. Which is why I asked whether I could trust you. I haven't committed any crime, but if what I'm about to say became public in the West, then I could pretty much kiss my career goodbye. I've no doubt your Stasi will have a file on me, so what I'm about to tell you may not come as a surprise.' Metzger let his arm hang loosely at his side, and then dragged his finger back and forth through the cool, dark water of the lake. Müller watched him give a small shiver. 'In my role with the West German Ministry for Economic Cooperation, as I've already told you, I have to travel regularly to the East. I'm away from my wife and family . . .'

Metzger's voice trailed off as he caught Müller's look of surprise. 'Yes, Comrade *Major*. I have a wife and two young children. It's the sort of thing that helps a political career. But when I'm over in the East – in Eisenhüttenstadt, or at trade fairs, for example in Leipzig – well, it can get lonely. And when men get lonely, they seek comfort. And sometimes, if that comfort is not readily found, it has to be paid for.'

'So you're saying you use prostitutes, Herr Metzger? You're not the first family man to be guilty of that, by any stretch of the imagination.'

The man closed his eyes for a moment. 'No, but it's worse than that. My particular preference, when I need comfort, is men.'

'So you're homosexual?'

Metzger shook his head. 'Not exclusively, no. As I said, I have a wife and children. I find women attractive too. So you might say I'm *bi*sexual.'

'All very interesting, Herr Metzger. But how does this relate to my inquiry?'

'Last month I was at the Leipzig Trade Fair. I was drinking alone in the Interhotel bar when I was approached by a young man – well, youth, I suppose – who made it very clear he was available . . . at a price. Initially, I laughed it off. Denied I was interested. But he was there the next night, we got talking, and one thing led to another.'

Metzger stared wistfully at the shoreline, and the Milch-häuschen café: the one Müller knew was a haunt for Stasi operatives. But she didn't think he was spy-spotting – instead, he seemed to be lost in his memories.

'Go on,' said Müller. 'I still don't fully see the relevance.'

'The relevance is that during our encounter in my hotel room, I clearly saw something that linked him to Eisenhüttenstadt. Something that I quite recently learnt – from gossip at the EKO steel works – also linked him to the body your police colleagues found by the shore at Senftenberger See.'

'What?' asked Müller, though she'd already guessed the answer to her own question.

'A tattoo. A partial tattoo of the local Hütte football team, BSG Stahl.'

23

The news that Dominik Nadel had been working as a male prostitute at the trade fair was an important new angle. She wanted to discuss it with Tilsner as soon as possible, but she had other things she needed to do first. After saying goodbye to Metzger, Müller retreated to the Strausberger Platz apartment, hoping for some quality time with the twins, and Emil, once he was home from the hospital.

But as soon as she was through the front door, a resigned-looking Helga handed her a note.

'One of your colleagues just rang from police headquarters. I said I wasn't sure when you'd be back, but he asked me to get you to ring him at Keibelstrasse as soon as you returned. He said it was urgent. His name was *Kriminaltechniker* Jonas Schmidt. And here's his extension.' She handed Müller a page from the telephone pad with Schmidt's number scrawled on it.

'Thanks, Helga. I'm sorry about all this. How are the twins? And has Emil been back at all?'

'Emil? No, I haven't seen him since this morning. Jannika and Johannes are fine. They're sitting up in the lounge. But to be honest, I'm finding it a bit of a struggle. I'm not getting any younger. I was meaning to talk to you about it. I think we need to find them a nursery or a kindergarten. They'll be crawling soon. I didn't realise that you'd be away so much.'

Müller felt a wave of emotion pass over her. She was being selfish. Putting her job first. It was the wrong way round. It had taken years – a whole lifetime – to find her natural grandmother, the only blood link to her now dead mother. The twins had been a gift almost from heaven after years believing that the physical and emotional trauma of the rape at the police college had left her unable to conceive. Now she was in danger of tossing it all away. For the sake of her police career. It wasn't worth it. She felt her eyes begin to moisten. She didn't want to cry. Not in front of Helga. Not in front of the twins. It would just make things even worse.

Helga lifted Müller's chin, so they were looking into each other's eyes. 'Look, don't get upset. I'm not angry. I'm not saying you're a bad mother. I knew the deal when I moved in – I knew what your job would be like. Well, I had some idea. I just think, for their sakes, we need something a bit more formal. There's plenty of free childcare in the Republic. I'm sure through your position you have access to the best. Let's use it. Let's take advantage of it.'

Not trusting herself to speak, Müller simply nodded. Then she pulled herself free of Helga's hug, and went to see the twins.

She crouched down first in front of Jannika. Her daughter immediately started babbling and smiling at her. Then the girl reached across and tried to grab a coloured brick Johannes was playing with, prompting him to start wailing and screeching.

Helga rushed in, picked him up and started cradling him, with Müller rooted to the spot as though she didn't know what to do.

'That's not a very nice way to greet Mama, is it little Hansi? You can do better than that, can't you?'

Müller had to bite her tongue. She didn't want her son to be called Hansi. It reminded her too much of the man at the centre of her previous investigation. But she knew she had to be grateful. Everything was in danger of falling apart. She couldn't afford to anger Helga at this point.

Once Johannes was calmer, the older woman passed him to Müller. 'Why don't you let Mama give you a nice big kiss, you handsome boy?' Helga, in turn, crouched down to play with Jannika.

Johannes gave Müller a huge giggly smile as she blew raspberries on his tummy. Perhaps there *was* a way to make this work. She would just have to try harder, and investigate childcare options, as Helga suggested.

Schmidt seemed to be back to something like his old self, as much as anyone could be when their only son was missing. Müller didn't need to imagine what it was like – she had faced the same situation when Johannes was just a few hours old. But other than a slightly manic glint in his eyes, Schmidt seemed refreshed, and filled with new purpose. It must have given him some comfort for Reiniger to appoint a special police squad to look into Markus's disappearance, even though – in reality – little had changed. And what Metzger had told her about Dominik Nadel's activities before his murder – and Müller still most definitely regarded it as a *murder* – filled her with a sense of dread: had Markus Schmidt fallen into a similar lifestyle?

His father was currently busy scurrying from lab table to lab table.

'Ah, Comrade *Major*. I'm glad you managed to get here so quickly. I didn't really want to discuss this over the phone.'

'What have you got, Jonas?'

'The sock. I've finally got the tests back on the sock. Very interesting, very interesting.'

'Go on.'

'Well, the first thing to say is it's from an Italian manufacturer. And it *is* a long football or sports stocking.'

'Could you tell which team?'

'Unfortunately not. It's just a plain red colour. But I did check it against those worn by BSG Stahl Eisenhüttenstadt. The home and away kits. It's not one of theirs.'

'So we've no indication where it's come from?'

'From the pattern, the fabric used to manufacture it – some sort of polyester – unfortunately not. However, I have found something interesting. Can you come and look at the microscope?'

It was the way Schmidt usually operated. Something that infuriated Tilsner. Rather than producing a concise report, the forensic scientist showed off all his findings like a schoolboy brimming with pride at his latest science project.

Müller squinted through the eyepiece. 'Give me a clue, Jonas. I don't even know what I'm supposed to be looking for.'

'Well, you see the pattern. It's very distinctive. What you're looking at is the cross-section of a twig.'

'Hmm. And?'

'The pith is chambered. There are air spaces in it, and it's a pinkish brown in colour, agreed?'

'Seems about right to me. Why does that get you excited?'

'Well, obviously the sock itself was covered in all sorts of horrible body fluids. You'd expect that. What an awful way to go. But caught up between the fibres was this tiny bit of twig, which I took a section of.'

'And how does that help?'

'Well. I've managed to identify the species.' Schmidt pulled down a reference book from his shelf, and then leafed through it until he got to the relevant page. 'See here,' he said, pointing to a photograph. 'It's exactly the same as what we're seeing under the microscope. Well, not exactly, but near enough.'

'And?' asked Müller. Schmidt was leaning closer to her as she looked into the eyepiece once more. She could smell his usual Wurst-breath – his favourite snack food, probably acquired from a stall on Alexanderplatz at lunchtime. At least he was back to eating.

'And what you're looking at, Comrade *Major*, is a slide of *Juglans regia Carpathian*. More commonly known as the Persian walnut. It only grows outdoors in an area stretching from the Balkans across to the Himalayas and parts of China.'

'That's a big area, Jonas. A *very* big area.'

'I'll give you that, Comrade *Major*. On the face of it, it doesn't help us much. But if you combine that area with the area where Italian football stockings are commonly imported or worn, things narrow considerably.'

'To what?'

'It wouldn't be any of our friendly socialist nations, unless they had a particularly open trade policy. It's unlikely anyway. The most likely country outside the communist bloc would be Greece. Northern Greece, to be precise.'

'*Greece?*' Müller was confused. Her mind started racing. They already knew what the tattoo on Nadel's back was; surely Schmidt wasn't now going back to the Greek pi theory he'd discounted earlier?

'But,' continued Schmidt, 'there is one socialist country with a border neighbouring Italy – a land and sea border – which regularly trades with the West, and imports Italian-made football stockings.'

Geography wasn't Müller's strongest suit, although she trumped Tilsner at it by some distance. Nevertheless, she knew what Schmidt was going to say before he delivered what he hoped was his *coup de grâce*.

'Yugoslavia,' he announced in triumph. 'I am almost certain that the sock used to kill Dominik Nadel came from Yugoslavia.'

24

Later that evening
Frankfurt an der Oder

Müller managed to persuade Schmidt that the search for his son would be best served if he accompanied her that evening back out to Frankfurt where they would stay the night, and meet Tilsner for a debrief and a discussion of the best way forward.

His initial reinvigoration from finding key information about the sock which had been stuffed down Dominik Nadel's windpipe soon evaporated when Müller revealed in the car that she believed there was a link between Markus and Nadel – and that Nadel was involved in some sort of homosexual prostitution.

She turned briefly towards where her forensic scientist was sitting in the passenger seat of the Lada. Schmidt was holding his head in his hands. 'So you're now saying my son – as well as being missing – is possibly working as a male prostitute?' He shook his head slowly. 'I can't believe that, Comrade *Major*. I just can't believe that. It's too horrible to contemplate.'

They chose the same bar that Diederich had observed them in the previous time, but on this occasion he was nowhere to be seen. Perhaps the local Stasi were confident Müller and her team had been warned off. Or the news that they been assigned the missing persons search for Markus Schmidt hadn't yet reached their ears. Müller was sure it would only be a matter of time.

She had a few blank sheets of paper and a pen in front of her. Really, it would have been easier to set up a proper incident room. But given their recent brush with Diederich and Baum, staying off the radar was possibly the better option.

'So what are we now saying?' asked Tilsner. 'That Nadel was actually killed by one of BSG Stahl's former Yugoslav players who was bitter that the youth's whistle-blowing cost him his livelihood? However, our best guess tells us that he wasn't the *actual* whistle-blower, just the fall guy. Set up by someone. It's a bit of a mess, Karin. In fact, it's a huge, horrible mess. And where does Jonas's son fit into all this? Or does he?'

Schmidt had gone into silent, unresponsive mode. Müller laid her hand on his arm. 'Try not to worry, Jonas. I know that's easy to say. But the best way to deal with this is to work towards finding Markus with logic.'

'I know, Comrade *Major*. I will do my best. I'm grateful for the chance to be working with you here.'

'I still say we need to give Jan Winkler a bit of a shake-up,' said Tilsner. 'He knows more than he's letting on. And where was he off to that day those Stasi thugs stopped us following him? He didn't hang around the club, did he? It must have been somewhere important for the *MfS* to try to stop us.'

'You're right,' nodded Müller. 'I've been treading softly because of what Jonas said about his father. If he does work for the Stasi, I didn't want to irritate them more than necessary. But we need to up the ante. I'll check with *Oberst* Reiniger whether we can bring him in. At the same time, I'll ask the colonel to authorise a twenty-four-hour surveillance team using either *Vopo* or *Kripo* officers in Berlin.'

'Might not be a bad idea to do the same for your West German friend. It would be nice to know exactly what he gets up to.'

'Metzger? I'll have enough trouble getting Reiniger to agree to keeping a tail on Winkler. Metzger would be a step too far, especially with the potential for embarrassment with the Federal Republic.'

'We could still put a bit of pressure on him. Threaten to tell the Bonn papers about his secret life.'

Müller sighed. 'Maybe. I said I'd keep it a secret, but maybe. As a last resort. Come on. All of us – you too, Jonas – let's think up possible scenarios.'

Tilsner drained his beer. 'OK. Let's drill down to the basics and try to ignore the spin. What do we know for certain? We know that Dominik Nadel accepted money for sleeping with other men, at least once, even if he wasn't part of some sort of ring. If he *was* part of a ring, then perhaps it's worth putting a bit more pressure on Metzger. Does he recognise any of the other lads? Has he – and I'm sorry about this, Jonas, but it has to be said – has he seen Markus doing anything like that?'

Schmidt closed his eyes behind his thick-lensed spectacles, as though he was trying hard not to imagine those sorts of things.

'We also know,' said Müller, 'that Dominik Nadel was injected with something that changed the level of his sex hormones.

Why? And who would do that? As it was clearly a forced thing, because of the marks from the wrist restraints.'

'Unless they were consensual wrist restraints,' ventured Schmidt, wearily.

'Good point, Jonas,' said Tilsner. 'What if it was some sort of weird homo S & M practice? I can believe it of that sort. Maybe he got a kick out of it. Or maybe our swinging-both-ways politician did. Another good reason to give him a bit of a shake-up.'

Müller sighed. 'But then how do you explain the testosterone levels?'

'Maybe that's one of their funny games too. I don't know. Maybe you get an extra shot of that stuff, more than the male body usually produces, and it makes you harder.'

Müller shook her head. 'That's just guesswork. We need the science. Jonas, that's a job for you. Find out all the science behind it using your Berlin contacts. Talk to the universities, the relevant departments. Do we know of anyone conducting any similar research? Officially or unofficially. We should have done this already, really. It's been staring us in the face ever since Fenstermacher mentioned it. And I suppose, if you must, see if injections of testosterone are ever used on the fringes of the homosexual world.'

'Of course, Comrade *Major*. I'll get onto it first thing in the morning.'

'I'll set about arranging the tail on Winkler, and at least raise the possibility of bringing him in for questioning – I can make some calls tonight. Werner, you get on to the youth team coach again. It was his theory about a possible Yugoslav revenge attack.

Didn't he mention one of them ran a bar in Hütte? That might be a good place to start. And – whatever the Stasi say about their "honey trap" – we need to go down to that club again. Question everyone. Has anyone gone off the radar recently, like Nadel did?'

'Yes,' said Schmidt, sadly. 'My son has.'

'I know, Jonas,' said Müller. 'But we're going to find him safe and well, and you're going to welcome him back into the family, whatever has happened.'

25

I feel nervous. I don't want to mess up. This is my chance to escape the nightmare, get my life back. I just have to do what they want, however distasteful. It will only be the once, they said. I have no other choice anyway – if it goes to trial, that's me finished. My father already hates me for what I am.

The bar here is busy. So many deals going on around the trade fair. Such a buzz of excitement. If I do finally sort all this out, this is the kind of thing I'd like to do. Work somewhere exciting like this.

They've made me study photos of him from several angles, with different hairstyles. Different designs of spectacles. I wouldn't say he's particularly handsome, but he's not bad. I just have to remember my lines, play my part. And then – like any actor – I'll get my payment. Only in my case, payment will be freedom. Freedom from all this hell hanging over me.

And I feel confident. I'm not wearing my thick spectacles. Instead, the agents have provided me with the very latest soft contact lenses from Japan. It's like a new world for me. I keep on trying to push my glasses back up my nose, like before, forgetting they're not there. It gives me a new confidence, despite what I've been through.

There's some of the latest western pop music playing. I choose a stool at the bar. I've been told that's what he favours. As I shake my head in time to the music, trying to look cool, edgy, I subtly scout the bar with each head shake trying to find him.

At first, I think my luck's out. I can't see him. Then I see a nervous, bespectacled man, thin and tall. I prefer thin and tall. I don't know what I'd have done if they'd asked me to do it with a Wurst-scoffing lard-ball.

I don't try to make eye contact initially. That's what they said my strategy should be. Don't be too obvious. Don't be too easy.

But then, on one head shake, he catches my eye. I don't smile the first time. Instead, I turn away. Teasing slightly. That's what they like in the West, they told me. Then I turn back. He's still staring. But he looks sad. I smile. My best, friendliest smile. Still moving to the music. I turn away again, flick my fringe back, the fringe that used to sit on the thick spectacles, but now just hangs free – sexily, I know, because I practised in the mirror – across my eyebrows. On the third glance, when I'm sure he's interested, I pick up my drink, down it, and go to sit next to him.

When we get to his room things don't go as well as I'd expected. Sitting on the stools, I'd dropped my hand to his left thigh, edged it up slowly. I could feel him hardening under the lightness of my fingers – unseen, I was certain, by anyone else at the bar. It seemed promising.

But when we get into the room, and he locks the door, things seem to have changed.

'I just want to talk,' he says. 'Just talk for a while.'

He sees my disappointment, sees the tears welling in my eyes.

'Don't cry. Please don't cry,' he says, hugging me to him. Perhaps I can turn this round. Even this might be good enough for them. A West German politician in a clinch with a boy who could be a teenager. I know their surveillance cameras will be catching this. I drop my hand to his groin again, but he brushes it away.

'I meant what I said. I just want to talk. Really. But I'll still pay you. Whatever your normal rate is.'

'If you're sure,' I say. 'That's kind of you.'

I let him count out the notes, then take them from him quickly before he changes his mind. Half of me thinks, *What a sucker*. But the other half feels sorry for him.

Maybe he's in a desperate situation too, like me.

'So what do you want to talk about? Sexy talk?' I ask hopefully.

He shakes his head. 'I'm not really one for that. I'm just getting over someone else.'

'A boy?'

He nods, looking slightly shamefaced. I glance down, see his wedding ring. He hides it self-consciously with his other hand.

'Married?'

He nods and sighs. I try to move close to him on the bed, so that our thighs are touching. He doesn't try to move away. *There's still a possibility.*

Although he says he wants to talk, he doesn't seem to be starting a conversation. It's strange, as he must know payment is by the hour, not that I'm going to be counting. My job is just to get him in a compromising position in front of the cameras. But maybe it's a case of playing the slow game still.

'So come on. We can't just sit here. If you don't want to do anything with me, we need to start talking. What do you want to talk about? You haven't even asked me my name yet. What's yours?'

'Georg.' I already know that, of course. At least he's not giving a fake one like I will when he asks me. 'You?' he asks.

'Tobias. Tobias Scherer.'

'And how did you get into this game, Tobias? Isn't it dangerous here in the East?'

'Why does anyone do it?' I reply, my confidence growing. 'Money. To get out of trouble. And no, it's not so hard in the East. As long as you don't do it in the full view of the authorities.'

'And tell me, do you know any of the others?'

'The others?'

'The other boys who do business here.'

This is starting to turn a bit strange. I hope he's not one of those weirdos you hear about on the western news. I shake my head. 'I'm not part of a group. I just work on my own.'

'And where are you from?'

For some reason this question throws me. I don't want to tell the truth. 'Frankfurt,' I lie, thinking of where I was arrested, the first town that comes into my head. 'Frankfurt an der Oder, of course, not the other one.'

'Of course.' He manages to raise a weak smile.

'Do you know Eisenhüttenstadt?' he asks. *Scheisse.* I start to panic. I can't remember where that is. But I seem to remember it's somewhere in the east. The east of the east. The eastern edge of the Republic. 'Of course,' I lie. It's easy, this lying game. Another world. Another world you can build and live in. It must be so tempting. 'It's right near us. I've plenty of friends there.' That's a lie, of course. I don't have any friends, actually, I want to say. And the only friend I had turned into my betrayer. But I know if I say that, the game will be up. The Stasi will make good on their promise. Bautzen or Hohenschönhausen. I don't want to try either of them, thank you.

He looks me straight in the eyes, as though he can tell I'm lying. I suppose a lot of prostitutes – because that's what I am now, a common prostitute – choose to lie.

'I was wondering if you might know my boyfriend,' he asks. 'He's from Hütte.'

Hütte? Where the hell's that? Panic rises in my throat again, I don't know if he can sense it. It's clearly somewhere I ought to know if I really did live in Frankfurt an der Oder. Then the penny drops. *Hütte.* The middle part of the name Eisenhüttenstadt. It must be a nickname. I hope he takes my blank look for me searching my brain to see if I remember his boyfriend. I don't of course, because I've never been to this Hütte in my life, and don't even really know where it is – though my guess that it's near Frankfurt seems to have been a lucky one.

'What's his name?'

'Dominik. Dominik Nadel.'

I shake my head slowly, and frown. 'Sorry. No.' I wonder if this Dominik has been stupid enough to give his real name, as the Stasi wanted me to. They claimed it would mean I'd be less likely to get caught out by forgetting my own fake name. I'd stood my ground and insisted I wanted to operate under an alias.

He looks even sadder now. Maybe I should have kept on lying, said I do know this boy. Spun it out. Arranged another meeting where hopefully we wouldn't just be talking.

He gets up, paces again. 'Look, I'm sorry. Maybe this was a mistake.'

'Are you sure you don't want me to just sit with you?'

'You just seem very young. Perhaps too young.'

'I'm eighteen,' I say. 'It's legal here, in the East.'

'Well, look. Let's leave it for tonight. I think it's just me. I'm just in one of those moods. It's been a tiring day. Perhaps if you're in the bar tomorrow?'

I try to smile my most winning smile. 'Of course. And you've already paid. Tomorrow's for free. Though it might be nice if we did more than talk.'

'No. I'm not promising anything. I'll pay – whether it's to talk again, or what, I don't know. Let's just see what happens.'

I realise I actually want to see him again. I want him to want me. Even though I've fulfilled my deal with the Stasi, even though I could stop now, I don't want to.

26

The next month (October 1976)
Wilhelm-Pieck-Stadt Guben, Bezirk Cottbus

Müller's plans to try to focus the investigation, to try to stop simply reacting to events and take control, were ruined with the news that came early the next day.

Another body had been found – near Guben. *Wilhelm-Pieck-Stadt Guben.* Müller tried – mentally at least – to give the town its official name.

But, as she knew only too well, sometimes in a homicide case it took a development like another murder to provide that missing piece of the jigsaw puzzle. To provide the breakthrough. The trouble was, this time she – and particularly her forensic officer Jonas Schmidt – had a personal involvement in the case. She hoped and prayed the body wasn't that of Markus, his son. That would be too much to bear. So far there had been no news on the victim's identity, other than that it was a young male.

They had to get down to Guben fast.

Schmidt had insisted on coming with them, despite his and Müller's fears. They all went in the Lada, Tilsner driving like a madman. Overtaking on blind corners, the blue light flashing. They wanted to make sure they got there before Diederich and Baum. Strictly speaking, of course, this was another administrative region – Cottbus, rather than Frankfurt. It shouldn't really concern the Frankfurt regional Stasi . . . but Müller had no doubt it would.

Schwarz had beaten them to it, to the banks of the Neisse, a couple of kilometres or so north of Guben. The body had been washed onto a mud bank on the western side of the river, the Republic's side – the opposite bank to Poland. As a matter of courtesy, Polish officers had also been invited to attend – Müller spotted their distinctive blue-grey uniforms as they waited at the bankside. Schwarz was already wading around in gumboots.

'Careful where you put your feet,' he said. 'It's easy enough to sink in right up to your middle. There should be some local uniform back in a few minutes. I sent them off to get duckboards.'

'What's it look like?' asked Müller. They couldn't see because a small tent had already been erected over the body to protect it from the elements. It was starting to rain. Schwarz must have seen the forecast and acted quickly.

'On the face of it, same sort of thing as Senftenberg. Naked. Restraint marks around the wrists again. Although maybe they weighed the body down in a different way, because I can't see any marks from ropes wrapped round it, or anything like that. That said, a lot of the corpse is covered in mud, so I can't really tell. And I didn't want to try washing it till the pathologist gets here. But, given the similarities, I took the precaution of calling in Fenstermacher. The local bloke's a bit put out. Is that OK?'

Müller smiled and nodded. It was more than OK. It was exactly what she'd been planning to do if the *Kripo* Hauptmann hadn't pre-empted her. 'When are you expecting her?'

'She'll be here in about thirty minutes. And by then we'll have a proper-size tent up – uniform are bringing one with the duck-boards.' He gestured towards the small camping flysheet which was the only thing currently protecting the dead youth from the downpour. 'That's just an emergency one I keep in the back of the car.'

Müller saw Tilsner rolling up his trousers. 'Your shoes will get ruined, Werner. Why not wait?'

He jerked his head towards Schmidt who'd been hanging back from the scene. Müller could tell he was trembling. She moved towards him, put up her umbrella to shelter them both, and pulled him into a hug.

'Is he OK?' asked Schwarz.

'His lad's missing and might be caught up in all this. Can you see the face without disturbing the body?'

'It's partly turned to the side. You can see some of it. Do you want to take a look?'

Tilsner nodded.

Schwarz started to take off his gumboots. 'I'm not sure what size you are, but you're welcome to try these. I wouldn't go in that mud without protection. It's badly polluted.'

Taking the local officer up on his offer, Tilsner took his shoes off and pulled the boots on, hopping from one foot to the other to try to keep his feet clean and dry, as Schwarz did the same in reverse with his own shoes.

As Tilsner lifted the flap to the makeshift tent, Müller held her breath. She could feel Schmidt, too, tense up in her arms. She squeezed him, swaddled him with her body, like you would with a child.

They were both hoping desperately for the same outcome.

They waited.

Time seemed to drag. Müller could see, though the gap in the tent, Tilsner peering at the body from various angles. Crouching down, examining.

Then he came out.

Schmidt was trembling.

Tilsner shook his head. Not a sad, slow shake. But a vigorous one. Then he was shouting.

'It's OK, Jonas. It's not him. I can't see all the face, but it's definitely not your son.'

Schmidt seemed to slump against Müller. She struggled to hold his not insignificant weight.

She could hear him sobbing, the tension easing from his body.

'It's OK, Jonas, it's OK,' she soothed.

He gave a heavy sigh. 'It's not, though, is it, Comrade *Major*? Hanne and I might have been lucky this time. But some poor mother and father, somewhere, have lost a son. And we still haven't found Markus.'

Schwarz's estimated time for Fenstermacher's arrival proved reasonably accurate, and within half an hour she was bustling around in a huge hooded rain cape. The larger tent and duckboards were now in position and they were all able to gather round the body as Fenstermacher examined it with her gloved hands.

She looked up briefly as one of the Polish officers entered. 'Goodness. There are even more of you this time. You must have been breeding like rabbits.'

'He's one of our Polish comrades,' explained Schwarz. 'In case the body's theirs, not ours. But there seemed to me to be some similarities to the one at Senftenberg. What do you think?'

'Some similarities. Some differences,' she replied gruffly. 'Same story everywhere, really. No dead body is ever exactly the same. That's why the job is such riotous fun. Although why you pulled me off my patch to come here, I'm not very sure. What did Dr Neudorf say about it? He won't be too happy. This is his manor. I'm trespassing. So if I get into trouble, it's you I'll be blaming, Helmut.'

'I'm sure you won't get into trouble, Gudrun.'

She continued her examination, without sharing any conclusions with the others – if indeed she'd reached any as yet.

'I wouldn't be too sure, Helmut. There's so many of you here, I bet some of you are Stasi, aren't you?'

Müller was about to say that, no, the Stasi hadn't arrived yet, when the flap of the tent opened and – as if on cue – Diederich walked in. He smiled warmly at Müller, as though the fact that her team had ignored the Stasi's orders to stay away from the case was of little consequence.

'Well, you could hear a pin drop in here now,' continued Fenstermacher. 'I wonder why?'

Müller could see Tilsner and Schwarz smirking at each other.

Fenstermacher sighed. 'Can I move him slightly? Have you got all the photos you need?'

Schwarz nodded. 'Go ahead. We got them before you came.'

'Right then, heave-ho.' Müller could see the strain on the pathologist's face as she lifted the dead youth on one side, just as she had with Dominik Nadel. There was a sucking sound as the torso was freed from the mud bank. Immediately, Müller could see a difference when his left shoulder blade was exposed, once the pathologist had wiped away the mud: there was no tattoo.

The pathologist let the body drop again into its muddy resting place. 'It's a bit like a newspaper spot-the-difference competition, really, isn't it?'

'What can you tell us so far?' asked Müller, given no one else had posed the question everyone wanted an answer to.

'All right. Similarities. Dead, obviously. Naked, obviously. A late teenage or early twenty-something person – and a male, obviously.' She batted away his floppy penis to emphasise her point. 'The similarities continue with these.' Fenstermacher lifted one wrist, then the other. They were partially covered in mud, but as Schwarz had said earlier, the marks were still clear. The youth had, in some way, been restrained. 'And then there's this.' She lifted the body again slightly, to show off the upper left arm, which she'd cleaned slightly. 'Injection marks. So, yes, there are plenty of similarities, and I can see why you brought me all the way from Hoyerswerda.

'However, there are also important differences. I can't see any evidence of anything being tied to the body – other than the wrists, of course, which we've already mentioned. But there are more fundamental differences, which may or may not help you with your inquiries. Ask me how long the body's been in the water.'

Tilsner took up the challenge. He seemed to enjoy Fenstermacher's wordplay. Müller would rather she just got to the point. 'How long has the body been in the water?' he asked, theatrically.

'I'd say just a few hours. Certainly less than a day.' There were looks of surprise all round, including from Müller. Diederich, she noticed, seemed to be maintaining a poker face. 'Ask me how I know that?'

Tilsner again batted it back. 'How *do* you know that?'

'Because there is no degradation of the body. Bit of wrinkling of skin, yes, but nothing more than you'd get after a long bath. And he hasn't yet been attacked by fish or other animals. And that usually happens *very* quickly. So, let's say less than a day to be on the safe side, at this stage. I suggest we do the autopsy quickly; here in Guben there should be the necessary facilities, unless Dr Neudorf starts getting territorial. Or am I supposed to say Wilhelm-Pieck-Stadt Guben these days? Anyway, you're doing very well, captain, with your questions. I'm impressed. Presumably I don't have to tell you the next question to ask.'

Tilsner play-acted, as though taking a long time to think. 'Umm, how about . . . what was the cause of death?'

'At last. Bravo! Well, if the police do finally realise that they're ridiculously overstaffed, and you're out of work, I might be able to find a bright lad like you a place working for me. Exactly. *What was the cause of death?* You'll remember that with our lake boy, it was asphyxiation, although a particularly nasty variant.

There are early signs of asphyxiation here too. I think he was probably on the cusp of drowning.

'But no. What finished this one . . .' – Fenstermacher made a dramatic swipe across the dead youth's chest, cleaning it of what Müller thought was just mud, but now in the smears left behind, she could see was mud mixed with blood – 'was this.'

The entry wound was now obvious.

They didn't need Fenstermacher's final words, but she said them anyway.

'He was shot.'

27

Wilhelm-Pieck-Stadt Guben, Bezirk Cottbus

Müller was keen to gather all the police officers together for a debrief as soon as possible. Schwarz offered to use his *Bezirk* Cottbus connections to secure a room at the Wilhelm-Pieck-Stadt Guben People's Police office, to avoid everyone having to go back to Frankfurt or Eisenhüttenstadt.

But as they were gathering to leave in their cars, Diederich approached Müller.

'I'm surprised to see you in these parts still, Karin.'

Müller studied his face. His expression was deadpan. 'We're not investigating Nadel's death any more – unless it overlaps with our current investigation.'

'Which is?'

'I'm sure you're fully aware, Comrade *Hauptmann*.' She wasn't going to play the first-names game with him. He and Baum had revealed their true colours.

'Well, yes, I'd heard it was about a missing youth. Markus . . .?'

The vagueness appeared faked to Müller. 'Schmidt. The son of the forensic scientist attached to the Serious Crimes Department. He has links to that "club" near Frankfurt, as did Nadel. And this death –' Müller gestured over her shoulder to the tent, where a couple of uniforms had stayed on guard until the body could be removed to the mortuary – 'in turn appears to have similarities to Nadel's death. You heard what the pathologist said. So it's perfectly reasonable for us to be involved in the investigation. I might ask why *you're* here. I thought you worked for the regional *MfS* in Frankfurt, not Cottbus.'

Diederich smiled, looking unconcerned. 'We, too, have a strong interest. If this death is indeed similar to Nadel's, then there may be another link to our drugs gangs. And clearly, if the victim was indeed shot—'

'I don't think there's much doubt about that, is there? You saw the entry wound yourself.' As Müller spoke, she saw Fenstermacher climbing into her car at the roadside. Ideally, she wanted the woman to join them for the debrief, and needed to catch her before she drove off. Diederich was blocking her path. 'Look, I'm in a hurry. Shall we just agree to disagree and accept we'll both have teams working on this – and try not to get in each other's way?'

'Suit yourself, Karin. I shall be referring this upwards – I doubt those above me will agree to that.'

Müller – who was already walking at a rapid pace towards Fenstermacher – turned back to the Stasi captain and shot him a withering look. 'I've already referred this upwards. I have the full backing of a colonel at Keibelstrasse.'

Diederich gave another thin smile. 'Let's see about that,' he said. 'In my experience, the Ministry for State Security usually gets its way . . . in the end.'

Müller was fortunate enough to catch up with the pathologist before she'd driven off. She seemed to be scrawling some notes on a dog-eared pad – probably her initial findings from the first view of the body. At first she looked doubtful about Müller's suggestion that she join them at Guben police station to discuss the case, but then demurred.

'I suppose if we're going to hold the autopsy here, I might as well hang around these parts. So, why not? Shall I follow you all?'

'Well, if you don't mind giving me a lift, I could ask you a few more questions as we drive along.'

Fenstermacher glanced down at Müller's shoes, eyeing them with distaste. 'That's fine, but if you could wipe those first, please, I'd be grateful. I like to look after this little beauty.' She caressed the steering wheel of the car as she said this, and Müller – while wiping the mud off her shoes on the grass verge – examined the vehicle more closely. She wasn't a car expert like Tilsner or Schmidt. But she knew this was an early, old-fashioned Wartburg – from the fifties or early sixties, before the more modern-looking, boxy ones commonly used by the police were introduced. It was in a rather fetching peppermint green, and it looked like the pathologist had kept it in near-perfect condition.

Müller signalled to Tilsner and Schmidt – who'd been waiting for her in the Lada – that she was getting a lift. Once she felt her shoes were clean enough, she moved round to the passenger side and climbed in. The inside of the car had a reassuring smell – a combination of old leather, petrol, and a tweedy middle-aged female.

'It's rather unusual this,' said Fenstermacher. 'My coming to one of your meetings. Why did you ask me along?' Fenstermacher checked her rear-view mirror, then signalled to pull out and follow Tilsner, the indicator giving a reassuring tick like an old mantelpiece clock.

'Well, it seems to me that what you can find out from the body at the autopsy, and what you've found so far, could help us to narrow this search down – significantly,' said Müller.

Fenstermacher nodded, but continued studying the road ahead.

'If the body had only been in the water a short time, then presumably it entered the water somewhere near here,' said Müller. 'Let's look at some of the local maps with the Guben police and see if we can pinpoint anything. If there is a link between Nadel and this latest youth's body, and they *were* both being restrained, were they being held somewhere around here? And if they were, are there others – and are they in danger?' *In particular, Markus Schmidt. Markus, the nervous, awkward son of my forensic scientist.*

'The gunshot wound obviously puts things in a different light too,' said Fenstermacher.

'But you say the body was already showing signs of asphyxiation, even before the shooting?'

Fenstermacher nodded.

'So he must have been shot in the water, while probably already struggling – and failing – to survive.'

'Someone obviously wanted to make absolutely sure he didn't,' said Fenstermacher. 'It's a wide river. It flows into the Oder and then to the Ostsee. I think it's just luck the body got caught on that mud bank. There's a bend in the river there. Otherwise the boy could have got all the way to Eisenhüttenstadt, Frankfurt – or even out to sea.'

The clock-like ticking of the indicators began again as Fenstermacher turned off the road, following Tilsner in the Lada into Guben's police office car park. She manoeuvred into the parking space next to Tilsner and switched off the engine. They didn't immediately climb out though. Müller had a couple more questions.

'The trouble is,' she said, 'that you said the body had been in the water a maximum of twenty-four hours. Your best guess was a few hours at most. It could have travelled a long, long way downstream in that time. Perhaps we need to be concentrating the search much further south.'

Fenstermacher sighed. 'Look, I can't say anything for definite until the autopsy. Once I've sectioned the lungs I might have a better idea. And I don't really like entering the realms of speculation. But –' Fenstermacher paused, stroking the steering wheel again with her calloused hands – 'we pathologists tend to be conservative, err on the side of caution when we're giving you visual findings from the first look at a body. It's a bit like a very rough sketch, and then we fill in the details later. I was giving you the uppermost parameters of length of immersion. We could – for example – look at it the other way.'

'What do you mean?' asked Müller, frowning.

'What if we looked at the lowermost parameters. How *few* hours the body could have possibly been in the water, given what I observed.'

Müller felt a lightness in her chest.

'Go on,' she prompted.

'Well, the answer would be very different. The *least* amount of time that body could have been immersed – based on what I saw just now – is probably round about half an hour . . . just thirty minutes.'

'Jesus,' said Müller. 'So whoever we're looking for . . .'

'Could be very close to here, *Major*, they could be very close indeed.'

28

The next night I have to wait even longer before I see him. I assume he isn't coming and finish the one drink I've been trying to make last as long as possible. Then I head for the door.

He walks in just as I'm about to go out, and we nearly collide with each other. There's a wild look in his eyes, and I can immediately smell the alcohol on his breath.

'You're not leaving, are you?' he whines. I keep on walking. Play hard to get sometimes, the agents said, it keeps them interested. 'Please,' he shouts, running after me. 'Come and have a drink with me.'

He tries to grab me, but I recoil. 'You already stink of drink,' I say. 'You shouldn't have any more. And I need to get back.' This last bit is a lie. I have nothing to go back to, except prison if I fail. The agents weren't satisfied with the pictures of kissing. They need him to be photographed in flagrante, in a position where there can be no doubts. But with the amount of alcohol it smells like he's consumed, I bet he won't be able to perform – so my night, and his money, would be wasted. He might not be willing to pay again.

'Come to the room, then, please.' I see him look quickly round the bar. He's wondering if anyone has seen our little exchange. When he's satisfied no one is paying any attention, he pushes me into a shadowy corner and then takes my hand, rubbing it against the front of his trousers. I can feel he's already hardening. Perhaps I've misjudged things. Maybe he's just recently downed a schnapps or something, but isn't yet too drunk.

'OK,' I say. 'But I don't want to end up just talking. I don't want to waste my time.'

'Feel me,' he whispers urgently. 'You won't be wasting your time, I promise.'

In the room, he immediately pounces on me, trying to get my clothes off.

'Easy,' I say. 'We've got all the time in the world.'

'I thought you said you had to get home?' He's kneeling on the floor, unbuckling my belt.

'I've changed my mind.'

I close my eyes. For a moment, I feel ashamed. I'm trapping this man – ruining him – even though I quite like him. My brain is torn between enjoying this and calculating the best angle to be standing in to make sure the photos being taken at this very moment show his full face. Soon, though, the pleasure centres of my brain take over.

We're in a new position. I hear him behind me, taking a long sniff of something. Then he's holding a small red-wine coloured bottle under my nose too – I pull away at first, worried what it is, repelled by the vile smell that's like old sweaty socks.

'Try it. It smells horrible, but it's harmless. And it makes you feel great.'

I don't really want to, but I don't want to annoy him. I need to keep him onside as photo after photo is taken secretly, automatically, by cameras the agents have hidden away. Or maybe they're in the next room and have drilled tiny holes in the walls. I have no idea.

I relent and take a long sniff. I nearly gag and retch from the disgusting smell, but then I feel the rush, an incredible horniness, and I understand now why there's a white lightning bolt on the label of the squat, miniature bottle.

I start to enjoy it. Even though, all the while, I know the Stasi are taking their photographs.

That last thought nags at me, and a new feeling starts to well up. I think of my father. How I've let him down. How he used to ruffle my hair. How we used to try to fish by hand in the lakes. And I begin to feel terribly ashamed.

29

October 1976
Wilhelm-Pieck-Stadt Guben, Bezirk Cottbus

Gathering in the small room at the People's Police station with Tilsner and Schmidt at her side felt like old times to Müller. The conversation in the car with Fenstermacher had been useful. Yes, there was no certainty the body had been in the water for less than an hour. Hopefully more precision might come at the afternoon post-mortem. But it made sense for the time being to start the search in and around Guben. It was a centre of population. Someone might have heard the shooting, unless, as Müller suspected, a silencer was used.

The local police had pinned a series of maps to the noticeboard on the office wall. Alongside were photographs of Dominik Nadel – living and dead; the best image they had of the unidentified body found that morning by the riverbank, and also – spaced some way apart, as they couldn't be sure he was caught up in any of this – a portrait photograph of Jonas Schmidt's son. She could only guess at the torment her *Kriminaltechniker* was going through, seeing a photograph of his only son in these circumstances.

She was happy to let Schwarz question the local officers.

'Do we know anything about the currents and flow of the river, here in the town and where the body was found?' He pointed to the bend in the river, where the body had washed up.

'Well, it's obviously not at its fastest flowing at the moment,' said the local *Vopo* captain. 'That would be in the spring, after the snow melts. But summer's over, it's starting to rain more. There's plenty of water in there. How fast it's actually flowing, I've no idea.'

'We could drop something off one of the bridges, perhaps?' suggested Schmidt. 'Maybe a piece of wood. Or even a fake body – something of similar size and density. I should be able to mock something up. Then time how long it takes to get from position "A" to position "B".'

'Good idea, Jonas,' said Müller. 'Get onto it straight away.' Keeping him busy would take his mind off his son. She thought for a moment. 'Could there be some sort of scientific laboratory around here?'

'We'd have heard about it, surely?' said the captain. 'Unless . . .'

'Unless what?' prompted Müller.

'Unless it's on the Polish side of the river. In Gub*in* rather than Gub*en*. I can liaise with our Polish colleagues if you like.'

'Good idea. Please get onto that.'

'OK,' said Schwarz. 'But what if it's somewhere anonymous?'. Are there any old industrial areas or disused buildings, any hidden basements that could be used?'

The uniform captain held his hands up in the air as though in surrender. 'There must be tens, hundreds, perhaps thousands.

There was a lot of heavy fighting here towards the end of the war when the Red Army was advancing. The Nazis deliberately destroyed a lot of buildings and infrastructure, but some of it was only partially destroyed. And it could equally be somewhere in plain sight.'

Fenstermacher, at the back of the room, cleared her throat. 'If I could just interrupt a second, I think you might be getting a little carried away with the idea of the body entering the water somewhere near Guben. I was only giving an estimate. I would counsel that some of this ought to wait until I've performed the autopsy.'

Müller nodded. 'You're right, of course. But there are still some things we can start investigating now. Comrade *Hauptmann* Schwarz, could you and the captain here organise a uniform team to go house to house, showing people the photos of Dominik, Markus and the face from the body today?'

'Isn't that going to alarm people?' said the captain, frowning.

Before she answered, Müller looked around the room to make sure Schmidt had left to begin his task. She was relieved to see that he had. 'They have every right to be alarmed. This *is* a worrying situation. At least one youth is still missing – he's the son of one of ours, and time may be running out for him.'

30

The next day
Eisenhüttenkombinat Ost

In the end Fenstermacher's autopsy was disappointing – at least to Müller – in that it didn't really provide any of the clarity she'd hoped for. The pathologist – whom Müller felt had opened up in their one-to-one conversation in the car – seemed to be back to her grumpiest self, and insisted that the parameters she'd already given for the duration of immersion were the ones borne out by a more detailed examination of the body. In other words, the minimum time the body had been in the water was thirty minutes. The maximum, twenty-four hours. It was a yawning window, which translated into tens, perhaps hundreds of kilometres difference in how far the body could have travelled. Nevertheless, Fenstermacher had implied she was leaning towards a shorter period, so Müller hoped the efforts they were making in Guben and neighbouring Gubin wouldn't be wasted.

Once she'd set the teams to work locally, she radioed Keibelstrasse to alert other police districts further upstream: Forst, Görlitz, and even right down to the Czechoslovak border

near Zittau, though the further away, the more unlikely. Then –
satisfied she'd put as much in train as possible to try to follow
the new lead – she retreated to the Hauptstadt for a long-over-
due reunion with Emil, the twins and Helga. The seriousness
of the new development – another murder – lifted some of her
guilt, but she still felt the weight of the shame of, in effect, aban-
doning her children, the children she'd yearned for for so long.

Her hopes for some quality time with them, though, were
shattered almost as soon as she was through the apartment door.
Metzger had got in touch again. He wanted to meet urgently.
At the steelworks, in Eisenhüttenstadt.

The man looked even more nervous – even more harried – than
before, if that were possible. And his mood darkened further
when he saw Müller hadn't come alone.

'I said this had to be another discreet meeting. I meant you,
Comrade *Major*, on your own.'

'Anything you can say to me, you can say to my deputy,
Hauptmann Werner Tilsner. He's equally trustworthy.' Tilsner
extended his hand, but the West German minister declined to
take it, and instead shooed them inside a low, corrugated-iron
building. Müller and Tilsner had had trouble finding it. Number
1 Work Street – the main entrance for the EKO complex – was
easy enough to find. No one in Eisenhüttenstadt could miss it.
Just follow the chimney smoke in a straight line down Hütte's
main shopping street. But this part of the works was round the
back, fenced off, and dated – Müller assumed – from when the

plant was first built at the beginning of the fifties. It hadn't aged well in the subsequent quarter century.

The shed Metzger took them into was in semi-darkness. It seemed to add to his sombre mood.

'I didn't tell you the whole truth before,' he said, sitting down on a rusted metal pipe, holding his head in his hands. 'There wasn't just one youth in Leipzig.'

Müller could see the man was tormented by having to reveal this news, but for her – and evidently for Tilsner too, judging by the way she'd seen him roll his eyes even in the dim light of the shed – this was no revelation, and hardly relevant either.

'So?' said Tilsner.

'There was another, who I had a deeper relationship with.'

'*A deeper relationship?*' Tilsner's repetition of the phrase seemed to drip with sexual innuendo. But Metzger ignored him and carried on with his story.

'I fell in love with this second youth, even though I was paying him. In the end he refused payment. He said he loved me too.'

Tilsner snorted. Müller gently shook her head and silently mouthed: '*No, Werner.*' She didn't want her deputy's prejudices encouraging Metzger to clam up. Perhaps he had something useful to say, after all. She did have some sympathy for Tilsner's cynicism though. It was an age-old story – a lonely man thinking he'd fallen in love with a prostitute. A prostitute who was probably playing him.

'We were seeing each other virtually every night. He seemed troubled.'

'Did he give you a name?' asked Müller.

'Yes,' said the politician. 'Tobias. Tobias Scherer.'

Müller felt a sense of disappointment. Although she hadn't wanted to think of Markus Schmidt prostituting himself, at least if it had been Jonas's son they would have had a more recent sighting.

'Troubled in what way?' asked Tilsner.

'Well, I'd noticed after the first couple of our meetings the lad had tried to talk more about what was going on at the trade fair, particularly about the steel price, contract negotiations, who the potential buyers were, that sort of thing. At first I wasn't suspicious about this. We were on the fringes of the trade fair. I'd already told him I was involved in the steel industry. It just seemed part of normal conversation.'

This time it was Tilsner's turn to shake his head. Müller knew what he was thinking. Why would a common prostitute have any interest in the steel market? Metzger seemed to have been incredibly naive.

The West German politician kept his eyes downcast, staring fixedly at the floor, strewn as it was with rusted bolts and other random pieces of old metal.

'But things changed after seeing him – every night – for a week or so.'

'A week!' exclaimed Tilsner. 'How much money was this costing you?'

'I told you,' the man continued, bitterly, 'I was lonely. Trapped in an unhappy marriage. Anyway, as I say, after about a week things changed. His questions started to become much more specific. I began to suspect that this was some sort of honey trap. At the same time, we were becoming more affectionate towards each other. I think there was love there – on both our parts – it wasn't just a financial exchange. So I was confused. I didn't initially let on that I'd realised he was using me, or *trying* to use me, trying to pump me for information. But eventually it started to become so obvious I had to say something. He broke down in tears. He was an absolute wreck. Clearly there was some terrible secret he couldn't tell me. I comforted him as best I could.'

'I bet you did,' said Tilsner. This time, Müller didn't admonish him. She was as fed up with the man's whining as Tilsner, and was continuing to wonder how relevant this was to her investigation.

'Please carry on, Herr Metzger,' she said.

'Well, as I say, I comforted him. Told him I loved him. That – if necessary – I would help him escape to the West, to live with me. Perhaps I wasn't being entirely truthful at that point. It wouldn't do for me to be seen to leave my wife and children. I'm sure you can understand that.

'But up to a point I was being honest. If I could have helped him to escape somehow – and with my being a politician that would be easier for me than some others – then I could have set him up in a flat in Bonn. We could have had some sort of a life together, some of the time at least. I think that was the tipping point. He started to talk. To explain what had happened to him. He'd been caught up in some drugs sting. Caught red-handed by the Stasi with amphetamines. But framed, he said.'

'Ah,' said Tilsner, throwing down one of the old metal bolts he'd been using like a worry bead. It hit the floor of the shed and then bounced off it with a crack like a bullet ricochet. 'That old chestnut. *Framed*. It's amazing how many drug dealers have been framed. In fact, I would hazard a guess that there aren't any actual drug dealers in the Republic.'

'I can understand your scepticism, officer. I'm just telling you the truth. I'm just trying to help you, and I hope that you will try to help me in return.'

'How?' asked Müller.

'I'll come to that, Comrade *Major*. Let me just finish the story. He said it was the Stasi who were insisting he try to find out confidential details about the steel contracts. Unless he did, he said, they were going to make sure he was jailed for the drug dealing. So he was under duress. Basically, your secret service had forced him to become a prostitute. Surely you can't be proud of that?'

Müller wasn't proud of it. She didn't like the sound of what Metzger was saying at all. But she wasn't entirely surprised about the Stasi's methods. 'It's not a question of pride, Herr Metzger,' said Müller. 'Secret services all over the world operate in a covert way. Sometimes their methods are – shall we say – not as clear-cut as those of my organisation, the police. The *BfV* – your West German domestic intelligence service – probably operates in similar ways. There's nothing I can do about it. I'm just trying to do my job.'

'That's what the Nazis used to say.'

The comment seemed to send Tilsner into a frenzy. He leapt up and grabbed the man by the lapels of his anorak. 'Don't you dare compare us to Nazis, you *Arschloch*! You're in no position to hurl insults around, or moralise. You'd just better hope none of these boys you were fucking – oh sorry, *that you were in love with* – are underage. Because if they are . . .'

Müller laid a restraining hand on Tilsner's shoulder.

'S-s-sorry,' the man stammered. 'I. . . I don't know what I was thinking. It was wrong of me to say that. I'm just so desperate, I'm not feeling myself.'

Tilsner had sat back down on a pile of old wooden pallets. 'Yes. That's the problem. Stick to *feeling yourself* next time. You might not end up in such a God-awful mess.'

'Anyway,' said Metzger, now looking even more downtrodden, 'we were making plans. We were in love. He said he wasn't going to help the Stasi any more. They'd insisted, got angry. He'd still refused.'

'How do you know he was telling the truth?' asked Müller.

'Because he revealed everything – everything that had been going on. He came clean to me. He said it had been a set-up from the start. At first, he was supposed to trap me into compromising positions, so that the Stasi could secretly take photographs.'

Müller frowned. 'The room was bugged?'

'That's what he said. Although if that was the case, why haven't they used them against me? Why haven't they released them to the West German press or TV? I was hoping that perhaps they'd messed up. Perhaps the photos didn't develop properly, or the automatic equipment failed to fire.'

Tilsner let out a loud guffaw. 'Ha! Don't count on that. They'll just be biding their time, you mark my words.'

Her deputy's warning seemed to finally silence the politician. The man just sat there, eyes down again, wringing his hands.

'The trouble is,' he said, finally, 'Tobias has disappeared. Since that night, since that night he said he loved me and he'd refuse to do any more work for the Stasi, I've not seen him again. First I looked in Leipzig, and then Frankfurt. That's where he said he was from. I even found this secret club – you know – where our sort go. No one's ever heard of him. What I wanted was to see if you could find out where he is. He and Dominik Nadel seemed to be doing the same thing, working for the same organisation, targeting me. There must be a link.' In the gloomy light, he looked at the two detectives hopefully.

'Did Dominik ever ask you about the steel contracts, anything like that at all?' asked Müller.

Metzger shook his head. 'No, nothing like that.'

Tilsner sighed. 'Then why do you think there was a link? There may be none.'

Müller reached into her inside coat pocket and brought out a photo of the unidentified youth found on the riverbank. It was just his face, after Fenstermacher had cleaned it up.

'Can you take a look at this photo, Herr Metzger. Is this the youth you know as Tobias Scherer?'

The man took the photo and started squinting at it. Müller reached into her pocket again, and this time pulled out her miniature pen torch, and clicked it on. Metzger shone the beam on the picture.

He shook his head. 'No, absolutely not. I've never seen this person before.'

Müller was more reluctant to do what she did next. Again, she reached into her inside pocket. Another photo for Metzger to examine.

Again he shone the torch on the image, then immediately exclaimed.

'Fantastic. This is him. This is Tobias. You know where he is, then?'

Müller, of course, didn't share the West German's enthusiasm. In fact, his reaction filled her with dread, even though she'd long had her suspicions.

'No, Herr Metzger, I'm afraid we don't know where he is. We're worried about him. Very worried indeed. And – I'm afraid – his name's not Tobias Scherer. That was a lie. And he's not from Frankfurt either. He's from Pankow in Berlin. And his father is a dear friend of mine.'

31

The way events had accelerated had meant some aspects of the inquiry had been ignored, Müller was aware of that. They now had solid information about Markus, but all roads there led to the Stasi. She couldn't imagine Diederich and Baum being cooperative, given what had gone on. And they may well be mixed up in all of it. If what Metzger had said was true, and the Stasi had followed through on their threats, it looked like Markus Schmidt might well not be missing at all – but languishing in some Stasi jail, having gone back on his deal of cooperating with them. There was only one Stasi officer she trusted enough to find out the information she needed.

Oberst Klaus Jäger.

The man who'd been central to the case of the *Jugendwerkhöfe* teens. The man who'd given her the information that had led to her discovering who her natural birth mother was – even if it was years too late for a reunion – and who had enabled her to be reunited with her natural grandmother, Helga. But her trust in

Jäger only went so far. If she went to him for help, he would want the favour returned – with interest. Of that she could be certain.

One aspect of the inquiry that had been put on the back burner was the sock used to kill Dominik Nadel by stuffing it down his windpipe. So far, the house-to-house searches in Guben, the hunt for potential medical research establishments, none of it had borne fruit. Now they were about to enter the bar of one of the former Yugoslav players for BSG Stahl. Even though Müller had her doubts, the youth team coach had insisted they might hold the key to Dominik Nadel's murder, and Schmidt's sock research had pointed in the same direction.

Slobodan Stefanović stood guard behind his bar, much in the way he used to protect his goalkeeper as one of Stahl's key centre backs in their *Oberliga* stint. A giant of a man, who looked more like a nightclub bouncer. A misshapen nose was testament to the number of times he must have put his head in the firing line to save his team. His reward? Cut loose. No pay, no prestige, no prospects. *Could a man like that be driven to kill?* Müller wondered. The trouble was, while the Stahl defence would have been kept perpetually busy, now that he was a barman, Stefanović had little to do. The bar was empty and looked like it had seen better times: dated wallpaper, dirty tables, and an array of trophies on virtually every shelf, all covered in a fine layer of dust.

He didn't appear particularly welcoming either, which might explain his lack of customers. Müller and Tilsner stood at the bar for a few seconds before he deigned to look up from his Serbo-Croat sports paper, even though he must have heard them approaching. And even when he did look up, he didn't say anything, just raised his eyebrows and flicked his head.

Müller and Tilsner showed their IDs. 'I'm *Major* Müller, this is *Hauptmann* Tilsner. We're from the serious crimes department in Berlin.'

'Oh yes,' said Stefanović, sounding bored, his German tinged with a strong Slavic accent. 'What *serious crimes* have been going on in Hütte? Nothing ever happens here. Wish it did. It might give the locals something to talk about. They might then want to come to a bar to discuss it, rather than sitting in their flats behind net curtains drinking cheap *Kaufhalle* beer.'

'We want to talk to you about your time with BSG Stahl,' said Tilsner.

'Ha ha. I don't suppose you want my autograph.'

'Not until we need you to sign your statement,' said Müller.

'Very funny. I haven't done anything wrong, so I won't be needing to sign any statements, thank you. Although if business continues like this – or rather *doesn't* continue, like this – I might have to rob a bank soon. But even then, I'd just end up with more of your shitty East German marks, so on second thoughts, I won't bother. I don't suppose you two are buying a drink either, are you?'

'I'll have a beer, if you're offering,' said Tilsner. 'On the house, of course.'

The man sighed, but despite his affected surliness, pulled out one of his largest beer glasses and started to fill it with draught Pilsner. He nodded at Müller. It was about as near as he was going to get to asking her if she wanted anything.

'I'd love a coffee, if that's OK?'

'Oh God! There's always one, isn't there?' he complained, half to himself, half to Tilsner. 'How about a juice instead?' He looked round at an almost empty shelf. 'I can offer you apple juice or . . . apple juice?'

'Apple juice would be lovely.'

Stefanović opened two juice bottles, added them and some ice to a glass, and plonked it down in front of Müller.

He sighed. 'So. BSG Stahl. A sad story. A sad, sad story.'

'Do people still feel cut up about it?' asked Tilsner.

'I guess so. The supporters especially. Some of the players. Particularly those directly affected.'

Müller gave him a quizzical look. 'So, the foreign players? The Yugoslavs?'

'I think that's a fair comment. I've no particular axe to grind, mind. I was at the end of my contract anyway, my knees were shot, I was already heading towards my mid-thirties. Your legs start to go then.' He gave a throaty laugh. 'The writing was certainly on the wall for me. Ah, look. I enjoyed it. I've got a fair few trophies, as you can see. I just wish my last contract hadn't been in a dump like Hütte.'

'So why didn't you go back to your homeland?' asked Tilsner.

'Now that, young sir, is a very good question. I can see why you've risen through the ranks as a detective. The answer, as is often the case, is I got a local girl pregnant. She's now my wife, she's in the kitchen, and no doubt if you hang around you'll be trying to cadge a free meal from her soon just like you've blagged a free drink from me.'

Tilsner smiled. 'Maybe. You never know your luck. Anyway, getting back to the illegal payments scandal. Who was blamed for it?'

Stefanović frowned. 'I'm not that well up on it. As I say, I'd have been leaving at the end of the season anyway. I think it was some youth team player, but that always sounded like a lot of nonsense to me. And it was never really a scandal. The only scandal was that BSG Stahl was the only team punished. Every team in the league was paying their foreign stars when they shouldn't. Why would they come all that way otherwise? To be honest, there *was* no scandal. It was just that we were a little team who happened to have been promoted to the big league. That didn't sit too well with some of the others, including the Wine Reds.'

'The Wine Reds?' queried Müller.

'Dynamo Berlin,' explained Tilsner. 'My team – it's their nickname.'

'*Your* team,' said the barman. 'And of course *Mielke's* team. The *Stasi* team. It wouldn't surprise me if he was the one behind getting Stahl ejected. So you support them, do you? You're not *one* of them are you?'

Müller laughed. Tilsner glowered and fell silent.

'Whoops,' said Stefanović.

Müller's face grew serious. 'Would it surprise you to know that that same youth team player, Dominik Nadel –'

'Ah, that's the one. Correct. Sorry, it had slipped my mind.'

'Would it surprise you to know he'd been found murdered?'

Stefanović's jokey manner changed abruptly. 'Jesus! It certainly would surprise me. Poor boy. What's all that about, then?'

Tilsner shrugged. 'That's what we'd like to find out. That's why we're talking to people . . . like you.'

'This isn't common knowledge,' continued Müller, 'but a sock, we believe from Yugoslavia, was instrumental in the murder.'

'Instrumental in what way?' asked Stefanović.

'In the way of being stuffed down his windpipe so he couldn't breathe,' said Tilsner, taking a long drink of his beer.

'Ouch,' said the flat-nosed former defender. 'Not nice. So how do you know this sock was made in Yugoslavia?'

Müller knew they'd already said too much to the bar owner, but he seemed to have a knack of finding out information, without it seeming obvious that was what he was doing. *He'd make a good detective if his bar venture does fail.*

'It wasn't made in Yugoslavia. It was Italian. But it had some vegetable matter trapped in it which we believe came from Yugoslavia.'

Stefanović leant back, laughing his head off. 'Well, that's it, then. Proof positive. Either me or one of my fellow Yugoslav ex-Stahl players obviously murdered this whistle-blower. It's as plain as day follows night.' Then he frowned. 'Sorry, I shouldn't laugh. What's happened to the kid is terrible. But come on, even if one of us had brought one of our football socks from Yugoslavia, why would there still be Balkan vegetable matter in it after so long? It's either a fairy story, or someone has obviously – and quite deliberately – planted some evidence. Now who would do that, do you think?'

Müller maintained a stony face. But she knew what was coming next. Judging by his sour look, Tilsner did too.

'Mr Wine Red supporter, I think you might have a very good idea, don't you think? The same outfit that protects your team, and makes sure it only gets the finest players.'

Stefanović didn't have to spell it out. Müller – her face burning – knew very well what he meant. She finished her juice, and tapped Tilsner on the shoulder. It was time to go. Stefanović might be mocking them – but she knew he was right.

32

Two months later (early December)
Strausberger Platz, East Berlin

The direction of the inquiry – which had seemed so clear when the second body was found, and when Metzger had confirmed the second youth he was involved with was Markus – now seemed to be meandering again, and the successful conclusion Müller had been hoping for just a few weeks earlier looked further away than ever.

The first flurries of wet snow had begun to fall on Berlin, and Müller knew Christmas wasn't far away. For her, Emil and Helga it would be the first Christmas with the twins, both of whom were now in a crèche, and at nine months old were crawling and causing mayhem when not in childcare. She knew, though, that Jonas Schmidt and his wife faced a much bleaker, more desperate Christmas – the first without their only son. Still missing, and despite Reiniger and Keibelstrasse assigning Müller's supposed Serious Crimes Squad to the case, still no nearer to being found. It was a horrific situation for Schmidt – and an embarrassing one for Müller.

Tilsner was even grumbling about having to spend so much time away from home. Things with his wife, Koletta, and his two teenage children hadn't been great since – with some justification – Koletta had accused him of having an affair with Müller some eighteen months earlier. Müller felt guilty she was putting too much of the drudgery of the investigation on his shoulders, while she used her new promotion as an excuse to spend more time at the People's Police headquarters at Keibelstrasse – which also meant more time with Emil and the twins.

They'd still failed to locate any possible medical research centre. Schmidt's body-floating experiments had produced a flow rate for the river, but without a more precise time of death, virtually any stretch of the Neisse that bordered the Republic upstream of Guben could have been an entry point. They hadn't even been able to identify the second body – and had no matching report of a missing person. That didn't seem to make sense, unless the victim wasn't even from the Republic. But then they'd checked with their Polish colleagues too, without success.

Her one hope of getting some information from the Stasi had yielded little so far either. She'd tried to contact *Oberst* Klaus Jäger several times at Normannenstrasse, but had drawn a blank every time.

When Jäger did finally respond to her request for a meeting, Müller was perhaps filled with more gratitude than it merited. But she'd felt powerless in her attempts to help her friend and colleague, Jonas Schmidt. At least now there was an opportunity to possibly get some information about Markus's welfare and whereabouts.

Just as Müller had chosen one of Jäger's favourite haunts for her meeting with Metzger, Jäger selected one of Müller's favoured meeting places: the fairytale fountains. The Märchenbrunnen in Volkspark Friedrichshain.

She took the tram, as she had before, and saw he was already waiting for her, sitting on the low wall in front of the fountains. Sleet was forecast, so Müller wore her red waterproof coat, but made sure she put on two layers of tights under her woollen skirt, and several layers under the coat. Even so, by the time Müller sat down next to him, she was already shivering.

'I see you've got yourself a new coat since the last time we were here, Karin. It's still not really the thing for this sort of weather though, is it?'

Müller looked into his face and smiled. He was still tanned, still had the sideburns, the shoulder-length sandy hair. In short, he was still the spitting image of one of the smooth TV presenters on the West German news.

'I know,' she answered after a moment. 'I put on extra layers too. And I can't moan. This time I *have* been promoted, so I could afford a new coat.' She looked at the sheepskin lapel of his. 'Maybe one like yours. It's the real thing, isn't it?'

He laughed. 'Only the best for the best.'

'Have you moved departments or something? I've been trying to get in touch with you for a while.'

Jäger shook his head. 'No. Still working for the foreign service – the Main Intelligence Directorate. But based here in the Hauptstadt.'

Müller fell silent. She felt slighted. He'd obviously been deliberately ignoring her calls. But it wasn't as though they were close friends. He'd been helpful over tracing her natural family. But in the graveyard girl case the previous year she'd always felt he was controlling her, toying with her, if not even outright undermining her.

'I can see that's not the answer you were expecting. But I work for the Ministry for State Security, Karin. Ultimately, you and I know we're on the same side. But our short-term goals aren't always going to coincide. I have been following your progress though. No doubt we'll be seeing more of each other, or at least you'll be seeing more of one Stasi officer or another. That goes hand in hand with a senior role in the police, I'm sure you're aware. Anyway, what was it you wanted? You didn't request a meeting just to find out how I am.'

Müller hunched down in her raincoat, pulling the lapels up. Stupidly, she hadn't brought an umbrella, and the sleet had started again. She didn't mind snow. It was a fresh, fun reminder of her childhood in the Thuringian forest with her adopted family, a reminder that she was once a top schoolgirl winter sports athlete. She didn't even mind the rain – it often had a cleansing effect on the Hauptstadt's thick, choking smogs. But she didn't like sleet. It seemed almost colder than snow, wetter than rain, and neither one thing nor quite the other.

Delving into his briefcase, Jäger pulled out a retractable umbrella. He unfolded it, and held it over both their heads. It felt a surprisingly intimate gesture to Müller, and she found herself blushing.

'Has the cold robbed you of the power of speech?' he chided gently.

Müller sighed. 'No, sorry. I was thinking. You're right, of course. I wanted to see you to beg a favour.'

'Another one? If I remember correctly, you're already in my debt after our chat in Halle-Neustadt. You're sure you want to ask another favour before you've paid the last one back? I'm renowned at Normannenstrasse for having an elephantine memory.'

'It's a favour for a dear friend.'

'Jonas Schmidt?'

Müller shouldn't have been surprised. Jäger's stock-in-trade was knowing everything about everyone.

She nodded, wary now.

'It's a difficult one, Karin. There are other – shall we say – *interests* involved. Sometimes regional branches of *MfS* have their own agendas. I don't think you enamoured yourself to the Frankfurt branch by circumventing their ban on investigating the drug addict's death further. Reiniger didn't either. He probably needs taking down a peg or two.'

'I see you're toeing the Party line, then, Comrade *Oberst*.'

'I shouldn't have to remind you, Karin, that in this Republic that's what we're all supposed to do. *Major* Baum in Frankfurt felt you were almost opposing him outright. That's a dangerous game to play. So my room for leeway may be slim. They won't want to be doing me – or you – any favours.'

Müller sighed. She'd had enough of pussyfooting around. She eyeballed Jäger and dropped the unctuous honorifics. 'Klaus. You're a father. I'm a mother. Just imagine if *your* son went missing.'

Jäger's face reddened. He started to speak, but Müller held up her hand.

'My son *did* go missing, remember? He was stolen away from me at birth. *Before I'd even had a chance to hold him.*' Müller could feel the tears welling up. She tried to fight them back – crying wouldn't help her cause. Anger wouldn't help her cause either, but she couldn't help it. 'Now just imagine that your son goes missing, you have no news of him for weeks, and then it looks like he's involved in a revolting conspiracy involving the planting of drugs, enforced prostitution and murder. You wouldn't be very happy, would you? In fact, you'd be desperate, as desperate as Jonas Schmidt is at the moment. Yes, he wants his son back safe. But even if you can't achieve that, surely you can find out some information?'

Jäger started to stand up. 'I've listened to enough of this.'

'Please, Klaus. You're just walking away from your own con-science. I know that somewhere inside you, Klaus Jäger, is a half-decent man.'

Müller could feel her heartbeat pounding inside her head. She wasn't sure what was driving her on. But she'd had enough.

She ran after Jäger, caught him up, and then stood in front of him, blocking his way.

'Is there a decent man inside here?' she shouted. He was red-faced with anger by now, fighting to control himself. 'Because if there is, you need to show it. Now's your chance. There's a stinking mess behind all of this. I know there is. You've got the chance to do just a little bit of good by helping a father like yourself.'

Jäger inhaled deeply and slowly, and then let the breath out. He sucked his teeth, as though he were fighting some inner demon. Then he ran his hands down his face, as though to wipe away the invective Müller had aimed at him, stepped round the detective and headed for the park exit.

33

When she returned to her office in Keibelstrasse after her meeting with Jäger, once the adrenalin of the argument had worn off, Müller started to worry. Had she, in letting her emotions get the better of her, scuppered her best chance of helping Jonas Schmidt? She knew what Jäger thought of her. That she was over-promoted and too young for her position. He'd said that at the end of her last case. That had been his reason for recruiting her, and since then she'd been promoted another two ranks, so he no doubt still thought the same.

At least she had stood up for herself, and for Schmidt, and for his son. She couldn't just go on playing the puppet on a string for her whole career.

Her frustrations were eased a few moments later by a telephone call put through to her desk from Hoyerswerda. It was Fenster-macher, the pathologist.

'I've got some news for you,' the woman grumbled down a crackly line. 'In fact two bits of news. Are you happy for me to talk about it over an open line, or do you want to meet somewhere?'

The thought of another tiring drive, of more time away from her family, didn't fill Müller with joy – despite the fact that Fenstermacher seemed to be offering up important new information. She felt drained by the verbal battle with the Stasi colonel. But it was the knowledge that the Stasi were taking so much interest in the case, the fact that they were *involved*, that made up her mind.

'*Major* Müller. Did you hear me?' bellowed Fenstermacher.

'I heard you, yes. Let's meet. Where do you suggest?'

'I can't get away for long, I'm afraid, so Senftenberg is about as much as I can manage. But at least that's a bit nearer to you than Hoy. I don't really trust that bar at the hotel though. It's exactly the sort of place where people eavesdrop. How about that beach on the lake where the sailing club is, where the first body was found?'

The sleet had turned to light snow, but it wasn't settling on the motorway, and with traffic light and the Lada able to cruise at high speed, Müller managed to do the trip in little over ninety minutes, without needing to take a break.

When she pulled into the car park by the sailing club, she found Fenstermacher's beautiful vintage Wartburg already parked up, facing the lake, its peppermint-green paintwork providing a beautiful splash of colour on an otherwise dull grey day. Once again, she found herself admiring the car. She'd never really coveted material things, but somewhere at the back of her mind a little voice told her it would be rather nice to own a stylish car like that. Something a bit different to the box-like uniformity of the modern Trabis, Wartburgs and Ladas. Perhaps she'd look into it when this case was finally over.

She parked the Lada and opened Fenstermacher's passenger door.

'Is this all right for you?' the older woman asked. 'I've had the engine and the heater running. Been here about five minutes already. So it's nice and warm.'

Too warm for Müller, who still had her coat and layers on from the Märchenbrunnen. She took her coat off, then peeled off her uppermost jumper, and placed them both on the back seat. In doing so, her T-shirt and thin jumper rucked up, baring her midriff. As she turned back to face the front, she caught the pathologist appraising her – at least that's what it felt like. The way a man might look at her. Fenstermacher looked away quickly, but not before Müller noticed the woman's face reddening.

The pathologist had a file open, resting on the steering wheel.

'First things first,' she said. 'The second body. The boy we've still not managed to identify. Obviously it took a while for the test results on the samples to come through. Much longer than with our first one. My tests at the autopsy hadn't detected anything similar to those strange levels we found in the Nadel case, but my equipment isn't that sophisticated. So I sent the samples off to Berlin. They concluded there *were* elevated male hormone levels. Same as Nadel.'

'That's useful,' said Müller. It was, but it didn't give them a new line to investigate. It just confirmed their suspicions.

Fenstermacher closed the file slowly. 'Now the other bit of news is a little more sensitive, and perhaps it's best you don't say where it's come from. You know that the Republic is short of hard currency?'

Müller nodded.

'So sometimes there are some quite strange things going on to try to bring in those US dollars and West German marks that the powers that be seem to need to keep things ticking over. That's reasonably common knowledge.'

'Go on.'

'Because of the hormones involved, I got in touch with some of my old sparring partners at the Charité hospital in the Haupt-stadt. I was discussing our strange little case with one, a contact who works in the endocrinology department there. He was tell-ing me about a medical trial conducted a couple of years ago. It was funded by an American pharmaceutical company. The evil capitalist West and all that sort of rubbish. I'm sure you're as tired of having that rammed down your throat as I am.'

Müller wasn't so sure. She'd always believed in socialism, while recognising children in the East got fed as much propa-ganda about the evils of the West as those in the West were fed about the East. For Müller, though, there was a key difference. Everyone here in the Republic *did* have a job. Everything wasn't about earning as much money as possible, so you could show off your latest refrigerator or washing machine to your neighbours. To her, it just seemed fairer. What she was less happy about was the infrastructure needed to keep that system in place. She accepted she was part of that as a member of the People's Police. But she justified her role by telling herself she was just fighting crime, as police officers did the world over. The things that Jäger,

Baum *et al.* got up to ... well, that was something entirely different altogether.

She forced herself to concentrate on the issue at hand.

'So this was for hard currency?'

'That's right,' said Fenstermacher. 'Suddenly the West is not so evil when our Republic wants their American dollars. This trial was an extension of other controversial work by the endocrinology department, initially on rats. One of the research scientists essentially took his work a stage further, with financial backing from the Americans. The results were written up, but were discredited by the peers of this research scientist. He was hounded out of Charité.'

'OK, but I don't understand how that links to our case.'

'It's the reason for the discrediting by his peers. Someone found out he'd extended his trials from animals to humans, using university students as volunteers, initially in return for small payments – though I don't think they realised what they were volunteering for.' Fenstermacher fiddled with her hair, adjusting the rear-view mirror to look at her reflection. She seemed in an unusually nervous mood to Müller.

'That was the problem,' she continued. 'If they had been told the truth, then there is no way on earth any of them would have volunteered – unless they were very mixed up indeed.'

Müller frowned. 'Why not?'

Fenstermacher looked Müller straight in the eyes and held her gaze. 'Because the experiments were to change people's sexuality – the very essence of their soul. The Americans were funding it to try to "cure" homosexuals.'

Müller's mind was racing with all the possibilities this raised.

'But this rogue scientist was removed from the Charité endocrinology department?'

'That's right. But not everyone was against him. There were rumours some of the high-ups were backing him, they'd arranged the funding, they wanted the trials to continue.'

'But they didn't?'

'Not in the Hauptstadt, no. However my contact has heard other rumours too.'

Müller frowned in alarm. 'What?'

'That he's still conducting his experiments – somewhere else in the Republic. In secret.'

'I'll need the details of your contact at Charité. We need to try to find this place as quickly as possible. Boys – young men – are not just having their sexuality tampered with. They're dying. And my forensic officer's son may be one of them.'

Fenstermacher nodded gravely. 'There's one more rather disturbing thing, however, and I may be at fault for the delay in discovering this. I'd preserved the brain of each of our victims in formaldehyde – it makes a detailed examination easier as the tissue becomes firmer after a few weeks. When I eventually examined them in the last couple of days, what I found in both were microscopic lesions in part of the hypothalamus.'

Müller frowned. 'What does that mean?'

'It means, *Major* Müller, we're not just dealing with someone who's pumping these young men full of male sex hormones, though that's bad enough. We're dealing with someone who is operating on, *mutilating*, their brains.'

34

Sunday evening
Strausberger Platz, East Berlin

Müller had immediately contacted the Charité hospital as soon as she was back in Berlin, but Fenstermacher's contact was away and wouldn't be back till the Monday morning. She left a message asking him to get in touch as soon as he returned. That said, from Fenstermacher's account it sounded as though the man had no real knowledge where this rogue scientist was now conducting his experiments, if indeed it was true.

Tilsner and Schmidt had updated Müller on their latest activities. Schmidt had done more calculations on flow rates of the river, but with winter almost here, conditions had changed. He had tried to narrow down some possibilities, which they'd discuss once she could get to Guben. He seemed to be holding together remarkably well, even though he must now fear the worst for Markus. His wife, Hanne, was struggling though.

Tilsner had continued to plug away with the missing persons files, widening his search from *Bezirk* Cottbus and Frankfurt to the Hauptstadt and the rest of the Republic. But as the days

passed without the clear breakthrough they sought, both offi-
cers were being asked by Reiniger to help out on other matters.
And Müller's hope that Jäger would provide information about
Markus Schmidt had so far come to nothing.

'You don't happen to know anyone in the endocrinology
department at Charité, do you, Emil?'

All five of the family were sitting round the dining table in
the hall eating their evening meal, with Helga spoon-feeding
Jannika and Müller looking after Johannes.

Emil looked up from his plate. 'Not really, no. Why do you ask?'

'It's this case I'm working on.'

'The one near Eisenhüttenstadt?'

'Mmm – don't do that, Johannes,' shouted Müller, turning
her attention back to her son. 'It's not nice to spit out food.' She
wiped up the mess with his bib. Then turned back to Emil, who
seemed to be hurrying through his meal. 'I just wondered if
you'd heard about a clinical trial in that department sponsored
by an American pharmaceutical company.'

'Trials of what?'

'Something to do with sexuality. Adjusting people's sexuality,
specifically homosexuals.'

'No, nothing like that. But I can ask around if you like.'
He dropped his gaze back to his plate. He swallowed his last
mouthful, quickly finished his drink, and then started to put
on his jacket.

'You're not off out again, surely? I thought we could have a
nice evening in watching the TV.'

'I've got a late meeting at the hospital. Bit of a crisis. You know how it is. I'll be back late. Don't wait up.' He leant in to kiss her on the cheek, then kissed each twin on the top of the head. 'Bye, Helga. Make sure these two don't get into any mischief.'

Müller made a mock sad face to Helga. 'Bang goes my cosy night in with my boyfriend.'

'He does seem to have a lot of these meetings. Not much of a life for you two – what with your police work and his hospital duties. Couldn't you have chosen more compatible careers?'

'Well, my alternative career would have been a ski jumper. But they still don't allow women to compete, so that wouldn't have had much career progression,' laughed Müller.

They started to get the twins ready for their baths, this time swapping round, so Müller looked after Jannika, Helga taking Johannes. She didn't like to admit it, but both seemed happier with their great-grandmother. They were more used to her. Müller had been away such a lot in the last few weeks.

Once both children were in their cots with the light switched off, Helga whispered conspiratorially to Müller. 'I wouldn't mind watching TV with you in the lounge. We could have some nibbles, open a bottle of wine. I'd kept a nice bottle of *Sekt* for Christmas, but I quite fancy being naughty and opening it now.'

Müller smiled. 'That's sounds very appealing. Is there anything on?'

'You probably get annoyed by TV crime shows, don't you?'

'I don't mind. *Polizeiruf 110*'s actually quite realistic.'

'Ah. I was going to suggest being really naughty. *Tatort* is on at eight o'clock . . . on *Das Erste*.'

Müller gave a mock look of alarm. 'Helga! You'll have me arrested.' When she was with Gottfried she used to try to dissuade him from watching West German broadcasts. These days she was more relaxed.

'Sorry, I'm a bit of fan. We could keep the volume down though. Go on. You need a break – something to relax you.'

'I'm not sure a crime drama is going to do that. But OK . . . only because you're bribing me with the *Sekt*. I'd better not have too much though.'

Müller found herself relaxing into the programme – and the wine – despite having to get up a couple of times from the sofa to quieten the twins and rock them back to sleep.

She'd just started her second glass when the show was suddenly interrupted by a news flash graphic, and a voiceover from the continuity announcer saying they were crossing to the newsroom for an important announcement. Müller and Helga looked at each other quizzically. This was unusual, even for western TV.

A male newscaster came on. It was the one Jäger always reminded her of. Why had he been wheeled in on a Sunday evening? He was one of West German TV's most familiar faces – normally seen on weekdays only.

He was reading from a script, a bit like they still did on the Republic's TV news. For the West, the news was slicker and more rehearsed, with the presenter's words delivered straight to camera as they read from a teleprompter.

'*The bomb exploded as members of the federal cabinet were leaving a special emergency meeting at the new Federal Chancellery in Bonn.*'

The first moving pictures from the scene were then floated over the announcement, showing a still-smouldering, blackened car. After her meetings with Metzger, Müller watched with more interest than she might otherwise have done, seeing if she could spot him. She also knew that West Germany had held elections just weeks earlier – Chancellor Schmidt successfully fighting off the challenge of Helmut Kohl, clinging to power thanks to a coalition. She didn't even know if Metzger, as a junior minister, would actually be at a cabinet meeting – presumably it would just be Schmidt and the more senior ministers.

'. . . *the meeting had been called by the chancellor to discuss the current steel crisis. The drop in the worldwide price of steel has led to fears of significant job losses in the Ruhr industrial area* . . .'

The newscaster droned on, although the mention of the steel industry kept Müller's attention.

'. . . *measures to support the steel industry and to maintain price levels, including a review of current contracts with the DDR* . . .'

Now Müller really pricked up her ears. It was the first she'd heard of this. Was this what was behind Markus's liaisons with Metzger – and his attempts to get information on behalf of the Stasi?

The newsreader's smooth delivery suddenly became hesitant. A hand appeared on screen, passing another script to him. Viewers presumably weren't supposed to see that.

'. . . *and we're just getting this update from the German Press Agency in Bonn. Early indications are that there is one fatality as a result of the explosion. It's thought this is the driver of the car you're seeing now, a Mercedes-Benz saloon* . . .'

The same newsreel of the burned-out vehicle was repeating in a long loop, as the newsreader spoke over it.

The moving images suddenly faded to a still portrait image of a man in spectacles.

Müller dropped her wine glass in shock. It shattered on the wooden floor.

'What is it, Karin? Are you all right?' asked Helga.

'. . . *it's thought the vehicle belonged to Georg Metzger, a junior minister at the Ministry for Economic Cooperation. He was at the meeting to advise the federal government on the feasibility of breaking its contracts to import steel from the Eisenhüttenstadt plant in the DDR at prices fixed in . . .*'

'Oh my God!' cried Müller. 'It's him!'

'Who?'

'. . . *unconfirmed reports suggest Herr Metzger was using his own transport to get to and from the meeting, and that he was the only occupant of the vehicle. His family – a wife and two young children – have been informed. The German Press Agency is reporting no group has so far claimed responsibility; however the Federal Border Guard say they are treating it as a terrorist act.*'

The still of Metzger faded back to the presenter talking to camera.

'*We'll bring you more on that story in our main news bulletin at ten o'clock. Meanwhile back to the latest episode of* Tatort.'

Müller felt her throat constrict.

'You look like you've seen a ghost,' said Helga.

'I knew him. I met him just a few weeks ago.'

'Oh God! How awful.'

Müller started to get up from the chair. 'Sorry, Helga, I need to make a few phone calls, and to be honest I don't much feel like watching the—'

A sudden repeated ringing of the doorbell interrupted her mid-sentence.

Then a hammering on the door.

Helga frowned anxiously as Müller went to answer.

She hadn't even managed to get as far as the door when it exploded inwards, the frame surround breaking, sending splinters and plaster flying.

Müller was instantly surrounded by leather-jacketed heavies.

'Leave her alone!' screamed Helga.

The noise woke the twins, and their cries now added to the confusion and cacophony as one of the men began to speak.

'Comrade *Major* Karin Müller, you're under arrest.'

'No!' she cried, trying to wrench herself free. 'You can't—'

One of the men clasped his gloved hand over her mouth. Helga tried to grab her granddaughter but she was shoved back. She lost her footing and fell to the floor.

'Don't try to interfere, old woman.'

Another man thrust his ID in front of Müller's face as her hands were wrenched up behind her back and the cuffs put on. She didn't need to see it to know what it said. *Ministry for State Security.* The Stasi.

35

Müller wondered if this was what it had been like for Gottfried. Had his arrest been so brutal? At least – in meeting with the dissident groups – he had done *something* to warrant it. But she – she hadn't stepped out of line at all. She possessed all the necessary authorisations from Reiniger. She'd only been seeking the truth about the case she was involved in. Perhaps that was it. Perhaps she was getting too near the truth.

As they waited for the lift, Müller felt ashamed, guilty – although she had done nothing. One of her neighbours opened their front door, but then closed it again immediately.

Parked up outside the block's lobby, on one of the quarter circles of the roundabout that made up Strausberger Platz, Müller saw yet another Barkas van – in addition to the camper that had made regular visits here since she'd moved her family into the new apartment. The new vehicle was almost identical to the 'bread' van parked for so long outside her old Schön-hauser Allee flat. Despite her desperate situation, she laughed out loud when she saw it had the name of a fishmonger's on the side. Couldn't they be more original than disguising their prison vehicles as food delivery vans? The response from the agents holding her arms was to tighten their grip and shove her roughly through the van door.

She thought again of Gottfried. Her first reaction to him in Hohenschönhausen had been to view him as a slightly pathetic, broken figure. Now, as she was forced into the tiny, cell-like space, only just about big enough for her crouching body, she understood why he had appeared so.

Her sense of outrage and bewilderment was matched by a feeling of nausea from the lingering smell of urine and faeces.

Then the van started up. She tried to work out from the turns, the acceleration and deceleration, where they were going. There were only narrow shafts of light in the makeshift cell, and she couldn't see out to check the route; instead she tried to make a mental map in her head.

But after what must have been something like thirty minutes of twists and turns, and being rocked and banged from side to side, she was forced to give up. She desperately tried to think *why*. Why were they doing this to her? Was it her secret meetings with Metzger? That was nothing illegal . . . But now he was dead, blown to smithereens by a car bomb. That didn't make sense. Was it the fact that she'd stood up to Jäger, challenged him? She couldn't believe he would be that vindictive. Was it because of her meeting that had been scheduled for the next day with the endocrinologist at Charité? A meeting that the Stasi had now ensured would not take place. That made more sense: perhaps some branch of the Stasi – with the involvement of Baum and Diederich – was worried she was getting near to the truth and was determined to stop her.

The disorientating stopping, starting and driving in circles had finally ended. The prison van interior was now completely dark – even the weak shafts of light from passing street lamps had stopped appearing. Müller could tell, as she tried and failed to stretch her limbs in the confined, stinking space, that they were now heading in a straight line, at speed. It must be a motorway – but she had no idea which one, or in which direction they were travelling.

Or the intended final destination.

She found herself fighting back tears. What she did know was that it was far from the Hauptstadt, far from her home and the twins. They'd been stolen from her at birth – for however brief a time – and now she'd been stolen from them. Would she ever see Jannika, Johannes or Helga ever again? Poor Helga. Pushed to the floor in the mayhem at the apartment. She hoped her grandmother wasn't seriously hurt – and if she was, what had happened to the twins? They would be all alone until Emil returned.

Emil. A horrible thought was forming at the back of her confused mind. She'd always had a nagging suspicion about the coincidence of him ending up in Halle-Neustadt during her previous case, of the ease with which they seemed to get together. And then – just before her life gets turned upside down by the Stasi – he hurriedly leaves the flat. For a meeting at the hospital on a Sunday evening?

Müller tried to swallow. Her throat was dry from the wine. She needed water. But the thought of it started another panic. Because she also felt a mounting need to go to the toilet – and she knew that if this journey carried on much longer she would suffer the humiliation of wetting herself in her mobile prison cell. From the smell of the fetid air around her, it seemed many other prisoners had suffered the same way.

36

Earlier that day
Pankow

When Müller told Tilsner she was going down to Senftenberg to interview grumpy old Fenstermacher, he was slightly put out that he was going to have to tail Winkler on his own, and that – according to Müller – Reiniger had confirmed that, at this stage, he wasn't prepared to authorise the younger Winkler being taken in for questioning. Something about not embarrassing the father. Tilsner didn't care about that. He knew the father, had history with him – but he couldn't reveal that to Müller.

The uniforms had failed to produce any information of value when they'd been detailed to watch the son, so with no progress, Reiniger had scaled things back. It was left to Tilsner alone.

He waited in a café with a clear view of the Winkler house, pretending to read a newspaper, his bike helmet on the seat next to him and a steaming cup of coffee just placed in front of him by the waitress. It was one thing haring around on motorbikes in September. Now, three months later, with sleet driving down outside, he wasn't looking forward to it at all.

He warmed his hands on the coffee mug and breathed in the bittersweet aroma, feeling it wake up his taste buds. Then, just as he touched the edge of the pottery mug to his lips, before he'd taken his first sip, he saw the Winkler youth come out of the house.

Scheisse! Tilsner slammed down the mug, grabbed his helmet and raced outside to his bike – ignoring the shouts of the waitress complaining that he hadn't paid. She was a pretty thing, so it was a shame, but it would give him a good excuse to visit again to settle his debt.

He quickly fired up the bike, carefully watching which direction Winkler was heading in. Normally, all the youths gathered outside Winkler's house before setting off on their Sunday convoy. This solo venture had taken him by surprise. Where was he off to on his own? Maybe the weather had put paid to their usual jaunt to the club.

Before Tilsner had released the throttle, Winkler had disappeared round the next corner. Tilsner could feel that the machine he was on was even more powerful than the previous one, but he didn't want to test its full acceleration on such a slippery surface. He just hoped to God that young Winkler wasn't more reckless. Not because he cared about the youth's fate. He seemed a duplicitous little rat, and coming to an end squashed on a road, or with his body wrapped round a lamppost, might be no bad thing. Tilsner simply didn't want to lose him round the next bend.

The bike gripped the road well enough as the detective cornered. Straightening it, he risked taking one hand off the bars to wipe his visor and saw Winkler still just about in sight. Then the youth turned towards Mitte. Tilsner opened up the machine as much as he dared. If a car pulled out now he'd probably end up squashed like a fly on its front grille. But he got a clear run, and when he took the same right turn as the youth, he could still see him up ahead. Really, to do this properly, you needed two tails on separate bikes – one taking over from the other at intervals so the target didn't wise up.

He dropped into the slipstream of a Trabant. This way he was hidden from Winkler but could still see him through the Trabi's rear and front windscreens. He just hoped the guy driving the car didn't suddenly brake.

They were on Schönhauser Allee approaching the lights by Dimitroffstrasse U-bahn. If Winkler was heading to Frankfurt or Hütte, his favourite haunts, then Tilsner would have expected him to turn left, following Dimitroffstrasse itself, as it skirted Prenzlauer Berg and Friedrichshain. But he was in the lane to go straight on. The Trabi was doing the same, so Tilsner still had cover.

He used the pause at the lights to wipe the visor again. *Sauwetter! And on a Sunday too, when he should be home with Koletta and the kids.* The leathers, gloves and helmet were keeping off the worst of it, but he could feel the cold wetness of the sleet getting in at his neck and starting to slither down his back.

The Trabi suddenly started slowing down and signalling left. Tilsner could either stay hidden behind it and hope to catch up in a moment, or risk pulling out and showing himself to Winkler. He looked in his wing mirrors. The mixture of wet ice and rain had formed a smeary layer – he could see nothing in them, and therefore it must be the same for Winkler ahead. Tilsner kicked down a couple of gears, then swung out and accelerated, slowing again once he was two hundred metres or so behind the youth. Tilsner could barely make out the TV tower in the middle distance through the low cloud, sleet and gloom. Then Winkler suddenly dived off to the right, down Saarbrückerstrasse.

Had he been spotted? Was Winkler trying to throw him off?

Tilsner kicked down, opened the throttle again, then took the same corner as fast as he dared, narrowly missing a car coming in the opposite direction. He felt the tyres start to slip under him, but he managed to straighten as they found their grip again. Winkler was still there, up ahead.

Tilsner knew the youth's bike wasn't anywhere near powerful enough to outrun his own. But unless he kept close, Winkler could still give him the slip if he wanted. *If* he spotted him. Tilsner just had to try to make sure he didn't, hoping the awful weather would help.

They were now passing the entrance to Volkspark Friedrichshain, and when Winkler chose to take the south-easterly route by the park – along Friedenstrasse – Tilsner started to relax a little. He had a fair idea where he was heading now. And when the youth turned left at Karl-Marx-Allee and carried straight on past the Kosmos cinema and the Frankfurter Tor, the detective was even more certain.

The weather had eased by the time they approached Frankfurt, which meant Tilsner had to stay further back to avoid being spotted, particularly at the turning to Eisenhüttenstadt – if

Winkler was indeed heading where the detective thought. But in easing off, Tilsner had allowed a truck to get in front of him. At first he didn't want to risk overtaking, but after a few seconds, realised he had to. He kicked down and pulled out. But although the sleet had dropped, the road was still soaked. Tilsner found himself driving blind – straight through a cloud of spray – praying no one was coming the opposite way. When he finally emerged and wiped the visor with the back of one hand, he saw the road ahead was straight – and empty.

No sign of Winkler.

Tilsner knew there was one last chance, one hope, that this wasn't a wasted journey.

In a few hundred metres, as he passed the entrance to the club, Tilsner made sure he kept watch on the car park from behind the visor – without turning his head to make it obvious. Thankfully, he saw Winkler, with his distinctive thunder flash striped helmet, getting off his machine.

Tilsner kept going until he was out of sight, then pulled over to the verge and put the bike on its side rest. He pulled off his helmet, shaking his soaking back – then wished he hadn't.

The truck he'd just overtaken roared by, sending a huge plume of water from a muddy puddle straight into the detective's face. He shook his head like a drenched dog and made a punching motion at the back of the truck as it disappeared towards Hütte.

Tilsner found their usual hiding place, the old shed with a broken window whose door had either rotted or been kicked in years before. He had a clear view of the club. Winkler, he assumed, must have already gone inside. There was no sign of him, but his bike was still parked up where Tilsner had seen him get off moments earlier. There were no other vehicles in the car park, save for one battered Trabant. And no music booming through the low building's walls. Whatever was going on inside, it didn't look like it was the normal weekly club meet. Tilsner settled down for what he expected to be a long wait – hoping that when Winkler came out, he might actually see something that would make the long, uncomfortable ride worthwhile.

To try to keep out the cold, Tilsner had found some old sacks in the corner of the shed. He used them now as makeshift blankets, ignoring the varieties of dirt attached to them. The extra warmth must have made him doze off, and he woke with a start when the headlights of a vehicle turning into the car park illuminated his face. He ducked down, then raised his head slowly. The occupants got out and made their way into the club. Winkler's bike was still parked up in the same place. The first car was followed by several more – there seemed to be some sort of evening gathering. But who were they? And what was Winkler's involvement? Perhaps they should have raided the club, despite the Stasi's explanation that it was their 'honey trap'. For now, especially as he was on his own this time, Tilsner would just watch and wait.

The first few cars had males inside – most looked to be in their thirties and forties. He didn't recognise any of them. Then there was one he did.

Diederich. With another man.

Both made their way into the club, and when Tilsner got a partial glimpse of whoever was opening the door, he thought it was Winkler, but he couldn't be certain. More cars arrived, with a mixed age range. More men in their early twenties, accompanied by what looked like late teenagers. Then he saw at least two of the youths from the motorbike group he and Karin had originally followed to this place earlier in the year – both brought in cars by older men.

The arrivals slowed. Tilsner was just about to settle down in his sackcloth bed again, knowing he would have a long wait until everyone started to leave, when a final car arrived. He did a double take when he saw the occupant get out. *Surely not?* The lighting in the yard was weak – perhaps he was mistaken.

He took another look.

It was definitely him. *Good God!*

He'd have to tell Karin – but really he needed her to see for herself. The man had gone inside the club now. It was definitely Winkler at the door because this time he saw him face-on as it opened. And Winkler obviously already knew the man. Their greeting of a warm hug was one of at least friendship.

Perhaps even more.

Tilsner couldn't believe it. He glanced down at his watch. There was still time for Karin to get here if she was back from her meeting with Fenstermacher – which surely she would be by now.

Climbing out of his hiding place as quietly as possible, Tilsner made his way out of the car park and down the road a short way to where he'd hidden the bike in the undergrowth. He wasn't sure he'd get a signal from the radio with all the undergrowth. But he had to try.

The line was crackly, but he managed to make contact with Keibelstrasse.

He couldn't say much over an open radio connection. His message was terse but to the point.

'*Please get this urgent message to Major Karin Müller. Send someone round to her home if necessary. Tell her Hauptmann Tilsner says she must come to the club in Frankfurt immediately and without delay. There's something she needs to witness.*'

He couldn't say more than that.

He knew Karin would be as utterly shocked as he was.

37

Later that night
A Stasi prison

The long, straight drive ended, and it was back to the stopping, starting and apparent driving round in circles. Müller didn't care where she was any more. Her whole body ached, the mobile cell stank, and she was sitting in her own dampness. Despite the stench, she found herself gulping down air to try to quell her panic. She'd assumed this was all a mistake. But what if it wasn't? *What if it's deliberate?* Images and memories of Jannika and Johannes kept flashing through her brain. She wanted to kiss them, hold them, rock them to sleep. This was all her fault. She should never have agreed to Reiniger's proposal to move to Strausberger Platz.

Finally, the van braked to a halt.

'Out, out,' shouted the guards, as one of them clambered inside, opened the door to her cell, and pulled her forward by her cuffed arms.

'I haven't done anything wrong. I'm a major with the People's Police criminal division. This is—'

'Be quiet!' shouted a second guard as she was bundled out of the van. Müller had to close her eyes because of the sudden blinding white light in the reception area – some sort of garage, with white walls that accentuated the brightness from the strip lights.

The guard jabbed her in the back with something hard, metallic. Müller had no doubt it was a gun. She wanted to continue to protest her innocence, but these were the foot soldiers. Just doing their job. There was no point arguing with them.

Then her world was plunged into blackness again, as some sort of hood was forced over her head and she was led away.

From the change in air temperature, she knew she was outside for a few moments. Then back inside an echoey building. Even through the hood she could hear the guards' boots reverberating on the concrete floor as they maintained a rapid pace, jabbing her in the back if she failed to keep up.

They stopped for a moment, keys were turned in a lock, a door creaked open and was then clanged shut behind her.

She was pushed forward again. After a few more paces, they turned a corner, and then finally the hood was lifted clear.

Müller didn't quite know what to expect. The journey had gone on long enough for them to have crossed the Republic's borders. But the guards at the garage had been speaking German, wearing the uniform of the Republic. She'd thought perhaps the long drive had all been a ruse, that she might have been taken from Berlin, out onto a motorway, and then brought back again, perhaps to Hohenschönhausen.

But this wasn't the Stasi prison in Berlin where Gottfried had been held, where she'd visited him. Or if it was, it was another wing.

Ahead of her were metal steps rising three – perhaps four – floors, surrounded by wire cages. The same smell as in the Barkas van: piss, shit and sweat mixed in with the tang of disinfectant, as though there had been half-hearted attempts to clean up. And the same red and green light control system she'd seen in Hohenschönhausen.

She was half-jabbed, half-pulled up to the second floor, and then marched to another wing. Two doors with control lights, then a narrow white corridor, with the doors framed in beige. The pipework was on show, all highlighted in lemon yellow.

Cell 13. That was the door they opened, shoving her inside.

Müller had expected isolation. That was the usual trick, she knew. That was what broke Gottfried into the snivelling wreck she'd had little pity for in the Hohenschönhausen interview room eighteen months earlier. But she had a cellmate – an older, thickset woman, with a leathery face and grey hair. She was sitting on the bench that doubled as a hard bed, smoking.

Müller turned to the guards. 'I can't go in here. I haven't done anything—'

One of the guards clasped his hand across her face to shut her up. The other uncuffed her hands. Then both turned to leave the room.

Müller rushed towards the cell door. 'Please—'

The door slammed shut. Müller sank to the floor in despair.

38

The next day
Keibelstrasse, East Berlin

Tilsner had asked for a personal meeting with Reiniger after failing to get hold of Müller – no one seemed to know where she was, and attempting to phone her at the flat just got an operator on the line saying the number was out of order.

When he was finally allowed in to see the police colonel, Reiniger looked harassed.

'What's going on? Where is she?'

'Don't you mean, "*What's going on, Comrade Oberst*"?'

Tilsner fought back the instinct to grab the overweight, middle-aged man and shake him. Instead, he rested his hands on top of the desk and fixed the colonel with what he hoped was his iciest stare. 'Apologies, Comrade *Oberst*. But I know there's something fishy going on. I read about Metzger and the car bombing in the paper. Is it something to do with that?'

Reiniger dropped his gaze and stared at his hands. 'I don't know what it's about. All I know is that she's been arrested.'

'*Arrested?* Why on earth has she been arrested?'

He watched Reiniger's Adam's apple bob up and down as he swallowed. 'It's not *us* who've arrested her, obviously, *Hauptmann* Tilsner. It's the Stasi.'

'Well, surely you rank highly enough to get them to un-arrest her, don't you? Where is she?'

'Bautzen.'

'*Bautzen II?* That's the shittiest hellhole in the Republic. She's the head of your new Specialist Crimes Department. I thought she was supposed to be *liaising* with the Stasi. Not being arrested by them.'

The man looked defeated. He seemed frozen to his desk, as though he wasn't the same person who'd authorised their hunt for Markus Schmidt, even though that meant continuing their inquiries into the Nadel murder against Stasi instructions.

Reiniger sighed. 'My hands are tied, *Hauptmann*.'

Tilsner could see no amount of cajoling on his part was going to do any good. Reiniger seemed to have given up. There was only one person Tilsner had enough influence over to get this reversed. And the influence he had over him was a threat, a threat to expose something that would leave Tilsner himself equally exposed.

But Karin was worth it to him.

He would have to play his last card. Whatever the danger to himself.

'Could you perhaps get *Oberst* Jäger at the Ministry for State Security on the phone for me?'

'Whatever makes you think he would talk to you about it, *Hauptmann*? In any case, I've already tried speaking to him.

It seems to be out of his hands too. I'm told the arrest was authorised by the *Bezirk* Frankfurt regional Stasi office.'

'*Scheisse!*' spat Tilsner. 'So, Baum and Diederich.' Tilsner took a deep breath, then slowly emptied his lungs. 'I can't tell you why Jäger will listen to me, Comrade *Oberst*. But he will, I assure you. And that may just be enough to get this sorted out.'

Reiniger looked dubious, but slowly lifted the handset of the telephone and began to dial. After a few questions and answers, he passed the receiver to Tilsner.

'*Hello, Werner. I understand you want to speak to me.*'

'It's time, Jäger. I'm calling in that favour.'

'*I don't know what you mean.*'

'You know very well what I mean. And you know very well what will happen if you don't cooperate.'

'*Don't try to threaten me.*'

'It's not a threat. It's a statement of fact. Sort this out, otherwise you know what the consequences will be.' Tilsner watched Reiniger raise his brow, intrigued. This conversation ought to be taking place in private, but Tilsner didn't have the time, and if his boss knew he had something on Jäger, then Reiniger might be a little more wary of him himself in future.

Despite the crackly line, Tilsner heard Jäger give a long sigh. '*I can't make any promises.*'

'I don't want promises, Klaus.' Reiniger frowned now, hearing his subordinate casually using the Stasi colonel's first name. 'I want action and results.'

The line went silent.

'Did you hear me?' asked Tilsner.

'*I heard. I'm waiting for you to tell me what you want.*'

'I want Müller released from Bautzen, without any stain on her record and without any further action taken against her.'

The line went silent again.

'You do understand, don't you?

'*I'm not sure I can do that.*'

'Oh, I'm sure you can, Klaus. We go back a long way, don't we? You can sort this out if you want to, and I'm sure you *do* want to.' Tilsner looked down at his watch. 'It's now a quarter to nine. *Oberst* Reiniger and I will be travelling to Bautzen and we expect to see you there at . . . let's say at 1 p.m. prompt. With whatever authorisations you need to get this sorted – even if you have to go to the very top.'

39

Three months earlier (September 1976)
Frankfurt an der Oder

'You're disappointing us, Markus. You were doing such good work.' The agent – I still don't know his name – is twirling his pen round and round with his fingers.

'Look. You wanted me to get the photos. That was the deal. I did what was required.'

'You did a good job, yes. But the man you were consorting with is involved in important negotiations with the Republic. It is vital for our country that you continue your work as requested. Yet you refuse. You know what the alternative is, don't you?'

'You said, yes. That I'll be jailed. If that's the case, so be it. I've told you I was framed. I'll just have to hope the truth comes out eventually.' I pull my shoulders back, thrust my chest out and try to hold his gaze. Try to look confident even though inside I don't feel it. I'm standing in front of them, but I don't know if I can for much longer. I feel dizzy, as though my legs could give way at any moment.

The other agent – the older, round-faced one – has been silent up to now. He gets up, stares out of the window and begins speaking, even though his back is to me, with his hands clasped together behind it.

'You do *know* what happens to people like you in prison, don't you?'

'People like me?' I know what he's driving at, but I want to force him to spell it out.

He turns and eyeballs me. 'Yes. People like you. Homosexuals, queers, faggots. Without your glasses, in the contact lenses that *we* provided for you, you're pretty enough. Certainly pretty enough for some of the rapists and murderers we get in our jails. If you're lucky, one of them will take a shine to you. Even then, you won't be able to sit on your arse for months after you come out.'

'It's not a crime to be a homosexual in the Republic.'

'It might not be a crime, but the normal laws don't apply inside prison, I can assure you. Let's say you're *not* lucky enough to find some thug who takes a shine to you and will protect you. Do you know what will happen then?'

I stay silent. Why play his verbal games? Let them do their worst.

'You won't just be used as a toy boy. You'll be beaten black and blue. They'll probably stamp on your dick in the showers. You won't last six months, never mind the three years we're likely to jail you for.'

Three years? Oh God. They've never put a figure on it before. I had assumed it would be months, not years.

'I can see you look alarmed at that prospect. But let me tell you what else will happen. We have photographs of you in some very compromising situations with Herr Metzger . . . very compromising indeed. You did well with that part of your assignment. I think your parents will be very interested to see them.'

'*No!*' I shout. 'Please not Mutti and Vati. Don't involve them. Please.'

He responds with a thin smile that makes me shiver. 'We can easily send them under a plain envelope to your mother and father. And then we can raid them. Possession of pornography – that won't go down well with your father's People's Police bosses. And featuring his own son? I suspect that will be the end of his career.'

'*Arschloch!*' I make a move towards him. I want to tear at his round, mocking face, but the other one – the good-looking, younger one – leaps up and grabs me before I can.

'Careful,' says this second agent. 'Sit down, take it easy. I might have an alternative for you.'

I sit with my elbows on the arms of the chair, my fingers splayed over my eyes.

'Would you like to know what that is? If you cooperate you can avoid prison, avoid all that happening to your mother and father.' Both of them have sat down again, side by side behind the desk, under the portrait of Honecker.

I don't reply. They've failed to keep their promises before. Why would they this time?

'I'll tell you anyway, because I think you'll be very interested. This could be a way of wiping the slate clean with us. We'll forget about everything. We might even be able to ensure you get a university place after all.'

The other man nods.

I sigh. 'My results weren't good enough.'

'We can always make sure that gets overlooked, or provide you with certificates that *are* good enough. More than good enough.'

I still don't trust them. There is no reason to trust them. They are scum. Manipulative scum.

'All we need you to do is help one of our eminent scientists.'

'I don't know anything about science.'

'You don't have to. All you'll be doing is what several students have already done in Berlin: volunteering for a medical trial. It's an important one, being sponsored by an American pharmaceutical company. So it earns important hard currency for the Republic and you'll be doing your bit for the country at the same time. We could even classify it as your military service. That way, you wouldn't have to serve in the army.'

Although I don't trust them, he's piqued my interest.

'Go on,' I say.

'The trial involves testing a drug used to control and alter hormone levels. And in that way control desire. It's hard to find suitable volunteers. We can recommend you as suitable. That way, you don't have to betray Georg Metzger any more. When all this is over, if you still feel the same about him, then we might be able to facilitate your emigration to the Federal Republic to be with him. And, of course, there will be no jail. No photographs sent to your parents. No threat to your father's job as a police forensic scientist.'

I don't trust them. Of course I don't trust them. But do I really have any option? And it will protect my parents. I've let down my father too many times. For once, I can perhaps do something to make him proud of me.

'OK,' I say. 'Tell me more.'

40

Three months later (December 1976)
Bautzen II

It took Tilsner just over two and a half hours to drive the two hundred plus kilometres from Keibelstrasse to Bautzen. The quaintness of the town was at odds with the two brutal prisons Tilsner knew it contained. But from this approach they weren't visible – instead the skyline was dominated by the various towers of its historic buildings.

He glanced across at Reiniger, who had been uncharacteristically silent for most of the journey. 'You haven't been saying very much, Comrade *Oberst*.'

'You can imagine I'm not best pleased with you, *Hauptmann*. You undermined me during that telephone call – and if you make an enemy of Jäger, or make me an enemy of his, the world can start to get dangerous.'

'I really don't care, Comrade *Oberst*. What I care about is getting my boss out of jail and back on this case. That should be all you care about too. It seems obvious to me that we must be getting very close to solving it, and some people – possibly even the powers that be – don't want us to.'

'Don't try to tell me my job, *Hauptmann*. Treading on thin ice doesn't even begin to describe your situation.'

They waited in a side street, making sure they had a clear view of the entrance to the walled and razor-wire-topped prison compound. A few minutes before 1 p.m., a black Volvo drew up and slowly drove past. Tilsner signalled with his arm from the window, and Jäger pulled in behind them.

Once all three were out of the cars and walking towards the prison entrance, Tilsner addressed the Stasi colonel. 'Is it all sorted?'

Jäger eyeballed him with a deadpan expression. 'You'll find out soon enough.'

Müller paced the cell. The chain-smoking of her cellmate enveloped her in a cloud of foul fumes, and Müller's constant toing and froing was a vain attempt to try to circulate the air. The woman was pleasant enough, despite her dismay at discovering that she was sharing her incarceration with a *Vopo*. But neither of them had more than snatches of sleep. The light above the door had constantly flashed on and off, so that dozing for a few minutes was all Müller could manage.

'You should lie down while you can,' the cellmate said. 'They'll soon be putting you to work in the basement. Save your energy.'

'I won't be staying here,' insisted Müller. 'There's been a mistake. I'll be released today when they realise.'

'Pah!' snorted the woman, blowing out another cloud of white, suffocating smoke, and then coughing repeatedly. Müller slapped her back lightly. 'That's what they all say,' she rasped. 'But trust me, they don't make mistakes. You might not be guilty of anything, or you might not think you're guilty of anything, but you're in here for a reason. Because they want you in here. They want to break you.'

The rattle of the guards' keys in the metal door ended the brief conversation.

Two guards entered. 'You!' one of them shouted, pointing at Müller. 'You're coming with me, now.'

Müller made a futile attempt to wriggle free as the guard tried to cuff her hand to his. Then she closed her eyes, relaxed her arm and let him drag her out, as his colleague stood watch over her cellmate, who was smirking to herself.

She'd assumed she was being taken down to the basement work area, as her cellmate had mentioned. Either that or being dragged to the same sort of interrogation room she'd met a desperate Gottfried in during his confinement.

Instead, she was led through the prison, along the wire-caged first-floor landing, down the central metal steps, and out to what looked like the staff and administration area. She was shown into an empty meeting room, and as he unlocked the cuffs the guard told her to wait. Someone would be in to see her shortly. The guard then exited the room and locked the door behind him.

Müller took a few breaths of the cleaner air. People had been smoking in here too. There was a faint smell of tobacco, but compared to the constant choking fug of the cell, it almost felt like she was in the open, country air. The minutes ticked by with nothing happening – perhaps this was part of the process, the attempt to break you. But she had nothing to confess. She wrung her hands and tugged at her prison overalls, the starched material chafing at her skin. She tried not to let hope enter her mind: the hope that soon she would be free, and able to see her young family again.

When the door did open, she was surprised to see Jäger, followed by Reiniger. Both smiling, but their smiles seemed forced, as though there was an underlying tension. She felt a fluttering in her stomach; this had to be a good thing, surely?

'Sit down, Karin,' said Jäger, who himself pulled out a chair and sat across the desk, elbows on the table, and fingers steepled together under his chin. 'As you can imagine, there's been a misunderstanding. We're trying to sort it out at the moment. Your clothes should be arriving shortly, then we'll give you a lift back to the Hauptstadt.'

Müller gave a laugh, but even she could hear the edge to it. The heat of anger flushed through her body. 'A *misunderstanding*?' she said in a level tone. 'A misunderstanding that sees me arrested in front of my children and grandmother? An old woman knocked to the floor by thugs from your own ministry? That's some misunderstanding.'

Reiniger sighed. 'Clearly something's gone wrong, Karin. We're doing our best to help you. Your arrest was nothing to do with either of us, but Klaus has gone out on a limb to secure your freedom. There will be no further action—'

'Further action? Hah! Why was there any action in the first place? I've done nothing wrong, nothing at all.'

Jäger nodded in agreement. 'As I say, it was a misunderstanding. Some members of a regional branch of the Ministry exceeded their remit.'

Müller could guess who. Baum and his lackey Diederich. 'I trust that *they* will be punished?'

Jäger rubbed his hand across his face. 'Let's just concentrate on returning you to your family. We can talk about everything else another time. Your clothes should have been cleaned and will be here in a moment. You'll be taken to the changing room, and then brought back here. Then we'll get you home to Berlin.'

41

Müller had been surprised to see Tilsner, too, waiting for her as they left the prison. He attempted to speak to her, but Jäger ushered her away firmly. There seemed to be something her deputy was eager to talk to her about, but Jäger thwarted him by making sure she came back in his Volvo to the Hauptstadt, with Tilsner driving Reiniger.

Müller used the rear-view mirror to check her make-up. Minimal, as always. Just a dab of mascara. 'Now we're alone, are you willing to tell me more about what's happening?'

Jäger stared fixedly ahead. Snow was falling steadily, but although it was settling on the embankments and verges of the autobahn, so far it was little more than slush on the actual road surface.

'I've told you about as much as I'm allowed to.'

'So was it all at the behest of the Frankfurt Stasi? I'm convinced they don't want us to get to the bottom of our investigation.'

He sighed and turned to her briefly. 'Perhaps it was a warning to you. And perhaps you ought to heed it.' He turned his gaze back to the road. 'I had to go right to the very top to get you out. Pull in a lot of favours again.'

'So are you going to try to get Reiniger to take Tilsner off the case?'

'No, but I'll be taking a personal interest from now on.'

'I thought you worked for the Main Intelligence Directorate – the foreign branch. How does this possibly interest you?'

'Your meetings with Metzger. *He* concerns us . . . or rather did, though we still have to make sure there is no fallout that comes our way from his untimely death.'

Müller fell silent. Jäger appeared happy to let her think her arrest was Baum and Diederich's work. But what if it wasn't? What if the people who seized her were from Jäger's own department? What if he knew? *What if he authorised it?* And then had second thoughts when Reiniger intervened.

As Jäger wiped condensation from the Volvo's windscreen with his handkerchief, Müller hunkered down into her red raincoat. What had Tilsner been trying to say? Was he attempting to warn her about something? Was Jäger even taking her back to her apartment as he claimed, or were they actually on their way to Normannenstrasse for questioning?

But no, Jäger – this time – was true to his word and escorted her to the lobby door at Strausberger Platz. Müller didn't invite him in. There was, however, still something she needed from the Stasi colonel. Though now wasn't the time to ask him. So, although it went against her better judgement, she held out her hand and thanked him.

He nodded, but his expression remained grim as he made his way back to the car, the melted snow squelching underfoot on the pavement.

'Karin, Karin. My God, I'm so pleased you're back,' Emil pulled her into a tight hug and then Helga joined in, but Müller watched her grandmother wince as she did so. Müller pulled back and then examined Helga's arm. The purple blotch surrounded by yellow was the size of a plum.

'*Scheisse*, Helga, is that what they did to you?' she asked.

'*Ach*, it's nothing. Emil's had a look – nothing's broken.'

'What we don't understand, Karin, is why?' said Emil as he kept his hands on her shoulders. 'Why did they do this to you?'

Müller shook her head. 'I don't know. They didn't give me a proper explanation. They said it was a branch of the Ministry for State Security exceeding its remit.'

'Are there consequences for you, *Liebling*?'

She shrugged. 'I don't think so. I haven't been charged with anything. I was accompanied back to the Hauptstadt by senior police and Stasi officials. Unless told otherwise, I just get on with my job. Immediately.'

Helga gasped. 'Surely they can allow you some time off to recover? Where did they take you? It must have been awful.'

Müller pinched her brow between her thumb and forefinger. Then she lifted her head and smiled. 'I was in Bautzen. Just for one night. I was one of the lucky ones.' Her cellmate, in the little conversation they'd had, had revealed she'd already been in Bautzen for two months . . . with no sign of being released, and no real knowledge of her alleged 'crimes'. Only that some of her friends had been planning an escape attempt across the Anti-Fascist Protection Barrier, but the cellmate herself claimed she was not involved. She had no real reason to lie to Müller, except, of course, that Müller was a major in the People's Police, although evidently – from her very presence in Bautzen – one whose career had, at least temporarily, hit rock bottom.

'Where are Jannika and Johannes?' asked Müller. 'I've been so looking forward to seeing them.'

'They're at the crèche,' said Emil. 'We thought it best that life should carry on as normally as possible. Helga has been a rock.'

'It's the least I can do,' said Müller's grandmother. 'Shall I go and get them back early so you can give them a kiss and a cuddle?'

The thought was tempting for Müller. But she really did need to get back to work. If the Stasi *had* been trying to prevent her talking to Fenstermacher's contact in the endocrinology department at Charité, then she had to redouble her efforts to find him and discover exactly what he knew about these sinister experiments.

'I'll see them this evening before bed, in time – I hope – for tea, and their bath.'

'We could have a little party, perhaps?' suggested Helga.

'That sounds lovely,' said Emil. 'But I have to work this evening. I managed to get switched from my early shift to a late one so I could help Helga with the twins and take them to the crèche.' He glanced down at his watch and frowned. 'But I was just about to go in before you turned up. I'd better still do that, otherwise I'll be for the high jump.'

'Of course,' said Müller. She leant in to give her boyfriend a kiss on the lips as he reached to get his coat. He paused, and pulled her in for a hug.

'I'm sorry about this. Let's arrange an outing with the children – and Helga too if she'd like – as soon as we can. It's just things at work are a bit chaotic at the moment. We've got a couple of doctors and nurses off sick.'

Müller knew she was as guilty as he was of not making time for their relationship. She'd thought her promotion, taking charge of the new unit, might end up as a poisoned chalice. She didn't want that poison to seep into her family life. She'd already failed in one relationship – with Gottfried – and now there were the children to consider too. She had to make this work.

42

Müller's attempts to arrange a meeting with the endocrinologist were again rebuffed by officials at Charité. She'd been given the runaround over the telephone so had turned up in person at the department, only to be told the same thing: the doctor was away and wouldn't be back till the following Monday. However, they said he was aware of Müller's need to speak to him and would make sure he was available then.

When Müller had tried to talk to Tilsner at Keibelstrasse she got the same kind of stonewalling until, during their telephone briefing, Reiniger eventually revealed that her deputy had – temporarily – been assigned to other duties.

'As soon as there's a breakthrough in the current case you can have him back, Karin,' Reiniger had said.

'That's all well and good, Comrade *Oberst*,' replied a furious Müller. 'But I won't *make* a breakthrough if I don't have a deputy or anyone to help. I'll have to rely on the local People's Police at Eisenhüttenstadt – and I believe they might be compromised by their links to the *Bezirk* Frankfurt Stasi regional unit.'

'You still have Schmidt. I've kept him in Wilhelm-Pieck-Stadt Guben. It'll keep his mind occupied while we search for his son.'

'But you've just, in effect, scaled down the search for his son by taking Tilsner off the case.'

'He's not off the case, Karin, I told you. I'm just reallocating him temporarily because of a shortage of manpower elsewhere.'

Müller found herself grinding her teeth as she listened. It was a habit normally confined to night-time dreams, much to Emil's chagrin.

'One useful thing you could do is go to see Schmidt's wife. She could do with some womanly support. It's coming up to Christmas – it must be terrible for her with her son missing and her husband away on a case.'

Müller bit down on the tip of her tongue to try to stop herself saying something she would regret. The sentiment from Reiniger was perhaps admirable, but the chauvinistic way he phrased it – as though only another woman could give a desperate mother support – made Müller's pulse pound in her head.

She paused slightly to let her anger dissipate. 'I can do that, of course. But I'm supposed to be the head of a new Serious Crimes Department. You've just taken away my deputy. My forensic scientist is working on half power because most of his energy's spent worrying about his missing son. Are you sure you want me to carry on?'

'I'm quite sure, Karin. Quite sure. But remember, one of the aims of the new unit was to ensure better liaison with the Stasi at a high level. You don't seem to have got off to a very good start on that front. Perhaps you ought to arrange a meeting with your friend Jäger. See if there's anything you can do to get back in their good books.'

Müller sighed but said nothing. She was tempted to just hang up, but in the end let Reiniger cut the call. She was quickly beginning to lose respect for her police colonel. Perhaps Tilsner was correct after all. He'd always found the man pompous, ineffective. Müller had a better relationship with him, but was fast coming round to Tilsner's point of view.

An atmosphere of sadness was evident everywhere in the Schmidt family apartment. The Christmas decorations looked half-hearted, and although Müller was far from a stickler for housework, she noticed that what few there were – on the mantelpiece and the top of a bookshelf – seemed to have been put in place without being cleaned from the previous year. Wax residue from melted candles was still on the base of candlesticks that didn't have candles in them, and the tiny *Räuchermännchen* were still covered in a film of dust.

As soon as Hanne Schmidt had ushered Müller through the front door, she scurried into the kitchen, busying herself with making them both coffee – even though Müller had told her not to bother. It was as though she needed to be doing something constantly, to take her mind off Markus and the days, weeks and months that had gone by without tangible proof of his well-being.

'Jonas isn't here, I'm afraid, *Major* Müller,' she called from the kitchen, above the clatter of utensils. 'Though I suppose you must know that already.' Her voice sounded forlorn.

'I'm sorry about that, Hanne. It wasn't my idea. Perhaps he should be here with you.'

The woman popped her head round the living room doorway. She had her arms crossed over her chest, as though trying to give herself some comfort. 'Oh no,' she said. 'I'd much rather he was trying to do something useful, and he tells me this case might help you to find Markus. Although, as I understand it, it's a murd—'

The woman stopped herself before she uttered the word – the word that linked her only son's disappearance to a possible brutal death.

She clasped her hand to her mouth, as though astonished by what she was about to say. 'I . . . I'll just get the coffee . . . sorry.' She turned and ran back to the kitchen, but not before Müller saw the moisture gather in her already raw, bloodshot eyes.

After a few minutes Hanne returned with the tray of coffee and sat down on an armchair, while Müller perched forward on the sofa. She tried to pour the coffee into the cups, but her hands were shaking so much she had to put the pot back down on the tray. Müller laid her hand gently on the woman's arm, and then took over the pouring duties.

'Th-th-ank you,' she stuttered. She held her hands over her face and breathed in a long draught of air, before letting it out slowly. 'Do you have anything new to tell me?' she asked Müller. 'I don't think you do, do you? I could see it in your face when I opened the door.'

Müller thought back a few minutes. To the curious expression on Hanne's face. *Of course. She was expecting either the best or the worst – why else would her husband's boss visit her? I should have put her at ease straight away.*

Müller pulled the woman to her for a gentle hug, then pushing her away slightly, looked straight into her eyes. 'I'm sorry, Hanne. I should have realised you would have thought my visit was something significant. It was remiss of me. I should have explained immediately. But please believe me, I will leave no stone unturned to find your son. I will do whatever it takes. All the information points to him still being alive, and as far as we know, safe and well.' This last part – Müller was fully aware – was a partial lie. She feared very much for Markus's welfare after what Fenstermacher had told her. Given the needle marks and restraint marks on the bodies of both murder victims. But there was no point worrying the woman further – if such a thing were even possible.

'I still think that Jan Winkler holds the key to all this,' said Hanne. 'At first it seemed as though he was Markus's saviour. Gave him something to live for. But really, that's when his troubles started. Before that, the bullying, coming home crying from school with his spectacles broken, even though at eighteen he ought to be able to look after himself, well, all that pales into insignificance now. Can't you put more pressure on that boy to tell us where Markus is?'

'Believe me, Hanne, we've tried. We've had teams following him everywhere. My team and a uniform team from Keibelstrasse. We're working on it.'

'I bet his father is protecting him,' said Frau Schmidt with a bitter edge to her voice.

Müller knew that was the case. She also knew her hands were tied. But she wasn't going to admit that to Markus's mother. Her impotency in the face of the Stasi.

43

Müller decided she needed to see Jäger again – partly because of Reiniger's assertion that she ought to try to build bridges with the Stasi colonel, and partly because of Hanne Schmidt's gossip about Jan Winkler's father's real job. There was also something more personal she wanted to discuss with him. Perhaps it wasn't the time, in the middle of a murder inquiry, but it was something that had been nagging her for months.

The choice of the Soviet War Memorial at Treptower Park as a meeting place encouraged Müller to return to her apartment to get a thick winter coat. Even with several layers under it, the raincoat wasn't going to be enough to protect her from the cold. The visit also enabled her to pick something up from the flat that she needed to show Jäger. Something personal.

Now, as she walked through the crusty, frozen snow, Müller twirled her gloved hand round the small metal box in her coat pocket. The one given to her by Helga when she'd first met her in Leipzig. The one that had contained the photo of her natural, teenage mother cradling baby Karin in her arms. And discovered beneath the photo, at the bottom of the tin, a military identity tag from – as far as she knew – the Soviet Red Army.

This was a poignant place to meet. If the identity tag belonged to her father, as Helga intimated, had he been one of the eighty thousand Soviet soldiers killed in the battle for Berlin? Or had he survived, impregnated her mother, then moved on with his life? And if he was alive, where was he now? In the Soviet Union itself, or perhaps stationed in one of the friendly socialist states on that massive country's doorstep? Perhaps – though Müller scarcely believed it – stationed in the Republic itself? There were plenty of Soviet troops garrisoned here. It was possible. But equally, the Soviet Union was a huge country, had a huge army. Why would her father even be in the army now that war was a thing of the past? He would almost certainly be too old, however young he'd been when he'd met her teenage mother. And even if he were still a soldier, or even an officer, surely the chances of him being posted to the Republic were tiny?

She entered the memorial complex from the opposite end to the statue – the Soviet soldier holding a rescued German child, which she could see in the distance. Jäger had told her to wait by the eighth sarcophagus on the left-hand side of the central area of the vast monument. Müller glanced up at the giant red granite sculptural representations of Soviet flags – one each side of the entrance to the complex. The statues of kneeling soldiers beneath them were still adorned with snow.

She counted off the sarcophagi. She knew from her history lessons at school that there were sixteen of them – one for each of the Soviet Republics, or at least, the ones that existed in the late forties, when the monument had been completed. Even before she got to the eighth she could see Jäger in his sheepskin jacket hugging his body for warmth.

As she approached he failed to smile.

'I hope this is important, Comrade *Major*. I don't appreciate being dragged out of my office in this weather,' he hissed.

'And I don't appreciate being bundled out of my apartment and into a stinking prison van by Stasi thugs, Comrade *Oberst*.'

Jäger's stern features softened. '*Touché.*'

'So if we're still playing the game of who owes whom, I think I'm owed more than anyone here.'

'That's not the way I remember it,' said Jäger. 'And I had to take a considerable personal risk – a risk to my reputation – to get you out of Bautzen so quickly.'

'A prison where I was being held without any charge, or any accusation being levelled against me.'

Jäger laughed now, but the laugh had a cruel edge to it. 'You know very well what all that was about. Baum and Diederich. How you used Reiniger to, in effect, countermand their orders.'

'Perhaps,' said Müller. 'But it conveniently delayed the overall inquiry. And I suspect there is more than their interests at stake here.'

Jäger snorted. 'I don't think you've the slightest *idea* what's at stake here, Karin.'

At least he's using my first name again, thought Müller. *That's something.*

'I didn't come here just to trade words with you, Comrade *Oberst*. I need something.'

'You usually do.'

'Something personal,' continued Müller, pulling the small tin box from her pocket.

'Haven't I seen that before?'

Müller nodded. 'On Peissnitz Island. When we were on the miniature Pioneer train.'

Jäger sighed. 'So there is even more inside, is there?

Müller nodded. She pulled off her glove and prised the top away from the rusty container, her fingers almost immediately going white from the bitter chill in the air. She'd already removed the photo of her and her mother to a safer place – it was her most valuable possession. It was the link to her past, which now, thanks to Helga, she also knew in its flesh and blood form.

She took out the tag, with its strange Cyrillic characters and letters. Jäger moved to take it from her, but she kept it out of his reach. 'You can look, but I don't want you touching it. I'm the only one allowed to touch it. It's a Red Army identity tag.'

'Whose? And from where?'

Müller said nothing, but could feel herself reddening under Jäger's gaze.

Jäger rocked back on his feet, guffawing, momentarily forgetting the cold. As he exhaled, his condensed breath formed tiny clouds in the air. 'You think this belonged to your father, don't you? Why on earth do you think I'd be able to find out any information about him? Or want to?'

Müller wasn't going to try to answer him. But ever since she'd found out about her teenage mother, who died heartbroken after Müller herself was taken away from her as a baby, she'd felt a desperate need to complete the puzzle about her natural parents. Even though she was embroiled in a murder and missing persons inquiry.

She put the ID tag back in the tin that Helga had given her when breaking the news about Müller's mother, closed the lid, and returned it to her pocket. Reaching into the other side of her coat, she brought out a folded piece of paper. 'I've noted down all the details.' She handed the paper to Jäger, who took it and put it into his own pocket. 'I need you to find out who this relates to, and whether he is still alive.'

'And presumably, whether he actually *is* your father?'

'If there is any information to confirm that, which I doubt there will be, then yes – please. And I have another request.'

'Go on,' he prompted, warily.

'I want you to tell me all you can about Jan Winkler's father. For some reason we're not being permitted to take his son in for questioning.'

Jäger seemed to suck his teeth, and glanced up towards the steel-grey sky. Then he slowly lowered his gaze to meet hers once more.

'I hope you'll take my advice, Karin. Perhaps it could be the trade-off for me finding out what I can about this Red Army soldier who may or may not have been your father.'

Müller frowned.

'Be very, very careful taking on Winkler. Whatever you may think you know about him, he's a very powerful man. A very *ruthless* man. He doesn't take kindly to anyone interfering with his son's life – or way of life – either. However much you feel you've been through during the two years or so we've known each other, if you cross Winkler, you'll be in more danger than ever before.' Jäger's face was like thunder – more serious than she'd ever seen it. 'That's clear, I hope?'

'Perfectly clear, thank you, Comrade *Oberst*. While I can't give you any absolute undertakings, as long as Herr Winkler and his son haven't committed any criminal acts, then they have nothing to fear from me or my team.'

'That's not what I mean, Karin. I mean steer clear of him – *whatever* you think you know.'

Müller nodded. For her it wasn't a nod of agreement, merely an acknowledgement of comprehension. If Jäger understood things differently that was his problem.

She held out her hand to his to shake.

Jäger held it briefly. 'I mean what I say, Karin. I don't think I can make myself any clearer.'

'I heard you, Comrade *Oberst*, loud and clear. Please do let me know when you have any information for me about the other matter.'

With that they left each other, walking away in opposite directions.

Müller strode now towards the main statue of the memorial – the Soviet soldier, Nikolai Masolov, with the toddler he'd saved as a firefight raged in ruined Berlin, perched on top of the Kurgan – the domed warriors' grave in which several thousand Red Army soldiers were said to be buried. Müller wondered if there were any similarities between the heroic Masolov and her father – whoever he was. In all probability, he too had been a Red Army hero, delivering Germany from the evils of fascism, of Nazism, at the same time as siring a baby with a teenage German girl.

44

Sunday afternoon (mid-December 1976)
Strausberger Platz

Müller's much-delayed meeting with the endocrinologist had finally been confirmed for the next day, with the help of Fenstermacher. Despite the awkwardness of their last encounter, with little progress in her own attempts to pin the man down, Müller had asked the pathologist for assistance. Fenstermacher was coming all the way from Hoyerswerda to sit in and try to put him at ease. Whether or not the man would talk was an entirely different matter.

Kriminaltechniker Jonas Schmidt, too, claimed to have made an important discovery that he didn't want to talk about over the phone. So she'd promised to drive straight to Guben as soon as her meeting at Charité was over. Tilsner had also rung her to say he was back on her service. Her immediate thought to how Tilsner could help brought her back to the thorny problem of Jan Winkler – and his father. Whatever it was that Reiniger had needed her deputy to do so urgently had now gone on the back burner.

Tilsner gave a heavy sigh when Müller said she wanted him to follow the youth again on his Sunday adventures.

'I really think you should come too, Karin. There's something I've wanted you to see since before Bautzen. Didn't you get my phone messages? I left them at your apartment and at the office.'

Müller remembered Helga saying a work colleague had been trying to get in touch. Amidst all the confusion and tension after her arrest, it must have slipped her mind. But she didn't recall receiving any message at Keibelstrasse. Was that just inefficiency on the part of one of the phone operators – or something more sinister?

'You need to see it with your own eyes,' continued Tilsner. 'That's why I'd like you to come with me on the bike.'

'That was a disaster last time. And it's too dangerous now, what with the snow and everything.'

'Hah! Too dangerous for you to ride pillion, but not too dangerous for me to have to follow that bastard Winkler alone. Thanks a lot. Anyway, I'm asking you one last time. I assure you it's in your own interests. If you won't come with me, still come – in the evening. That's when they seem to be meeting now. It's a different crowd. Older guys too. There is something you must see.'

'And you can't just tell me what?'

'Just come. Honestly, Karin. I am swearing on my life. You need to see it for yourself.'

Despite Tilsner's pleas, she felt she owed it to her family to spend the day with them. And rather than watching *Tatort* with Helga in the evening, she wanted some cosy time with Emil on the sofa once the twins had been put to bed.

They'd had a lovely afternoon, strolling up and down Karl-Marx-Allee. Although it was still cold, the strong sun made it a beautiful winter's day. Johannes kept straining against the push-chair belts as though he wanted to get out and run, even though both he and Jannika were still at the crawling stage. When not having to carry one of the twins to keep them quiet, Müller had linked arms with Emil as he pushed the double buggy along. Helga stayed in the flat to give them some space.

'It seems to be better between you and Helga now, Emil. More relaxed.'

He smiled. 'She's not so bad. And she's a tough old bird. I was impressed with the way she bounced back after your arrest. It was a nasty fall she had—'

'Push, not fall,' insisted Müller.

'Of course.' He didn't seem in the mood to disagree. 'But she didn't mope about it – just started making as many phone calls as possible to your boss to try to find out what the hell had happened. She wouldn't let it rest.'

A spiteful thought wormed its way into Müller's head. *Shouldn't it have been you doing that, Emil?*

Perhaps, though, she was being unkind. At that moment, Johannes began kicking and screaming again, so it wasn't a thought she pursued.

But it was a thought that resurfaced at dinner time. Emil seemed to be rushing his food again.

'Emil. Why are you in such a hurry again? I've never seen anyone eat so fast. Can't we just relax and enjoy the meal?'

His face creased into a frown. 'What?'

'You seem to be rushing, that's all.'

'Have you started to police my eating habits now?'

'I didn't mean—'

Emil slapped his palm down on the table, provoking tears and screaming from Johannes. Helga picked him up and started rocking him.

'I think it was very clear what you meant.' Then he turned to Helga. 'Could you leave us, please?'

'Of course, I'll just put him down in his cot.'

'Helga, you don't have to—' Müller's attempts to defend her grandmother were cut short.

'And the girl too.'

'*The girl?* She does have a name, you know,' said Müller.

'Right, that's it,' he said, grabbing his coat. 'I'm not going to be told how to eat in my own home.'

'*My* home,' said Müller feeling her muscles quivering with anger. 'And where the hell do you think you're going?'

Helga, had by now moved both twins to their cots. Both were screaming, but Müller's grandmother ignored them and took refuge in her own room, slamming the door behind her.

'The reason I was rushing my food is that I'm behind on work. I was hoping to do some here this evening. I took time off to deal with your little drama when you got yourself arrested.'

'When I *got myself arrested*? How can you say—'

'You're always sailing close to the wind, Karin. That's your problem. There are rules in this Republic. Perhaps you should obey them once in a while.'

'That's outrageous. How dare—'

Emil was already at the front door. 'I dare. I'm going to the office at the hospital. It's the only place I can get some peace.' He slammed the door behind him.

Müller rushed into the twins' room and tried to calm them. She got them both out of their cots, turned the light on, and then got some toys out for them to play with. Soon they were gurgling happily again. But Müller knew it wasn't good enough. She and Emil shouldn't allow their differences to affect their children, especially at such an impressionable age.

Müller slumped down into Helga's antique nursing chair. She rocked back and forth. This wasn't the way it was meant to be. It was all so, so wrong. But she didn't want to give up on another relationship. Somehow, she and Emil had to make this work.

Helga knocked softly on the door.

'Come,' said Müller, surprised how shaky her own voice sounded.

Helga crept into the room, then saw the twins were awake and playing on the floor.

'Are you OK, Karin?'

The concern from her grandmother, when Müller and Emil had been at fault, was just too much. Müller cleared her constricted throat.

'I hope you'll forgive me, Helga. That should have never happened in front of you and the children. I'm so terribly sorry.'

Müller knew the only solution – for the time being – was to take refuge in her work. To increase her efforts to try to find Markus Schmidt and solve the murder cases. She still felt they were inextricably linked. But the priority was to get Markus home, safe and well, as soon as possible.

Helga tried to persuade her to watch television with her. She even offered another bottle of her dwindling supply of sparkling wine. Instead, Müller explained to her grandmother she had to go out. There was something she had to do.

'Good grief,' whispered Tilsner, as Müller crept into his hideout overlooking the Frankfurt club. 'I wondered who that was for a moment; thought I'd been discovered. What are you doing here? Mind you, I'm beginning to wonder what I'm doing here. I'm getting sick of just watching Winkler and his cronies, rather than arresting them. But I thought you wanted me to do this on my own?'

'Nothing better to do,' she said quietly. 'I thought I might as well get some fresh air. Although it isn't very fresh in here.'

'It's these sacks,' said Tilsner. 'They don't smell any better than when we first came here – worse, if anything. They're the only things keeping me warm though. Well, not exactly warm, but they stop me freezing to death.' He lifted the side of his make-shift blankets and motioned for Müller to join him. She could feel her teeth beginning to chatter as the cold started to get into her bones. She squeezed up against him, feeling his warmth.

'Just like old times, eh?' he said, in a lecherous voice.

'Don't get any ideas—'

Müller's low tones were cut off mid-sentence as Tilsner clasped his hand over her mouth. The headlight beam of another car swung into the car park.

Müller cupped her hands over Tilsner's left ear to whisper to him. 'I've only come here because you insisted there was something I had to see in person,' she giggled. 'Although it is quite nice being squashed up here.'

Tilsner sighed. 'It won't be anything to laugh about, Karin,' he said in a stern whisper. 'As I said, you have to see for yourself, but you won't like it. Though I can't guarantee it will happen just like last week.

'Can't you tell me what it is?'

She felt him shake his head as the car doors of the latest visitors slammed shut. A man aged about thirty, thought Müller, from what she could see in the light, and a youth. Aged twenty at the most. They waited at the door of the club, then it opened and they were let inside. In the illuminated doorway, Müller clearly saw the face of Jan Winkler.

'Is that what you wanted me to see?' asked Müller, *sotto voce*.

Tilsner shook his head again. 'No, Karin,' he whispered back. 'I wish it were, but it isn't.'

'What, then?' she asked.

Before Tilsner could answer, another vehicle pulled into the car park.

Müller was surprised when Diederich got out of the driver's side, and then opened the rear door for another young man to emerge. When the youth was upright, her surprise turned to shock. Diederich was pushing him against the side of the car, and they appeared to be embracing.

'Good God!' cried Müller under her breath.

'That's not what I wanted you to see either, Karin, I'm afraid,' hissed Tilsner.

She saw another man get out of the car's passenger side. For a moment, he looked like a doppelganger of Diederich. *The blond hair, the square jaw, the classic—*

'No! N—'

Tilsner clasped his hand across her mouth again, held her down as she fought against him.

'I'm sorry, Karin. I'm sorry. This is why you had to see it for yourself.'

Because there, facing them now, apparently hugging a younger man who'd also emerged from the back seat of the car, was someone who looked remarkably like Diederich. Müller had remarked on it before in the bar in Frankfurt at the start of this godforsaken case.

Müller tried to blink away her tears. The yard's lighting was weak. But there was no mistake. It was *her* partner, Emil Wollenburg. The father of her children. And Müller knew – as Tilsner continued to hold her back, and she continued to struggle – that her world had just fallen apart.

45

She was disgusted with him, disgusted with herself for not realising, *livid* with Tilsner for not telling her as soon as he'd found
out. As soon as the four men were in the club, she wrenched
herself free of her deputy's grasp.

'Don't do anything stupid, Karin,' hissed Tilsner.

She ignored him, ignored the club, banished all thoughts of
confronting Emil for now. That could wait. She didn't care what
Tilsner discovered now in his cold, lonely vigil. She wanted to
get home.

Müller knew she was in no real state to drive. Too many thoughts,
dark thoughts, racing round her brain. Thoughts as dark as killing
Emil, making him pay the ultimate price for his betrayal.

She could feel the tendons bulging in her neck as she gripped
the steering wheel of the Lada. She wasn't going to do anything
stupid. She was going to get back to Strausberger Platz and then
assess her options.

Once she got back to the flat it was quiet, save for the sound
of the occasional car or motorbike on Karl-Marx-Allee or on

Lichtenberger Strasse – the street they directly overlooked. Helga and the twins had long gone to sleep. Müller briefly toyed with the idea of waking her grandmother, but decided she was just being selfish. It was a problem – and what an understatement *that* was – that she would have to deal with alone. And at the end of the day, Emil Wollenburg would still be the father of her twins. She would still be linked to him in some way, whatever action she decided to take. And she was determined that, in whatever she decided, Jannika and Johannes's needs had to come first.

She suddenly felt a huge wave of tiredness wash over her. Her legs felt like lead and she struggled to even put one in front of the other as she made her way to the bedroom – the bedroom she shared with a man she now knew was a liar. A pervert even. Although as soon as she had this thought, she banished it. Markus Schmidt wasn't a pervert, so why was Emil?

Taking off her boots, Müller slumped down onto the bed. She didn't have the energy to take off her clothes. Instead, she pulled the duvet over herself and curled into a foetal ball. She didn't know what she could do; didn't know who she could trust, or who she could confide in. Perhaps only Helga, but it was unfair to lay all her troubles at her grandmother's door.

She didn't know how much later it was that she felt Emil's weight on the other side of the bed. He tried to reach across to her, but she pushed him away. He would think it was just a continuation of their earlier argument, that she still hadn't forgiven him. But it was something much, much worse. A betrayal of the absolute worst kind. As he lapsed into contented snoring, she remained wide awake, the images of him outside the club flashing in front of her eyes.

He'd arrived with Diederich. Had he been betraying her to him all along, discussing her secrets, the aspects of the case she'd let slip at home? Worse than that, was he one of *them*? A member of the Stasi. Were her original suspicions about his job in Halle-Neustadt conveniently coinciding with hers well founded after all?

If so, it meant everything was a lie.

Their whole life was a lie.

And the twins? What of them? They must – to Emil – have been a huge mistake. Perhaps he'd been relying on what the gynaecologists had told her repeatedly: that it was impossible for her to get pregnant. Yet she had. That was the irony of the situation. If Emil was a Stasi agent, if he was a homosexual, then he had still given her the most precious gift of her life: Jannika and Johannes. And he was still – for all his sins – their natural father. She would have to think very carefully about what she did next, and bide her time.

The next day, she made sure she was up before he was, leaving a note for Helga explaining she had an early meeting at Keibelstrasse. She hadn't, of course. Her first appointment was at 10 a.m. with Fenstermacher and her endocrinology contact at Charité. She just couldn't face Emil. She wasn't even sure she could face Helga or the twins – little though they knew about what was going on.

She just needed to get out of the apartment.

Her hopes and dreams for a happy future had been shattered.

46

Müller scanned the Charité hospital car park, looking for Fenstermacher's peppermint-green Wartburg, with its elegant, curved bodywork. Finally she spotted it, made her way over and opened the door.

'Citizen Fenstermacher, so good of you to come all this way. I'm very grateful. Do you think it's best if I'm in the front or the back?'

Fenstermacher tapped the passenger seat. 'Sit in the front with me. Poldi can go in the back. And then if he's brought any documents, he can spread them out next to himself.'

When Müller climbed in and settled herself, the older woman looked at her. 'You look tired, if you don't mind me saying so, *Major* Müller.'

'I am. Bad night's sleep, I'm afraid.' There was a grain of truth in that, but it was so far from what was *really* the truth it was almost an outright lie. 'But if Herr Althaus has anything useful to say, anything that helps us to crack this case, that might perk me up.'

'I'm sure he will,' said Fenstermacher. 'But he's a bit nervous, perhaps understandably. That's why he wanted to meet in my car rather than the hospital itself.'

Althaus, when he arrived, looked to Müller much as she'd imagined. A slight man, with wire-rimmed glasses, a bit like an emaciated Trotsky – a man out of his time, with unfashionable clothes that appeared to be from the fifties, never mind the sixties.

After the brief introductions, Fenstermacher asked Althaus if he was happy to talk here in the hospital car park, or if it might be better to go for a drive. When he indicated the latter, the pathologist asked him if he had any preferences.

'Well, if it's not too far out of your way, perhaps the Müggelsee? I'm rather fond of it, and you can park right by the lake.'

The pathologist's face fell. It was a good three-quarters of an hour's drive at least.

Müller smiled. There was a way to make the endocrinologist's suggestion work. 'If you drop Dr Althaus and myself at Köpenick S-bahn afterwards, we'll be able to make our way back from there, and you can pick up the motorway system at Bohnsdorf.'

The Müggelsee – what they could see of it through the mist, at least – was completely frozen over following day after day of plunging temperatures, with only a few hardy souls dressed in their warmest winter coats and boots actually walking on the ice. Müller didn't fancy that, and it seemed Althaus and Fenstermacher were content to stay in the car too. Fenstermacher kept the engine ticking over to ensure they were warm enough.

'So, Poldi, tell *Major* Müller here what you can about Dr Uwe Gaissler,' she said. She smiled conspiratorially at Müller. 'There's no love lost between them – but I have it on good authority from others that Poldi's account is correct.'

Althaus pushed his spectacles back up his nose, and then started talking as Müller and Fenstermacher turned in their seats to listen.

'Well, I don't like to speak badly of colleagues, but with Dr Gaissler I make an exception. He worked in the endocrinology department, and some of their work is controversial, but the basic thesis isn't bad: it argues that homosexuality in males is a result of androgen deprivation during a particular phase of foetal hypothalamic development. They had some success with rats in reversing this. The department's argument is that, although homosexuality isn't illegal in the Republic, many homosexuals are suicide risks, therefore anything that can be done to prevent this must be a good thing.

'So the initial idea was one of prevention, rather than a cure – if indeed we should talk of such things when discussing sexual orientation.'

'Pah,' snorted Fenstermacher. 'Of course we shouldn't. It's a fundamental human choice. If you start to talk about, or look for, these so-called "cures", you're little better than the Nazis with their so-called "experiments".'

Müller was inclined to agree, but she wanted to hear what the doctor had to say about the facts and about Gaissler, rather than listen to Fenstermacher's own views.

'Go on, Dr Althaus,' she said.

'The theory was that those foetuses at risk could be administered androgen therapy, thus preventing a homosexual adult developing. The foetuses unsuitable for treatment should be aborted.'

Fenstermacher gasped, although Müller was sure the woman must have heard this before, given she was the one who'd arranged this meeting. For Müller, the man's words were an uncomfortable and unwanted reminder of her own past – the abortion she'd had at the start of her career.

'But what about Gaissler? It's him we're concerned with isn't it?' prompted Müller.

'Yes,' agreed Althaus. 'There was a proposal to go as far as potential brain surgery as one part of a so-called "cure". As far as I know, it initially didn't go any further. But Gaissler decided he wanted to try to – with a lot of backers in high places.'

'Including the American pharmaceutical company?' asked Müller.

'Yes. That's what I'm coming to. Gaissler started talking at lectures about the possibility of extending it further, to try to find an actual "cure" for adults via surgery. And it was this that interested the Americans. I think it was a company with very traditional, religious backers, who believed homosexuals should burn in hell, that sort of thing.'

'Nonsense,' spat Fenstermacher.

'And of course the Republic's government was very interested in this pharmaceutical company's attention—'

'Because it brought in American dollars,' said Müller.

'Exactly, *Major*, exactly. Gaissler started these experiments in the cure phase a couple of years ago, using student volunteers. They were paid well. I'm not sure, though, that they really knew what they were letting themselves in for. There were some complaints at Charité. Some of his colleagues started questioning his methods, and conclusions. The end result – even though he had government and US financial backing – was that the hospital kicked him out. Although some of his colleagues have since allegedly suffered at the hands of the Stasi for that.'

'Were you one of those, Dr Althaus?'

'I'd rather not say. I'm here. I still have a job. Let's leave it at that.'

'But your suspicion,' continued Müller, 'is that Gaissler is still doing his experiments, somewhere?'

'It's more than a suspicion, *Major*. One of his assistants went with him. They were both given Stasi protection. But he and this assistant had some sort of falling out. This assistant came to me and urged me to try to stop Gaissler. He claimed the experiments were getting out of control. He said there had been an incident.'

'When was this?' asked Müller.

'About three or four months ago.'

About the same time Nadel's body was found in Senftenberger See. Was that the so-called 'incident'?

'I'll need the name of this assistant,' said Müller.

'I can't give you that, *Major*, I'm afraid. It wouldn't be too difficult for you to find out. But it can't come from me.'

Müller sighed. 'So what more can you tell me that Dr Fenstermacher has not already said?' asked Müller.

Althaus handed her an envelope. 'I can give you this – it contains the most recent photograph I could find of Gaissler.

That might be useful. And I've done a bit more digging since I last talked to Gudrun. I've uncovered something very interesting. Does the town of Wilhelm-Pieck-Stadt Guben – or indeed its Polish mirror image of Gubin – mean anything to you, *Major*?'

Müller felt her mouth suddenly going dry. *Guben? Our searches there found nothing. How can we have been so close all along?* When she started to speak, her tongue seemed stuck.

'Yes,' she said after a moment, try to calm her mounting anticipation. What was the man about to say? 'What about it?'

'What I found out was that Gaissler's family used to have a medical supplies factory there, before the war. It was badly damaged in the fighting. Not much use, I was told. So when other similar factories were taken over by the Soviet administration, and then by the Republic, theirs wasn't.'

'And it's actually in Guben itself?'

'That I don't know, I'm afraid, *Major*. But if Gaissler was to go anywhere to set up his new laboratory, my guess is it would be there.'

47

Müller put all thoughts of Emil out of her mind as far as she could. She would have to deal with it later. For now the priority was finding Gaissler before he could do more damage.

Rather than take the S-bahn from Köpenick, she flagged down a passing *Vopo* patrol, showed them her ID and then borrowed their radio to dial up Keibelstrasse. When she got through, she told Tilsner to bring the Lada and pick her up immediately. Then she tried to get through to Schmidt at Guben. He'd said he had important new information. What was it? She needed to know. But the police at Guben said they didn't know where he was.

Tilsner put his foot flat down on the accelerator as they hit the motorway. With the blue light flashing, they blared the horn at anyone who got in their way.

As Tilsner concentrated on driving, Müller desperately tried to get Schmidt on the radio again.

This time she had more luck.

'We're on our way, Jonas. But I need to know what you wanted to tell me.'

'I didn't really want to say over an open telephone line or radio link, Comrade *Major*. I still don't.'

'Don't worry about that, Jonas. Just tell me. Now.'

'Well, I was talking to our Polish coll—'

'Not the whole story, Jonas. A one-sentence summary. Quickly.'

'Rats. Dead rats. Lots of them washed up or dumped on an island on the Polish side of the river. They were frozen into a huge clump – well, the whole river is frozen over now – and found by an old Polish man out walking his dog. I tested one. Similar results to those Fenstermacher got at her autopsy. Sex hormones.'

'Which island? Where?'

'It's called Theatre Island. Middle of the river, but more on the Polish side. Linked by a footbridge. And now ice too.'

'But no road?' asked Müller.

'Not to the island itself, Comrade *Major*.'

The horn blared again as a lorry driver tried to pull out to overtake, but then thought better of it as he spied the Lada in his wing mirrors, speeding towards him.

'Have you been there?'

'Yes – of course.'

'What's there, other than dead rats?'

'Trees, grass and an open-air theatre. That's it.'

'Anything that looks like a disused factory?'

'Yes, yes!' shouted Schmidt. 'On the Gub-*en*, the German side of the river. There's a dilapidated building that looks like a factory. Slightly upstream from where the rats were found.

That makes sense. And they hadn't spread out, they were all clumped together – maybe they were all in a container that broke up or something like that?'

Müller wondered if she could trust her forensic scientist not to do anything stupid. He was currently wrapped up in his rat discovery, but behind all that he was a desperate father. By now, he knew as well as Müller did that his son was at serious risk, if – as Müller believed – he was being held at the factory with other youths.

'OK, Jonas. I don't trust either the Eisenhüttenstadt police or those in Guben.' Müller knew the Guben *Vopo*s might be listening in, but continued nonetheless. 'They've failed to put an end to this so far. But Schwarz from Senftenberg seemed reasonably sound. Tell him to get to that factory as soon as possible with as many officers as he can spare.'

'That might be harder than you think, Comrade *Major*.'

'Why, Jonas?'

'All roads in and out of Wilhelm-Pieck-Stadt Guben have been sealed. The bridge across to Poland too.'

How had that happened so quickly? They can't have known what Althaus told me.

'Do you know why, Jonas?'

Müller grabbed the dashboard as Tilsner swerved off the motorway at the Cottbus turning.

'No, not precisely, Comrade *Major*. But it happened soon after I told uniform here about my rat discovery. I'm very sorry. I should of course have reported directly to you.'

Müller swore under her breath. He certainly should have come to her first, or simply kept it to himself until he could. Instead, the local police had no doubt reported it straight to Diederich and Baum.

'OK. Well, see what you can find out about this factory. See if there's another route to it. But don't do anything stupid, Jonas.'

Müller ended the call. They'd now been slowed down massively by the traffic. There was no way to avoid Cottbus. That or Forst, further down the motorway. Whichever they chose, they had to drive almost right through the centre of town.

Tilsner had one hand on the wheel. The other was constantly jabbing at the Lada's horn. But still some drivers ignored them.

As they neared Guben, Müller attempted to raise Schwarz's team on the radio.

'Helmut, are you reading me?' she shouted again and again. Finally, she got through.

'I can hear you clearly, Comrade *Major*.'

'We need to get to a disused factory opposite what's known as Theatre Island in Wilhelm-Pieck-Stadt Guben, Helmut. But there's a problem.'

'What's that?'

'Someone – we believe the Stasi, possibly a local branch of the Stasi acting on their own initiative – has sealed off the town. Do you know any back roads, any lanes they might have missed that we can go down?'

'No,' said Schwarz. 'But I do have one idea.'

What he said next sounded horribly risky to Müller. She felt under her coat. Checked the Makarov was there. Then took it out, clicked the safety off and on again, and checked the gun was loaded.

'Is yours ready?' she asked Tilsner.

He nodded grimly.

They both knew what they had to do.

For the sake of their forensic scientist. For the sake of his son. And for the sake of other parents whose sons were perhaps at that very moment being experimented on as part of Gaissler's mad scheme.

48

'Don't try to struggle, boy. It was your choice.'

I feel my heart pounding in terror, but I'm not sure why. I can't remember. I just know that the soothing tones are dangerous for me. My brain tries to grasp the words, but they slip away before I can even touch the meaning, never mind decode it, the way you can never catch a fish by hand. I used to try that with Vati, on holiday in the Mecklenburg lakes. They were always too quick for us. The memory makes me want to smile. But then I remember it was before . . . before he came to hate me, hate what I am. Before all this.

I fight against the wrist restraints, try to cry out. But my arms won't move, and my jaw, instead of opening, is biting down.

'Prepare his arm, please, nurse.'

Get away. Get away from me. That's what I want to say. But although my brain tries to force my mouth to open, no words will come.

'We can't hear what you're trying to say, boy. This was your choice, remember?'

My choice? You liar! You gave me no choice. I wouldn't cheat for you and your kind any more. I wouldn't betray my love. And you call that a choice? A vision of his face torments my brain now. I could not, would not, betray my love.

The needle approaches my arm in infinitesimal slow motion. At least, that's how it seems to me … but my mind is playing tricks. Time has been slowed down to torture me further.

I want my father here. I want to forgive him. I want him to love me for who I am.

Vati, Vati. I am still your little boy. Why won't you help me when I need you?

The needle in the nurse's hand has nearly reached the end of its journey. Once it punctures the skin, once the chemicals are pushed into my bloodstream, then the very essence of me will be changed – for ever.

Never able to love again.

At least, never able to love in the way I want to love. And that, for me, will be a living death.

Is that what you wanted, Father?

Is that what you wanted for your little boy?

You and the precious Republic of Workers and Peasants that you so slavishly serve.

49

Müller calculated that their best chance of mounting a surprise raid on Gaissler's lair was from the north. She radioed that through to Schwarz.

A few kilometres outside Guben, Tilsner turned hard right following Müller's instructions, to the village of Grano. That way they could skirt the town and end up about four kilometres outside it, where one of the roads closely followed the line of the Neisse.

Schwarz came through on the radio. He'd caught them up and was now directly behind them, following with his team in two police cars. One marked, one unmarked. Müller turned her body slightly and acknowledged his presence with a wave.

Once they got to the road by the river, Tilsner kept a close eye on the left-hand, driver's side of the car. Searching for an opening.

Suddenly he saw it.

A slipway.

Müller had already warned Schwarz that their convoy would need to spread out. That they ought to leave a sufficient gap between each vehicle.

Although she wasn't religious, Müller found herself saying a prayer, asking, if there was a God, for it to look after her loved ones should anything happen to her and Werner. To look after Jannika, Johannes and Helga. Emil wasn't mentioned in this silent prayer. She still had to deal with that. If she survived.

Tilsner slowly edged the car down the frozen slipway.

Müller fully expected the car to simply break through the ice. But it didn't. The front wheels held, then the back, and then Tilsner was weaving his way forward, slowly but steadily. Schwarz had told her the best technique was to keep up a steady pace. On no account were they to stop.

Müller wound open her window. She wanted to be sure of what she thought she was hearing above the din of the engine. A bitter blast of air hit her in the face. She felt the pores in her skin constricting. But now she heard the noise clearer than ever. The rapid crack of the ice fracturing beneath the wheels.

'I don't like this, Werner,' she screamed, as the Lada jolted along. 'It's not going to hold.' She could see the cracks forming as they progressed. How thick was the ice? Schwarz's forensic scientist had calculated the river had been frozen for long enough that it might just be thick enough to hold one car. They had three in a convoy. And it wasn't even the depths of winter – that would come in February.

'Shut up,' shouted Tilsner. 'I need to concentrate.'

Müller knew that further north, where the Oder met the Ostsee, sea winds, melts and refreezes would have made this impossible. There she'd seen pictures of the jagged ice blocks frozen together. Here – apart from a few wind-blown ridges making the car shudder – it was relatively smooth.

She turned her head to view the progress of Schwarz and his team.

'*Scheisse!*' she shouted. 'One of their cars is stuck. They're trying to get out. We need to go back and help them.'

'We can't,' said Tilsner. 'It's too risky.'

She saw four police officers clamber out onto the ice. They had to abandon the car to save themselves. But Schwarz's own vehicle behind didn't seem to be stopping either. He was taking a long sweep round, trying to find thicker ice.

'How much further?' asked Müller, feeling as though a huge weight was pressing on her chest. She tried to swallow.

Tilsner glanced down at the speedometer briefly.

'It was four kilometres to Theatre Island. We've done two.'

Tilsner suddenly picked up the police radio handset.

'What are you doing? You need both hands on the wheel.'

He ignored her and started speaking into the radio.

'We're going in,' Tilsner shouted over the mouthpiece, the rapid cracking of the ice providing a staccato backdrop to his words. 'Make sure your lot are ready.'

'Who are you talking to?' asked Müller. Tilsner failed to reply as he concentrated on driving in a straight line. It must have been Schwarz, thought Müller.

She could see the river widening. Buildings on each side now – the Republic and Gub-*en* on one side, Poland and Gub-*in* on the other. Then she saw the ice-covered river diverge into two frozen channels.

'Have your gun ready,' Tilsner shouted. 'I can't shoot while I'm driving.'

She glanced over her shoulder again. Schwarz's Wartburg was still making progress a few hundred metres behind.

'*Scheisse!*' he exclaimed. 'I can't see anywhere to take the car. The riverbanks are too steep.'

Müller realised her deputy was looking at the Guben side of the river. Müller checked the other bank – the island. There was what looked like a snow-and-ice-covered beach of pebbles.

'There,' she shouted. 'Go that way.'

'But we need to be the other side.'

'There's a footbridge.' She pointed to it. Tilsner put his foot down for the last few metres of the ice. She felt the wheels sliding under them, more jolting and banging, and then the Lada came to rest, safely out of the river.

They drew their guns, then exited the car and ran towards the bridge. If the Stasi or anyone else was guarding it, then it was all over.

It looked to be clear. But on the main town bridge a few hundred metres downstream, Müller could see some activity. A man pointing a finger in their direction. Then she realised it wasn't a finger – it was a gun.

'Get down!' she shouted to Tilsner. They crouched under the iron railings as they ran across the footbridge. A shot rang out. She heard the ricochet against the metal bridge.

Panting now, they reached the East German side and raced towards the disused factory building, some six storeys high.

They didn't really know what they were looking for, or where exactly in the building they needed to search.

As they got near the entrance, they saw a man in a white scientist's jacket poking his head round the corner, alerted by all the shouting – and presumably the gunshot. He tried to run back inside, but Tilsner was too quick for him. He tackled him round the legs, and then brought his police Makarov up to the man's temple.

'Keep quiet and take us to the laboratory and you won't be harmed,' he hissed into the man's ear while wrenching his arm up behind his back, provoking a series of yelps.

When the man refused to answer, Tilsner pulled his arm higher.

'Stop!' the man cried. 'Please! Up there.' He nodded towards the dark, dilapidated stairwell.

'Quickly,' said Tilsner jabbing the gun in the man's back. 'Take us there.'

They raced up two of the several flights of stairs. Once they reached the second floor, they were suddenly in a more modern, ordered environment. But when Müller pulled the door, it was locked.

Tilsner jabbed his gun in the scientist's back again. 'How do we get in?'

'You have to use the intercom.'

Müller saw something in the man's eyes. 'Liar! You've got a key, haven't you?'

'Have you, you little bastard?' said Tilsner, wrenching the man's arms up again.

When that didn't work, Müller clicked off her safety catch and put her Makarov to the man's mouth.

'We don't have time for this. Let us in or I shoot.'

She pressed the metal barrel of the gun into the man's fleshy lips, then in slow motion started to squeeze the trigger.

The man suddenly whimpered and nodded his head. Tilsner allowed him to reach into his pocket. Müller grabbed the key as soon as it was visible and then opened the door.

'Take us to where the lads are being held. And keep quiet.'

Müller knew time was running out. The Stasi agents on the main town bridge had seen them. They'd been lucky the actual lab wasn't guarded, but at any moment they could be overrun and outgunned.

The corridor opened out into what looked like some sort of makeshift operating theatre.

Müller scanned the room of people, trying to recognise Gaissler from the photograph provided by Althaus. Somehow they hadn't been spotted yet.

Then she saw him, leaning over someone strapped down to an examination couch.

'Gaissler. Stop right there. People's Police. You're under arrest.'

The rogue endocrinologist looked round frantically and then raced towards a back exit. Müller ran after him. 'Stop, or I'll fire . . .' But Gaissler had already made his escape through doors at the rear. Müller was tempted to follow alone – but then remembered how it had ended in the Harz, when Tilsner had almost died trying to save her. Instead, she frantically looked round the room, trying to see Markus. Schmidt had now joined them, and she saw the panic in his eyes as he realised his son wasn't there.

Tilsner jabbed his gun at the scientist's temple. 'Where's Gaissler gone? And where are the other youths?'

He clicked off the safety catch.

'Talk. Now! Otherwise I'll very much enjoy shooting you.'

50

They raced down the back staircase all the way to the basement, Tilsner's Makarov pistol pressed against the scientist, as Müller, Schmidt and Schwarz followed.

At the bottom, Müller paused, panting.

'Where now?'

'Through there,' said the man. 'There's a tunnel through here.'

Müller tried the handle on the grey metal door.

'Where's the key?' shouted Tilsner, jabbing his pistol into the scientist's ribs.

The man got out his keys, selected one, and turned it in the lock. Tilsner pulled him out of the way, then opened the door and Müller rushed through, gun at the ready.

Ahead of them was a tunnel in semi-darkness. Müller replaced the gun in her shoulder holster and pulled her torch from her pocket. She shone it into the void as the others followed behind. A heavy Nazi-era typeface on the wall indicated this was tunnel 41 – but of how many?

'Where's this taking us?' shouted Müller, as she half-ran, half-stumbled along the tunnel's uneven ground, her boots splashing through puddles of green-black water.

'It goes under the river to the Polish side,' the scientist yelled back. 'To Theatre Island.'

After some hundred metres or so, the tunnel widened into a chamber. On one side were stone stairs leading upwards; opposite, another grey metal door, which the scientist pointed to. At any moment, Müller was expecting the Stasi to arrive. What she didn't know was what would happen when they did. Surely she, Tilsner and Schwarz were doing the right thing in trying to save these youths? But since the gunfire from the bridge as they'd approached Gaissler's lair, she was still worried it could all go wrong. That the Stasi would finally make an appearance and try to cover things up. What would the fate of the boys be then?

Müller pocketed her torch and drew the Makarov from its holster once more. She turned the handle of the door. This one was unlocked.

She kicked it open.

'*Kriminalpolizei!* No one move.'

As she edged round the door frame she saw Gaissler standing stock still, staring at her. He had a gun pointed at the head of a figure curled on a dirty mattress. Müller realised to her horror it was Schmidt's son, Markus.

More youths were lying on other mattresses scattered around the floor. At least ten, maybe more. All chained and shackled, but unresponsive – as though they'd been drugged.

'Don't come any closer!' Gaissler shouted.

'Drop the weapon,' Müller said calmly, 'and put your hands above your head.'

'No! Why should you stop my work? This is all approved at the highest levels. We're approaching a breakthrough.'

Müller heard a commotion behind her. Then another armed man entered the room, flanked by two cronies.

Jäger.

A look of recognition flashed across Gaissler's face. Then a nervous smile.

'Comrade *Oberst*—'

Jäger raised his gun and cut him off. 'Your work is over, Comrade Gaissler. Drop your gun.'

'But—'

Müller heard the click of Jäger releasing his safety catch.

'Now.'

Gaissler began to move his weapon. Müller felt a momentary sense of relief: it looked as though he was about to lay it down.

But instantly a shot rang out, then another. There was screaming, shouting. Müller – her eyes sweeping to the prone Markus – saw he was splattered in blood. Schmidt rushed forward, cradling his son.

'No! No!'

Then she realised Markus was still moving. The blood was Gaissler's, not the boy's. The endocrinologist lay splayed upon the floor, fatally wounded.

She glared at Jäger. 'What have you done?'

Jäger's voice was icy. 'He was about to shoot him, that is what your report will say, Comrade *Major*. Make sure I get to see it before you submit it.'

Müller was almost too shocked to move. It was Tilsner who had to order Gaissler's shaking assistant to free Markus and the other youths.

Schmidt meanwhile slowly raised Markus to a sitting position, embracing him gently.

Jäger went over to Tilsner and slapped him on the back.

'Good work, Werner. Excellent,' he said.

'Thank you, Comrade *Oberst* Jäger,' replied Tilsner.

Jäger glanced over to Müller.

'And you too, of course, Karin. Well done to both of you. You've both done work today to make the Republic proud of you.'

Müller stared at him hard. *How could the man have the gall to make out that the ending of Gaissler's operation – and the freeing of the surviving youths – was what his Ministry for State Security had wanted all along?* She'd seen the look of recognition from Gaissler. Heard him start to reason with the Stasi colonel, until he was silenced in the most brutal way possible. It suited Jäger to have Müller and her team help him close this down now – but she was certain that hadn't always been the case.

51

'Has everything been sorted out, Klaus?'

'It has, Comrade Generalmajor.'

'And Jan will not be involved?'

'No, of course not. I've made sure of that. Your son will be portrayed as an innocent party.'

'And my name – that will be kept out of things too?'

The colonel nodded and the Stasi major general offered his subordinate a glass of schnapps.

'So what will we say about what the Bezirk Frankfurt department were doing?'

'We will say that Baum and Diederich acted alone. That they were siphoning off money from the American pharmaceutical company for their own purposes. We will say they were in league with Gaissler, who in turn was keeping money back to rebuild his family's former property portfolio in Wilhelm-Pieck-Stadt Guben, and that he was killed when he attempted to thwart an armed police operation to free the patients.'

'So Baum, Diederich and Gaissler were all acting like the worst kind of capitalists?'

'Exactly, Comrade Generalmajor.'

The Stasi major general leant back in his chair, his hands clasped behind his head.

'And just to be clear, there is no paper trail? Nothing official that can be laid at our door?'

'Nothing, Comrade Generalmajor.'

'What about that infernal People's Police major? Can't we take her down a peg or two? You were saying she's been over-promoted.'

'Yes,' the colonel replied. 'But that's useful for our purposes.'

'You're not sweet on her, are you Klaus? She's an attractive woman – and I hear she may be about to become single again.' The major general took out a cigar box, selected one for himself, then offered the box to Jäger, who declined the offer, just as he had with the schnapps.

'Nothing like that, Comrade Generalmajor. As you know, I'm married. I have a young family. I wouldn't take the risk.'

'Well, I'm sorry you're not joining me in a celebratory drink and cigar.' He put the unlit cigar down and lovingly stroked the white bust of a sharp-faced, bearded man that was prominently placed on his desk.

'I think Dzerzhinsky would have approved of our operation, don't you? We've proved ourselves to be the German Cheka, even though some of our Soviet colleagues mock us.'

The colonel smiled.

'Getting back to this People's Police major,' the major general continued. 'This ends her inquiry, yes? She won't be sniffing round Metzger's untimely demise?'

'She has no reason to, and no authority to go to the West, so I don't expect so. They'll be patting themselves on the back at Keibelstrasse over this thing in Wilhelm-Pieck-Stadt Guben, without really realising what's gone on in Bonn.'

'And we're sure about the loyalty of our agent involved in the Metzger incident?'

'Absolutely. He was recruited in . . . shall we say, exceptional circumstances. He was shown the importance of being loyal, and the price of disloyalty.'

'And this policewoman, she doesn't realise who he is?'

'No. She has no idea. And we'll make sure we keep it that way.'

52

I don't really understand what's happening. The drugs they give us make our thoughts cloudy. Trying to find what I want to say isn't easy; it's like something is lost inside a huge, luxurious feather duvet, and I'm flailing round to try to find it. But then I can't remember what I'm looking for, and I realise it doesn't matter anyway.

Something *has* changed. The usual faces have moved away. There are happier faces now, smiling faces.

And then one of these, a round face, adorned with thick spectacles, like the ones I used to wear before they got me the contact lenses, emerges from the sea of confusion and lunges towards me.

Then I realise.

It's my father.

He's happy to see me. I'm pleased he's happy, but I'm not sure why he's crying.

'Oh Marki, Marki,' he slobbers, stroking my face like he used to when I was a little boy. I try to say something, something loving, but my mouth is just opening and closing, my face feels damp, and no sounds are coming out.

When I stand, and my father lets me lean on him, it feels nice. Warm. Comforting. Like those wet autumn days when you finally get home after school, and Mutti has a steaming mug of cocoa waiting for you. But when I try to move my legs, they wobble and shake like jelly. And then I feel I'm going down. My head hits something. There's more confusion. It doesn't matter, I want to tell them. Nothing really matters. And then they're strapping me onto something. I want to tell them not to, that I don't want any more of the injections, that I don't think they're good for me. But I can't summon the energy, and instead I let them carry me up the stairs and into the fresh air.

Outside, there are blue lights flashing. They're carrying me to a van with a red cross in the window. I try to remember what it is. Then the word comes to me through the fog. It's an ambulance. *An ambulance.* I toy with the word in my head, rather proud of myself. It's a nice word. It has a nice ring to it.

After a few days at home, my head begins to clear. And that woolly feeling starts to fade. I begin to feel very angry. I've been tricked, cheated and abused and yet my mother and father are trying to carry on as though nothing has changed. They want to talk about my future. The agent's promises of a university place, of adjusted grades, seem to have evaporated.

Towards the end of the first week, my father's police boss, *Major* Müller, comes to see me with her deputy. I don't particularly want to talk to them, but my father insists.

We sit across from each other in the lounge. I tell my mother and father I don't want them to stay in the room.

'How are you doing, Markus?' Müller asks, once they've left.

'Fine.' I feel myself flushing, my heart racing.

'Good. We're glad you're safe now, and back at home.'

Yes, I think. *But you know all about me now, don't you? You know about me and poor Georg. You and your Stasi friends will always be watching me.*

Müller explains what was going on in Guben. We were being experimented on to try to 'cure' our homosexuality with hormone drugs and implants, backed by some American company. We were human guinea pigs. Just the thought of that utterly disgusts me. When the police raided Gaissler's headquarters there were around ten of us there. Some had even had their brains operated on. But something went wrong with Dominik Nadel, and then his death was disguised as a sadistic murder, his body weighted down and dumped in a lake near Senftenberg. I never knew him, of course. But he knew Georg. In the same way I knew Georg. Blackmailed to be a 'Romeo' just as I was. So I feel a connection; almost like he's a brother I never got to meet.

'One of you managed to escape from the Theatre Island bunker,' she continues. 'We still don't know who he was – we think he was Polish or Russian. We're trying to check through all the records with them.' The major has this look of motherly concern – as though she cares. But she's just like them, the agents who got me to spy on poor Georg. She works for the state.

That was the start of the whole scheme collapsing, she explains. The escaped youth was already drowning in the treacherous waters of the Neisse when they found him. But they shot him – just to make sure. 'They'? I think. Who's 'they'? Why isn't she saying 'we'? Because that's the truth. She's one of them. She has blood on her hands just like the rest.

What an awful, rotten country ours has become. Was there ever a dirtier, darker, more disgusting state, ruled by liars and criminals? And tricksters – like my former 'friend' Jan, luring people to that club at the behest of the Stasi, and then planting drugs on them. One way or another, I'm going to get out of it. One way or another.

Not long after they leave, my father says he wants to have 'a talk'. Even Mutti looks worried about this, and says she'd like to be there too. But Vati says it's a father and son thing – just between us.

He drives us to the Weisse See in the Trabi and we sit in the car, looking out over the frozen lake. I remember when we used to come here when I was a little boy, all three of us, when they bought me some skates. Other kids would be skating round with their parents, but mine were never that sporty. They'd just help me put my skates on and then leave me to it. If I got teased by other girls and boys because of my clumsiness, then that was just hard luck. Once, after I'd had a bad fall and cut my face where my glasses severed the skin, I'd refused to go the next week. That was the only time Vati came with me – not actually skating, just holding my hand as he waddled around, trying to keep his balance.

I hear him sigh now, and focus back on the present.

'It's a pretty spot, isn't it? Especially when it's all frozen over like this,' he smiles.

I nod, but don't smile back.

'Your mother and I are very worried about you, Markus. We know you've been through an ordeal, and it will take time to get over it. But we need to have a chat about your future plans. To see if there's anything we can do to help you.'

I start humming. I know it infuriates him.

'Don't do that, Markus. You're not a ten-year-old boy now, you're an adult.'

'Why have we come here?' I ask.

'Because I need to have a serious talk with you.'

'About what?'

My father swallows. This is difficult for him, I know. But why should I make it easy? The difficulty is caused by his prejudices.

'Your future . . . and your lifestyle choices.'

I can't help laughing. I see his face start to redden.

'We will try to support you. I will try to see things from your point of view. But you know that if you continue with your current . . .' His voice tails off. He still can't bring himself to mention the unmentionable. 'All I'm saying is you need to understand the dangers. You know how much prejudice there is against—'

'Against what?'

I want to provoke him into uttering the word. But he won't. Behind the thick glasses, tears begin to form in his eyes.

53

The atmosphere in the Strausberger Platz flat was one of restrained hatred between Müller and Emil. She still hadn't confronted him. While the investigation had been under way she had just wanted to concentrate on her work. She realised he didn't really know what was wrong – for him, it was simply a continuation of their row from the Sunday night.

Müller had wanted time, too, to decide what she wanted to do. At the back of her mind, a constant refrain: *he is the father of your children*. He had the right to see them, and they may well in future years come to resent or even hate her if she denied them that right. Each time he'd tried to initiate sex, though, she'd pushed him away. He made her skin crawl. It wasn't the homo-sexuality, the bisexuality, or whatever. She had no proof of that, and he would probably deny it, or invent some sort of a story to explain his behaviour.

No. The problem, Müller told herself, was the lying. When claiming he had important meetings at the hospital, Emil had instead been travelling miles each Sunday evening to a club near the Polish border. You had to have a pretty strong reason to bother to do that. Whether it was to meet his Stasi agent friends, or to fuck youths, she had no idea. But it was clear – however you looked at it – that it was a betrayal.

Before she confronted him, she decided to approach Helga.

'Is there any way, if I paid, you could go to the cinema tonight, Helga? Or out for a meal, something like that? I need to have a serious talk with Emil.'

Her grandmother nodded. 'Of course, dear. But there's no need for you to pay. I've plenty of money of my own. I'm living here rent free, remember?'

Müller smiled. 'You more than pay your way by helping with the childcare, so I insist. I just need an hour or so to talk to Emil. And it might get a bit . . . fractious, shall we say. So I think it's better if you aren't here.'

'What about the twins? If you're worried about my being here, isn't it going to be a problem for them?'

'Don't worry,' said Müller. 'I'll wait till they're fast asleep. They're little terrors, but at least they're both good sleepers.'

Helga held her arms around Müller, and patted her back. 'I can tell things have been bad between you two. Do you want to tell me about it, or would you rather I kept my nose out of it?'

Müller took a step back but held her grandmother's hands in hers. 'To be honest, I don't want to advertise what's been going on, and I don't want you to hate him. He's still Jannika and Johannes's father, and always will be. So it's a delicate situation.'

'Another woman?'

'Something like that, but as I said, I don't want to go into the details. What I will say, though, is that Emil is going to be moving out, at the very least for a trial period, but I expect – to be honest – that it will be for good. He still has his flat in the hospital. He'll just have to move back in there.'

Emil was late back from work, if that was indeed where he'd been. Müller had no idea any more. At least it meant she, the twins and Helga had eaten. She'd already put the twins down and they were sleeping soundly, and Helga had set off for her night out.

There was no point delaying things further. As soon as Emil was through the door, before he'd even taken his coat off, Müller asked him to sit at the dining table.

He sighed and ran his hand through his hair.

'I'm tired, Karin. And I thought you weren't speaking to me.'

'Just sit down,' she ordered. Her tone brooked no argument.

He sat in his coat, his briefcase on the table.

She cleared her throat. 'I want you to move out. Immediately. This evening.'

'*What?* I know we haven't been getting on but—'

'This is my apartment, Emil. Not yours. I'm not negotiating. I'm telling you to leave. You won't be homeless. You still have the hospital flat, though goodness knows what you use that for.'

'Sorry? What are you trying to say? And what about the twins?'

'I'm saying that our relationship is over. You'll—'

'Over?'

'That's right. We're not compatible. You've been keeping secrets from me. I can't have that. You'll still have access to the twins, but it will be controlled access for the time being.'

'What do you mean?'

'You'll be able to see them, here, and I will go out. You won't be able to take them with you anywhere.'

'Well, that's ridiculous. I don't know what's brought all this on, but I'm certainly not going to agr—'

'You will agree to it. You'll sign all the necessary papers.' She sat down, and sighed, then, looking up, held his gaze. 'You see, Emil, it's not *just* that you've been lying to me. It's not *just* that you have been keeping secrets – pretty fundamental secrets – from me. It's that I know what those secrets are. And I have the evidence.' To an extent, this was a bluff. Yes, Tilsner had taken photos of those coming in and out of the club, but Müller had looked at them – there was nothing particularly incriminating in the ones of Emil, other than him going into the club with a younger man. It proved nothing. Tilsner hadn't managed to get any shots of Emil actually in a clinch with one of the youths. But Emil didn't know that.

His head slumped on his shoulders and he held his face in his hands. Eventually he raised his eye level to hers.

'How did you find out?'

'I'm a detective, Emil. Finding out is what I do.'

He sighed. 'I suppose I should have known this new job of yours would have had you liaising with the Stasi at a high level. Presumably that's where you found out? To be honest, I couldn't believe you weren't more suspicious when I followed you to Halle-Neustadt.'

Müller suddenly realised the conversation was taking an unexpected turn. But for the moment, she allowed Emil to continue to speak.

'But the children weren't my fault, Karin. You always insisted there was absolutely no way you could get pregnant. I took that at face value. Obviously on any close assignment like this we're trained to make sure things like that don't happen.'

'By the Stasi?' asked Müller, more as a prompt than a real question. She knew the answer now.

Emil nodded slowly. 'But you have to believe me. I care for you now, I care for the children.'

Müller fixed him with an icy stare. She wasn't buying this. 'Do you still care for us while you're gallivanting off to your club in Frankfurt on Sundays? You and your boyfriends?'

Emil leant back, looking up at the ceiling. 'Oh ... my ... God!' He gave a strangled laugh. 'You don't believe I'm one of them, do you?' His eyes widened. '*That's* what this is about!' He started shaking his head.

'I'm not laughing, Emil. When you were supposed to be doing urgent business at the hospital you were on urgent business all right. Urgent business to satisfy your lust.'

Emil just kept on shaking his head, still laughing. 'I've clearly overestimated your detecting abilities, Karin. Halle-Neustadt I hold my hands up to. I'm not telling you this officially, and I will deny it if ever challenged, but your suspicions there are correct. My job was to find out everything about you. Our chance meeting at Charité wasn't a chance meeting at all. You'd telephoned ahead to ask if it was OK to visit Tilsner in his hospital bed. It was known you were coming. But the Frankfurt club business has nothing to do with my sexual proclivities, I can assure you. It is a job – nothing more, nothing less.'

Müller tried to control her breathing. She'd gone into this thinking that Emil had a secret life – that he was homosexual, or at the very least bisexual. This, though, was even worse. Confirmation that her suspicions about their relationship had been a lie all along.

Emil reached across the table to take her hand. Müller snatched it away.

'You have to believe me, Karin. I have grown to love you. And I certainly love the children.'

Müller shook her head. 'Our children, to you, are little more than mistakes. Part of your sordid little surveillance operation that went wrong. To me, they're the world. Everything in the world. And I won't have you hurting them as you've hurt me. So I want you out of here, immediately. And you will sign whatever access arrangements I choose to present you with. Do I make myself clear?'

There was a pause. Müller could see Emil's hands shaking on his briefcase, tears beginning to well in his eyes.

'You're wrong, Karin,' he whispered. 'Our relationship isn't a sham, however it may have started. And I do love Jannika and Johannes. It will devastate me not being able to be with them as they grow up.'

Müller was unmoved, and got to her feet.

'I'm not saying that I won't allow you full access in the future, Emil. But for now, this is the way it's going to be, and that's what you're going to agree to. Otherwise the evidence I have will become more widely known.'

He looked at her in shock.

'So you're blackmailing me?'

'Call it whatever you like,' she said, surprised at her own icy calm. 'That's the way it is. And you don't have any choice in the matter.'

54

I can't stand the suffocating false bonhomie of Christmas. The decorations in any case look pathetic. There's a horrible atmosphere in the apartment. Mutti and I still get on just about OK, though I try to stay out of the way. I spend most of the time in my room with the headphones on, listening to records. I don't want an apprenticeship. I don't want to do my military service. My only interests are my music and my motorbike.

Finally, on Christmas Eve, I crack.

It's another comment from him that triggers it.

I've tried to stay out of his way, but he corners me in the kitchen. 'Have you thought about what I said, at the Weisse See?'

He holds on to my shoulders, but I try to wriggle free. I won't meet his eyes.

'Have you, Markus?' he repeats.

'Yes,' I say, wrenching myself free. 'Yes, yes, yes, yes. I agree with you. Of course you're right.'

'Don't be sarcastic, Markus.'

'I'm not being sarcastic, Vati. You'll see. I'll do what you want.'

I wrap up warm, though I don't really care. But I suppose for this bit, I might as well be comfortable.

I don't really know where I'm going, I just head south on the bike, following the TV tower to start with and then turn southeast, along Karl-Marx-Allee. There is an icy blast of fine snow against my face. I feel – I suppose – a bit like how those polar explorers must have felt. The ones who know they're never coming back.

I realise I could just turn into the oncoming traffic. That would be quick. The temptation is almost too much to resist, but there is one last place I wanted to see.

They dumped Dominik's body, hoping no one would ever find it. Someone did. If it wasn't for that, I wouldn't have been rescued. But was I really rescued? In reality, I was just taken from one trap to another. According to my father, I'm still not allowed to live the way I want to.

I stop for a coffee halfway. In the café, I get the feeling a man is eyeing me up. He's attractive, dark hair, tall. I glance back, hoping to feel something. But it's as though someone has numbed me, castrated me, taken away my life force. There is no reaction. Perhaps Gaissler's injections worked after all, despite all the fuck-ups. He's succeeded with me, and I hate him for it.

The wind is so bitterly cold, coming straight at me across the frozen lake. Was this the spot where Dominik was found – here by the sailing club? It's the easiest place to park up. I wonder if he knew what had happened to him. And what about Georg? He was a sweet man. I laugh to myself, surprised I still can. I'd set out to trick him – I'd succeeded in tricking him – and then ended up falling in love with him. If the Stasi hadn't forced us apart, would he have taken me with him to the West? I wonder what it's like there. You see it on television, of course, you can see it from the top of the TV tower, like I did all those years ago when my father took me up there. But I wonder what it's *really* like. You know, to live there. They say it's even harder for homosexuals, queers, faggots, whatever name I used to be called in the playground that turned out to be true. Even harder there than it is here. More persecution. More nastiness.

The act itself. I could still give pleasure, I know. But I don't think I can be properly aroused any more. Gaissler has done that to me. The people at Charité insist it's all in my mind – that I was only given the placebo, according to Gaissler's records. I know differently. I feel differently. I will never be able to love that way again.

I pick up a flat stone, so cold it almost sticks to my fingers. And then I skim it across the surface of the ice. It bounces a couple of times and then skids along, like an ice hockey puck. On top of the frozen, artificial lake. On top of the fish, who I assume are still swimming in the water underneath. The fish in the lake that you can never catch by hand. The lake that was once an opencast mine, feeding the hunger of this Republic for dirty brown coal, the dirty brown coal that drives our industry, our factories, lights up our homes. And covers our capital city in a choking blanket of smog.

I head back the way I came on the bike with no real plan, thinking I may delay things after all. But when I see it, it seems to be calling to me, in the same way the onrushing traffic did. It's a huge – no, *gigantic* – structure. It's almost as if the Eiffel Tower has fallen down, and then been dumped here in the Lausitz lignite belt.

It's like a giant metal animal from a science fiction film. Eating the earth and excreting what it doesn't want. Laying waste to huge tracts of land to keep the heart of the Republic pumping. And it's calling to me. I know it's calling to me. And I have to answer its call.

55

Müller was determined there should be no air of sadness lingering from Emil's departure, spoiling her first Christmas with Jannika, Johannes and Helga. They were all having huge fun round the tree. Both of the twins had recently taken their first steps, and they were obsessed now with the tinsel and baubles on the branches. It meant they had to be watched constantly to avoid any mishaps.

Having cut short her maternity leave to start up the new unit, Müller had managed to negotiate extra leave over Christmas. She wasn't going back till early January – as long as there were no serious murders that, in Reiniger's opinion, the local *Kripo* couldn't handle.

When the hotline to Keibelstrasse rang, she assumed that's exactly what had happened. Christmas was going to be ruined by work. But it was worse than that. And it wasn't even anyone from the People's Police on the line – it was Jäger. The Keibelstrasse switchboard must have re-routed his call.

What the hell does he want?

'Hello, Karin. Happy Christmas. Sorry to ring you on your day off, but I have just received some news, and I thought you would want it immediately.'

'What is it?' she asked, warily.

'Meet me outside your apartment block in ten minutes. There's something I need to show you. I can't talk about it over the phone.'

They drove north along the motorway, Jäger refusing to say what this was all about. Müller was taken back nearly two years to early 1975, when Jäger had taken her to Colonel General Horst Ackermann's house in the forest settlement – the place she now knew was home to all the Republic's high and mighty. Honecker lived there. Mielke. By western standards, the detached houses might be modest. But by the Republic's standards? They were detached houses. That was enough to set them apart from most homes in the East.

Instead they took a different turn off the motorway, and then – almost immediately – Jäger pulled over to the side of the road. He opened the glove compartment of his Volvo and took out a hood.

'I hope you're joking,' said Müller.

'No, I'm not, Karin. I've discovered something you will want to know. I promise you. I want to show you the place, but to do that I cannot let you see exactly where it is. Its location is classified.' He held the hood, hovering over her head. 'Don't you trust me?'

'I'm not sure I do, no.' What was this about? The last time she'd been hooded, it was by Jäger's colleagues as she was led into Bautzen. Were they going to another jail? She didn't think so, but she still flinched away from the black, sack-like hood.

It looked like something they might place over an execution victim's head.

'Trust me,' he murmured.

She knew she should say no. Nothing was worth this humiliation. But curiosity is a powerful driving force. After all, she was a detective. It was her job to discover things. Things that people often didn't want to be discovered.

She gave a small nod and allowed her head to be covered.

The journey became something like the one she'd endured to Bautzen. Stopping, starting, going round in circles. She knew that Jäger was making certain she couldn't make a mental map of the route. There was one big difference though. Here, she was in a comfortable seat, in a luxury car. The smell was of leather, cigars, Jäger's cologne. An intoxicating mixture. On the way to Bautzen it had been piss, shit and puke.

The car finally came to a halt and Jäger gently pulled off the hood. They were on a forest track. Ahead of them, a clearing. But on all sides, a thick blanket of trees. The only light – and that only the dim light of winter – was from above. Each side, thick with trees, was in deep shadow.

Jäger reached over to the back seat and grabbed his sheepskin coat. He put it on inside the vehicle. Müller was already wearing a thick coat, but she knew as soon as the doors were opened they would be enveloped in a shroud of bitter, winter air.

Climbing out of the car, Jäger made his way towards the clearing, and Müller followed.

When he got to the centre, he breathed in deeply, and then exhaled.

'I love the smell of the forest,' he said. 'Especially in winter. Don't you?'

Müller nodded, warily. *What is this all about?*

'I have a confession to make,' he said. 'It concerns your ex-husband.'

To Müller, Jäger looked nervous – as though he was apprehensive about her reaction to what he was about to say.

'I know you've divorced. But you may still have feelings for him. That's why, when I learnt this news, I thought I should bring you here. As you know, I was told he was allowed to emigrate to the Federal Republic. I believe you even received a letter from him.'

'That's right,' said Müller. She didn't ask him how he knew. By now, she expected the Stasi to know everything they wanted to. There were no secrets in this Republic. 'The letter was signed – it was definitely his signature.'

'And the rest of the letter?'

'It . . . it was typed.' That had always nagged at the back of Müller's brain. It wasn't Gottfried's usual style. Usually, any letters from him would be handwritten – from start to finish.

'Do you know how easy it is to fake a signature, Karin?'

She stared at him in horror. What was he about to say?

'State leaders, heads of companies in the West, they all have machines that can fake a signature. It looks genuine, because in some ways it is. You get the subject to sign his or her name with the machine, the machine records the pen movements, and can then recreate that signature exactly. Again and again and again. You didn't seriously believe that Comrade Honecker hand-signed all his responses to letters and petitions, did you?'

Müller felt a tightness in her chest. She wanted Jäger to stop speaking now. She didn't want to hear any more.

'I did my best for Gottfried, tried to use any influence I had to secure his release. I was told I had been successful, that he had indeed been allowed to go to the West. I'm sorry to say I was lied to.'

The news hit Müller like a sledgehammer. 'What?' she shouted. 'You mean he's still in the Republic, in prison somewhere, and you never told me?'

Jäger shook his head and sighed. 'I'm afraid not, Karin. The charges your husband faced were very serious. The maximum sentence was the death penalty. That is what a court could have imposed.'

Müller frowned. 'He was tried in court? Why was I never told? I would have been a character witness.'

Jäger turned away. He began speaking, but wouldn't meet her eyes. 'The Ministry for State Security, as you're probably now aware, doesn't always abide by the court system, particularly when it's carrying out a death sentence. Your former husband was brought here. Hooded, as you were just now. I'm afraid he never left.'

Müller felt herself drop to the icy ground. It couldn't be true, she told herself. She'd received the letter. All right, it was typewritten. But it was Gottfried through and through. The tone of voice, everything.

Kneeling on the forest floor, she began beating it with her fists. Yes, they were divorced. But she still cared for him. Hoped to see him again sometime. And he had been her first true love. Had nursed and nurtured her after the horrors of her rape at the police college. They had spent so many happy times together. The thought of him meeting such a terrible and lonely end was unbearable.

They'd driven back to the Hauptstadt in silence. Müller felt desperate. She realised she wasn't even sure whether to believe Jäger. Their relationship was strained at the best of times. Müller wasn't sure it would ever recover. The Ministry for State Security had – in effect – murdered her first true love. A man she was sure was innocent. Schmidt had proved that the Stasi had faked the photographs of him in compromising situations with the reform school teenagers. What if everything he had been accused of was false?

56

'Did she accept your account, Klaus?'

'Yes, without question, Comrade Generalmajor.'

'So the identity of our agent is secure? And she believes he is dead?'

'Yes, Comrade Generalmajor.'

'This time I insist you join me in a cognac, Klaus. Before you go back to your family for the remainder of Christmas. Would that be acceptable?'

'Very acceptable, Comrade Generalmajor.'

57

The hotline was ringing again. Müller tried to stop herself lifting the receiver, but in the end she couldn't resist.

As she picked up the phone, she had a strong sense of déjà vu – with good reason. It was Jonas Schmidt on the line.

'Karin, Karin, you have to help us, please. He's missing again.'

Schmidt insisted on travelling with them, even though they didn't know where they were going. The Lada seemed none the worse for its ice drive, so they were sitting in it now, paralysed, trying to work out where Markus might have gone.

'Would he have tried to go after Gaissler in jail?' asked Tilsner.

'He wouldn't know which jail he's in. He'd have no idea,' replied Müller.

Schmidt held his head in his hands. 'We have to do something – please!'

Müller turned towards him. 'We've put out an all-bulletins alert, Jonas. I can't see the point of chasing round anywhere until we get a sighting back from that. We might just end up further away from where we need to be when someone does spot him.'

'We can't just sit here waiting, Comrade *Major*. I'm sorry, that's not good enough.'

'What about Winkler's house?' asked Tilsner. 'Could he have gone to have it out with him?'

Müller was still angry they hadn't been able to make a charge stick against Winkler. He seemed to be under the protection of people in very high places – presumably because of his father, who she now knew was a major general with the Stasi. But she knew Markus wasn't with Winkler. 'I asked for a watch on their house as soon as Jonas told me he was missing. If he'd gone there, we'd have been told.'

'How about that club?' asked Tilsner.

'The one near Frankfurt? We could try, but as I say it might be a wild-goose chase, and then if we have a sighting in Berlin we'd be miles away.'

Schmidt's tone was firm. 'I'd like to take that risk, Comrade *Major*. We've got to do something.'

Thankfully, just as they joined the motorway system near Rüdersdorf, a call came across the radio.

'Sighting of suspect . . .' Müller groaned inwardly at the use of the word. He wasn't a suspect, he was a poor, confused boy. '. . . at the Klettwitz-Nord mine near Lichterfeld.'

Müller looked at the index for their road map.

'That's not far from Senftenberg. In the Lausitz. What on earth's he doing there?'

'Let's not worry about that,' said Tilsner. 'Let's just get there, fast.'

Müller was thrown back in her seat as her deputy kicked down hard on the accelerator.

She reached out of the passenger window and attached the magnetic blue light to the roof. She switched on the siren, then turned back towards Schmidt, placing her hand gently on his leg.

'Don't worry, Jonas. I'm sure he's going to be OK.'

By the time the three of them got to the mine, a group of other police cars, an ambulance and even a fire engine with a ladder were all in place, their blue lights rotating.

They soon identified one of the officers as Schwarz.

'He's warning us all to stay back or he'll jump.'

'Where is he?' demanded Müller.

'There.' Schwarz pointed to what looked like a small dot at the end of the massive structure. 'Right at the end of the conveyor belt. It's an overburden conveyor bridge – it moves all the earth from above the lignite layer, and then dumps it in terraces on that side of the mine.'

'Haven't they at least stopped it from mining, till we can get him down?'

'They say they can't. They've got government targets to reach. They're in competition with other mines. I've tried reasoning with them. But they insist he's in no more danger, whether they're continuing to remove the overburden or not.'

'I'll have to go up there,' said Schmidt. 'I owe it to him. This is all my fault. Let me through.'

Tilsner grabbed the forensic scientist. 'Hang on. You're not going alone. And what do you mean, it's all your fault? If that's the case, we don't want you spooking him.'

Schmidt hung his head. 'There was a misunderstanding about . . . about a personal matter.'

'What did you say to him, Jonas?' asked Müller.

Schmidt breathed in heavily. 'I may have given him the impression that I didn't want him living at home any more because . . . well, because of his lifestyle choices. But it wasn't what I meant. I just wanted him to consider everything carefully . . . for his own sake, not mine.'

Müller watched Tilsner roll his eyes. 'If we let you up there with us, Jonas, you have to promise me that you're not going to say anything negative. All I want to hear from you is reassurance that you love him. Do you understand?'

Schmidt nodded.

Müller eyeballed Schwarz. 'Is there an elevator?'

'No. You have to climb. Up the stairs and along the walkway. It's half a kilometre long and two hundred metres off the ground. And he's virtually at the highest, furthest point.'

Müller knew she didn't have a head for heights, not since the ski jump incident as a teenager, where she'd frozen in fear. But she'd faced her fear once before when she'd had to, on the roof of the Interhotel Panorama, when the life of her own son was hanging by a thread.

Now it was the son of her *Kriminaltechniker*.

She knew how desperate Schmidt must be feeling. She and Tilsner would do all they could to try to save Markus, although perhaps, given what he'd been through, he just didn't want to be saved.

They let Schmidt go first, so Markus could see his father was coming. Müller felt that would be the best way.

Before he'd even climbed halfway up the first set of stairs, Schmidt seemed to be struggling, panting and out of breath. Müller began to wonder if her decision was wise – an emotional father and a suicidal son meeting in a highly charged, highly dangerous situation, with an icy wind howling all around.

'Jesus,' cried Tilsner. 'He's going to die from the cold if we don't get him down, never mind anything else.'

Müller motioned angrily, a single finger raised against her lips. Luckily, the wind had almost certainly carried Tilsner's stupid comment away with it.

As they edged along the walkway, still climbing to the peak of the conveyor bridge, Müller tried not to look down at the ground. The bridge itself was high enough already. But underneath it, the earth and lignite had been excavated away. There was now a giant hole beneath them, and a drop of nearly a hundred metres more, even after ground level.

Soon they got close enough to hear Markus above the roar of the machinery.

'You two, don't come any closer,' he shouted. 'Vati, you can approach.'

Schmidt went another ten metres before his son ordered him, too, to halt.

'That's close enough. You'll be able to hear clearly enough from there.'

'I'm sorry, Markus. I'm sorry. I didn't mean what I said.'

'Oh, but you did, Father. You meant every word. It's too late now anyway.'

Markus started to lever himself up to the top of the railing that protected the end of the walkway.

'I didn't mean it, honestly,' pleaded Schmidt. 'You live your life how you want to. Your mother and I both love you, unreservedly. I'm desperately sorry if what I said to you led to a misunderstanding. We'll always support you, I promise. We love you.'

Markus was now sitting at the top of the railings, his feet dangling over the massive drop.

'Do you remember fishing in the Mecklenburg lakes?' he shouted towards his father.

'Of course, Marki. Of course. I'd like to do that again. As soon as the ice melts. You and me together. We could go camping.'

'You've never time though, have you? Your police work always comes first.'

Müller noticed from the corner of her eye that Tilsner seemed to have found a ladder taking him to a lower level, and was using it as Schmidt spoke to his son.

'I will make more time for you, Marki. Honestly. I will support your lifestyle choices. I will see you through this – whatever it takes.' Müller noticed Markus straightening his arms and back, as though he was preparing to jump. She edged forward, as Schmidt continued to shout to make himself heard above the roaring, bitter wind. 'You'll always be welcome in—'

'No!' shouted Müller, rushing forward. 'Don't, Mark—'

Too late.

The boy had jumped.

Müller and Schmidt leant over the side of the walkway, expecting to see the worst. But Markus had landed just a few metres below, his fall cushioned by the rubberised, overburdened conveyor belt and its load of earth.

His arms and legs were flailing around. Müller wasn't sure if he was trying to stand or to jump again. And then she realised. He'd seen the end of the chute.

The plume of earth being sent hundreds of metres to the ground below.

And Markus was about to be sent with it.

The youth was frantically trying to stand again, to run against the direction of the belt and save himself from certain death.

He wanted to live, she realised now.

He wanted to be with his father.

'I'll get him,' shouted Tilsner, as he leapt from the iron ladder onto the conveyor, and then started scrabbling towards the youth. Unless he reached him in time, they would both be sent flying over the edge. 'Karin,' Tilsner shouted over his shoulder. 'Run down to the control room. Get them to stop it!'

Müller had been frozen to the spot, but she ran now until her lungs were bursting, as though it was the most important race of her life. She waved her arms, hoping Schwarz below would see what was happening.

She risked one look back.

Tilsner had reached Markus, hauled him to his feet. But they were now just a metre or so from the end of the belt.

Müller shouted at the top of her voice towards the control room but knew the sounds wouldn't carry on the wind, and she was still only halfway there.

She tried her utmost to go faster, but her body wouldn't let her.

No one was responding.

She knew she wouldn't make it in time.

And she knew what that meant for Markus . . . and Tilsner.

58

I'm not really going to do it, I tell myself.

And when my father says he wants to take back what he said, that my sexuality is my own business, I tell myself to climb down from the railing. But my body seems locked on its course.

Instead of scrambling back, I'm falling.

I don't understand at first what's happened. Then I realise. I've fallen just a few metres onto the earth-carrying conveyor. The soft earth and the rubberised belt beneath it have cushioned my fall. But I can't seem to stand. I'm not injured; at least I don't think so. I just can't right myself.

Then I hear the female detective, Frau Müller, and my father scream. At first I don't understand why. Then I do. I'm moving. Being carried with all the waste earth, about to be dumped to my death hundreds of metres below.

Then I feel the belt judder, and see the male detective has jumped onto the conveyor from a maintenance ladder. He's coming towards me, swaying slightly as he climbs across the earth, half-crouching, trying to keep his balance.

And he's nearly reached me. But we're both nearly at the end of the belt. Just a few more metres.

I hear my father shouting, screaming. 'No, no, Marki!'

The male detective is pulling me up into a hug, trying to haul me backwards, but my legs won't work.

Then more juddering, screaming and groaning of metal.

Then silence.

We sway together in the wind, at the end of the giant arm. Holding each other.

The belt has stopped.

We've been saved.

And as the handsome detective still holds me, finally gets me walking, I realise two things.

I'm glad to be alive. I want to give my father another chance to accept me.

And also something else.

Something totally inappropriate in this life or death situation.

The closeness of this handsome man, this stubble-chinned man who's saved me, has produced an embarrassing reaction.

Dr Gaissler's injections haven't worked.

They haven't worked at all.

I feel my life force running through me. I am what I am. Take me or leave me.

My name is Markus Schmidt.

And I'm alive.

59

There was an empty place setting for Christmas supper at the Strausberger Platz apartment. Intended for Emil.

'I didn't know if you'd invited him or not,' said Helga.

Müller shook her head, sadly. 'No, Helga. It's too soon. Maybe next year. Let's see if he agrees to my proposed access arrangements first.'

Helga nodded. 'By the way, there's some good news. Aside from the delightful fact that we're spending Christmas together for the first time. Jannika said her first word yesterday.'

Müller felt a momentary stab of jealousy, but then dismissed it. It had been her choice to return to work, and despite the time apart from the twins, she didn't regret that choice. She just had to accept that some milestones she would miss. So she hid any upset as well as she could.

'Did you, darling?' she said to her daughter. 'What a clever girl. Are you going to show Mutti now? Or do you only talk for Oma? Can you say "Mutti"? "Mut-ti". Will you do that for Mutti?'

Jannika smiled and looked down at her toy doll, then lifted it up proudly. 'Vati! Vati!' she shrieked, a devilish smile on her face.

For a moment Müller felt affronted, though she knew that was ridiculous, and then almost slightly tearful, thinking about how things had turned out with Emil. Of the horrifying way things had ended for Gottfried.

Helga laughed at Jannika's mischief, but must have seen the shadow cross her granddaughter's face.

'Then, earlier today, your little man did something very clever too, didn't you, Johannes?'

Johannes widened his arms, as though inviting his mother to pick him up from the floor. But when she did, he started fretting and pointing at something. Helga reached down to pick up one of his toy cars, and handed it to him.

As she cradled her son under one arm, Müller saw it was the scale model of a Wartburg squad car she'd got him for Christmas. Complete with olive green and white livery, and the silver star of the *Volkspolizei* on its doors and bonnet.

'Who's that, Johannes?' asked Helga, gesturing towards the miniature figure inside the toy.

The boy stayed silent, and instead threw the car at the wall.

Helga rolled her eyes. 'He's not going to do it for you, but a few hours ago I'm sure I heard him saying "Mama, Mama".'

Müller laughed. 'All in good time. They always say girls are more advanced than boys anyway.' But as she said it, she felt a tinge of regret. About how Johannes – and Jannika – would need a father figure, and how she had failed them.

She went over to pick up the car – it was undamaged. Then she noticed where it had struck the wall there was a small tear in the wallpaper. Müller pushed it back into place – with a bit of glue, it would hardly be visible. But as she held her finger over the damaged area she felt something else, just to the side. Some sort of wire. The electrics? *But electrical wire wouldn't be just below the surface, directly under the wallpaper, would it?*

Müller traced the line of the wire, up and across, moving the side table out of the way. Helga was too busy calming Johannes down to notice what she was doing.

The wire reached some sort of node that had been hidden behind the table edge.

Immediately, she realised what it was.

A microphone.

She felt a darkening of her soul – like a heavy storm cloud passing over. She clutched her arms to her chest.

It wasn't a surprise, but it still disturbed her. Reiniger's assertion when she'd originally moved in that this new apartment was 'clean' was either an out-and-out lie, or something had been installed later, perhaps when she was in Bautzen.

She glanced back at her grandmother playing with the twins. Calm had returned. They hadn't noticed anything wrong.

Smiles, laughter, happiness. Müller was determined that was the way it would be for them, always.

Darker forces in this Republic might want to track her every move, listen to her every conversation.

But she would protect what remained of her fractured family.

Come what may.

And in any way she could.

GLOSSARY

Ampelmann	East German pedestrian traffic light symbol
Anti-Fascist Protection Barrier	The euphemistic official East German term for the Berlin Wall
Arschloch	Arsehole
Barkas	East German manufacturer of the B1000, a small delivery van or minibus
Bezirk	District
BfV	*Bundesamt für Verfassungsschutz*, West Germany's domestic intelligence service
Deutsche Demokratische Republik (DDR)	The German Democratic Republic, or DDR for short, the official name for East Germany

Duroplast	Fibre-reinforced plastic similar to fibreglass, used in the body panels of Trabant cars
Eisenhüttenkombinat Ost (EKO)	Ironworks Combine East (the main steelworks in Eisenhüttenstadt)
FDJ	Socialist youth movement (*Freie Deutsche Jugend*)
Fernsehturm	East Berlin's TV tower
Fernverkehrsstrasse	Main (long-distance) road
Goldbroiler	Grilled or roasted chicken
Ha-Neu	Short form for Halle-Neustadt
Hauptmann	Captain
Hauptstadt	Capital city (in this book, East Berlin)
Hohenschönhausen	An area of north-eastern Berlin infamous for its Stasi prison
Hütte	Short form for Eisenhüttenstadt
Interhotel	East German chain of luxury hotels

Jugendwerkhof	Reform school or youth workhouse
Keibelstrasse	The People's Police headquarters near Alexanderplatz – the East German equivalent of Scotland Yard
Kriminalpolizei	Criminal Police or CID
Kriminaltechniker	Forensic officer
Kripo	CID (short form) – also known as the '*K*'
Liebling	Darling
Main Intelligence Directorate	The Stasi's foreign arm – the East German equivalent of MI6
Major	The same rank as in English, but pronounced more like My-Yor
Ministry for State Security (*MfS*)	The East German secret police, abbreviated to *MfS* from the German initials, and colloquially known as the Stasi – a contraction of the German name
Mutti	Mum, or Mummy

Neues Deutschland	The official East German Party newspaper
Oberleutnant	First Lieutenant
Oberliga	The top division of the East German football league
Oberst	Colonel
Oma	Grandma, granny
Ostsee	Baltic Sea
People's Police	The regular East German state police (*Volkspolizei* in German)
Plattenbauten	Concrete slab apartment blocks
Polizeiruf 110	East German TV crime drama (literally 'Police Call 110', the equivalent to 999)
Räuchermännchen	Incense-burning figurine
Republikflüchtlingen	Official term for people who escaped or tried to escape from East Germany
Sauwetter	Dirty/rotten weather

S-bahn	Rapid transit railway
Scheisse	Shit
See	Lake
Sekt	German sparkling wine
Śnieżka	Snowball (a popular name for a female dog or bitch in Poland)
Stahl	Steel
Stasi	Colloquial term for the Ministry for State Security (see above)
Szkopy	A pejorative Polish slang term for German soldiers (literally 'castrated rams')
Tatort	West German TV crime drama (literally 'Crime Scene')
Tierpark	East Berlin Zoo
Trümmerfrauen	The 'rubble women' who helped clear up and reconstruct Germany and Austria at the end of the Second World War
U-bahn	Underground railway

Unterleutnant	Sub-lieutenant
Vati	Dad, or Daddy
Volkspolizei	See People's Police above
Vopo	Short form of *Volkspolizei*, usually referring to uniformed police officers, as opposed to detectives
Wohnkomplex	Housing estate
Wyspa Teatralna	Theatre Island (in Polish)

AUTHOR'S NOTE

Some of the science in this novel is based on truth, but most of it is a fictional extrapolation from that truth.

Dr Uwe Gaissler is a totally fictional creation and is not meant to represent anyone, living or dead.

However, real-life research was undertaken at Humboldt University endocrinology department which was seen as part of a campaign to prevent homosexuality. This advocated the manipulation of the hormone levels of pregnant women to prevent them giving birth to homosexual offspring. A central part of that research was based on experiments on rats, and argued that sexual drive could be changed by hormonal implantations through the administration of androgens. The theory was defended because of high suicide rates amongst the homosexual population. Based on rat experiments, brain surgery was also proposed as a method of altering the sexuality of adult humans – although as far as I know, never actually carried out.

My story, though, is entirely fictional. Again, as far as I know, there were no experiments on humans and no financial support from any American pharmaceutical companies in relation to changing people's sexuality. However, a report commissioned by the Charité Hospital released in 2016 confirmed that more than 900 other medical experiments were carried out by western pharmaceutical companies on East Germans between 1961 and 1990, including 320 clinical trials in the 1980s. The Stasi kept a close eye on the studies, and an office under Stasi control negotiated the contracts in order to raise hard currency for the communist state.

East Germany legalised homosexuality in 1968, apparently to show how progressive and egalitarian socialism could be. This was five years before homosexuality was fully decriminalised in West Germany. Nevertheless, East German homosexuals interviewed in a 2013 film denied that the state was indeed progressive in this way. 'It was ultra-conservative,' they said, and there were numerous examples of discrimination against, and active targeting of, gays.

The use of heterosexual 'Romeos' by the Stasi (more often than not, female secretaries) to glean information from West German politicians and businessmen is well-documented. But what is less well known is that the Stasi also used gay Romeos. The same 2013 documentary mentioned above, *Out in East Berlin* (by Jochen Hicks and Andreas Strohfeldt), includes an interview with Romeo victim Eduard Stapel. It wasn't until Eduard accessed his Stasi file after the fall of the Wall that he discovered the full extent of the Stasi's surveillance of homosexuals. However, the target of my Romeos, Georg Metzger, is a wholly fictional creation.

When the archives were opened after reunification in 1990, another major discovery was the Stasi's links to the Red Army Faction (RAF). The Stasi trained RAF members responsible for the 1981 bombing of the US air base at Ramstein. And the *Guardian* reported in 2011 that one of the RAF's founders had been a paid Stasi informer.

I should point out that the winter of 1976/77 was not – as far as I know – especially harsh, so Müller and Tilsner's drive over the iced-up river is a bit of authorial licence. Although the Neisse at Gubin does freeze over completely in some years (and locals say it would be strong enough to hold a car in the coldest years – which included some during the DDR era), I don't know if it did when the novel is set. Nevertheless, weather records show that in nearby Cottbus the minimum temperature recorded that winter was minus 17.5 ° Celsius, which was colder than the normal minimum, and the weather station at Ueckermünde – near the Polish border – recorded twenty-two days when the temperature never rose above zero.

Another bit of cheating by me for plot convenience concerns the footbridge connecting Guben and Gubin – it's actually a modern construction and there wasn't one in DDR times, although there was a road bridge. The Nazi tunnel under the Neisse linking Guben to Theatre Island is also fictional.

The Stasi's Special Commissions – units that took over investigations from the People's Police to keep them under wraps – were very real, and the subject of another German TV documentary in early 2017. And a special serious crimes squad with a national remit was indeed set up by the People's Police, although not until the early 1980s.

Eisenhüttenstadt's football team, BSG Stahl, did once play in the East German *Oberliga*, and was forcibly relegated in an illegal payments scandal. However, it actually happened a few years earlier than the fictional events in this novel.

The massive overburden slag-removing machine known colloquially as the 'reclining Eiffel Tower' does and did exist at Lichterfeld, although it's now a museum piece (and well worth a visit). You can also still visit a working lignite mine in the Lausitz at Welzow Süd, which I'd thoroughly recommend. It's like being on the set of a science fiction film.

Another visit that's worth making is to the pretty little town of Bautzen, home to the hated Stasi prison of the same name, which is now preserved as a memorial. There was a women's section, but I don't think it included Cell 13. When you visit, pay attention to your fellow visitors and be respectful towards them. When I was looking round, I spotted a man lying down on one of the prison bunks, and began talking to him in my halting German. It transpired he was a former prisoner, jailed for some fairly trivial anti-state activity, making his first visit since he was incarcerated there in the 1970s.

ACKNOWLEDGEMENTS

Many thanks to the various people who have helped to make my Karin Müller series a success so far – especially readers, reviewers, bloggers and library and bookshop staff.

Former East German and ex-BBC World Service colleague Oliver Berlau very kindly once again checked my initial manuscript for errors, particularly things about the DDR. As always, any remaining mistakes are wholly my fault.

Stephanie Smith also kindly read an early draft and provided useful insights, as did fellow crime writers Steph Broadribb (aka Stephanie Marland) and Rod Reynolds.

Some of this book and its plot were run past the writers' group set up by past students of my year (2012–14) on the City University London MA in Creative Writing (Crime Thriller option) – including Steph and Rod. It's been great this year to see another in our number – Laura Shepherd-Robinson – agree a publishing deal. What a fantastic historical crime novel *Blood and Sugar* is. Watch out for it in 2019!

Many thanks to the other members of the group: Rob Hogg, James Holt and Seun Olatoye. I'm sure they'll all have books on the shelves before too long.

For embarrassing themselves in helping to promote my last book around launch day, I'm very grateful to John Cornford (giving out promotional postcards at various motorway service stations), Pat Chappell (doing the same at Richmond station) and Jat Dhillon (bombarding the BBC newsroom with flyers).

Huge thanks are also due to my departing editor Joel Richardson, who's gone to pastures new at Michael Joseph – and to the editor who took over from him, Sophie Orme, ably assisted by Rebecca Farrell. All three played important parts in the development of this novel.

And many thanks indeed to my fabulous literary agent Adam Gauntlett of Peters Fraser and Dunlop, who first spotted the potential in *Stasi Child* and managed to secure a new deal for the series this year – meaning there are now a total of five novels under contract. So at least two more after this!

Also, well done to the foreign rights team at PFD (Alexandra Cliff, Marilia Savvides, Rebecca Wearmouth, Laura Otal and Silvia Molteni) who've so far sold the Karin Müller series to eleven territories around the world, with hopefully more to come.

Read on for an exclusive letter from
David Young and a chance to join
his Readers' Club . . .

A message from David . . .

If you enjoyed A DARKER STATE – why not join the DAVID YOUNG READERS' CLUB by visiting **www.bit.ly/ DavidYoungClub**, or you can order the first and second books in the Karin Müller series now.

By joining my Readers' Club, you'll get access to exclusive content – including an unpublished chapter from my debut, and the first in the series, STASI CHILD.

Hello,

First of all, I'd like to thank you for deciding to read A DARKER STATE, and I very much hope you enjoyed it. Although it's part of a series, I've tried to make sure each novel has a distinct story within it, so that new readers will not feel they've missed out by not having read my previous two novels, STASI CHILD and STASI WOLF. There's no need to go back and read them – but I really hope you do. Both were longlisted for the Theakston Old Peculier Crime Novel of the Year award, and STASI CHILD won the CWA Endeavour Historical Dagger.

People often ask me why I decided to set my series in East Germany. The idea came from a tour I arranged for my indie-pop group at the end of the noughties. I'd started the 'band' – really it was just a singer-songwriter project (and I can't sing, although some of the songs are OK!) – as an escape for an increasingly unfulfilling day job as a news editor in the BBC's international TV newsroom. Someone I met at a party, who was in a Ska band, mentioned that German venues loved booking UK bands, no matter how good they were (or weren't). So – in my fiftieth year – I had one of my many mid-life crises and decided to book a little tour for myself. It was one of the best experiences of my life – a dream come true.

Only one of the regular members of the 'band' was available, but we managed to cobble together a group via adverts on Gumtree. We had just one day-long rehearsal before we set off – horribly under-prepared – for six dates, five of them in Germany. Things went from bad to worse, when at the first venue – in the Netherlands – the other musicians decided sampling the delights of a Dutch coffee shop was more interesting than sound-checking or helping me set up the equipment. The gig was awful – we played to about two people. But the next night, in Berlin – what was once the Mitte area of East Berlin – was much better. We supported an up-and-coming band who'd had loads of Radio 1 airplay. There was a good turnout, and we thoroughly enjoyed it. I adopted the once trendy but now defunct Bang Bang Club as the fictional headquarters of Karin Müller's murder squad in *Stasi Child*, under the arches of what was then Marx-Engels-Platz S-bahn station (now Hackescher Markt).

In between gigs, I read Anna Funder's excellent non-fiction account of the victims of the Stasi, and that – together with my feeling that the ghost of the GDR still, in some way, lived on in the east – was what inspired the idea for the Karin Müller series when, a few years later, I began a creative writing MA at City University London.

I wanted a feisty female lead, and that wasn't so very far off the truth as women had a much greater role in the workplace in 1970s East Germany than they did in the West. But I didn't want a clichéd East equals bad, West equals good approach. So Karin – to some extent – still believes in the socialist system, even though during the course of the series those beliefs get challenged at virtually every turn.

A DARKER STATE – like the previous two novels – was inspired by real-life events, although it's a fictional story. Fans of *The Same Sky* on Netflix will be well aware of the Stasi's use of heterosexual Romeo agents to gain information from female secretaries in West Germany. But there were also reports of homosexual Romeos, and I thought that was an interesting counterpoint to real-life research that was carried out at Humboldt University into the possibility altering sexuality. So, although my stories are fictional, I do try to be honest and ensure that my East German world has at least some flavour of authenticity.

Book 4 – working title, *The Burning East* – will follow the real-life story of a World War Two massacre even more closely, although my extrapolation of events into East German times is fictional. In it, Karin's faith in the system she works for is challenged to breaking point, as she discovers dark truths about those working within the Stasi and the People's Police. It is – I think – an exciting novel, but it's also perhaps my darkest yet. Watch out for it in 2019!

I hope there will be many more Karin Müller adventures to come. If there are, it will be thanks to you, my readers, and I want you to know that I'm incredibly grateful that you're allowing me to fulfil another of my lifelong dreams. Remember, you can join the DAVID YOUNG READERS' CLUB by visiting **www.bit.ly/DavidYoungClub** and you can order STASI CHILD and STASI WOLF, the first two books in the Karin Müller series, now!

All the best,

David Young

Read the very first gripping cold war thriller featuring
Karin Müller . . .

STASI CHILD

Winner of the CWA Endeavour Historical Dagger Award
Longlisted for Theakston Old Peculiar Crime Novel
of the Year Award
The Times **Crime Book of the Month**
Telegraph **Pick of the Week**

East Berlin, 1975

A teenage girl's body at the foot of the wall. The Stasi say she
was shot while escaping – but *from* the West.

Oberleutnant Karin Müller in the People's Police suspects
otherwise.

But in East Germany, there is nothing more dangerous than
asking questions.

Especially when the answers lead very close to home . . .

AVAILABLE IN PAPERBACK AND EBOOK NOW

1

February 1975. Day One.
Prenzlauer Berg, East Berlin.

The harsh jangle of a telephone jolted *Oberleutnant* Karin
Müller awake. She reached to her side of the bed to answer
it, but grasped empty space. Pain hammered in her head. The
ringing continued and she lifted her head off the pillow. The
room spun, she swallowed bile and the shape under the blankets next to her reached for the handset on the opposite side
of the bed.

'Tilsner!' The voice of her deputy, *Unterleutnant* Werner
Tilsner, barked into the handset and rang in her ears.

Scheisse! What's he doing here? She began to take in her
surroundings as Tilsner continued to talk into the phone, his
words not really registering. The objects in the apartment were
wrong. The double bed she was lying in was different. The bed
linen certainly didn't belong to her and her husband, Gottfried.
Everything was more ... luxurious, expensive. On the dresser,
she saw photographs of Tilsner ... his wife Koletta ... their two
kids – a teenage boy and a younger girl – at some campsite,

smiling for the camera on their happy-family summer holidays. Oh my God! Where was his wife? She could be coming back at any moment. Then she started to remember: Tilsner had said Koletta had taken the children to their grandmother's for the weekend. The same Tilsner who was constructing some tall tale at this very moment to whoever was on the other end of the phone.

'I don't know where she is. I haven't seen her since yesterday evening at the office.' His lie was delivered with a calmness that Müller certainly didn't share. 'I will try to get hold of her and, once I do, we will be at the scene as soon as possible, Comrade *Oberst*. St Elisabeth cemetery in Ackerstrasse? Yes, I understand.'

Müller clutched her pounding forehead, and tried to avoid Tilsner's eyes as he replaced the handset and started to get out of bed, heading for the bathroom. She wriggled about under the covers. It had been cold last night. Freezing cold. She'd kept all her clothes on, and her underwear now chafed at her skin under the tightness of her skirt. Before that, Blue Strangler vodka. Too much of it. Her and Tilsner matching each other shot for shot in a bar in Dircksenstrasse; a stupid game that seemed to have ended up with them in his marital bed. She could still taste the remains of the alcohol in her mouth now. She wasn't entirely sure what had happened after the bar, but just the fact that she'd spent the night at Tilsner's was something she knew she could never let Gottfried discover.

Tilsner was back now, proffering a glass of water with some sort of pill fizzing inside.

'Drink this.' Müller drew her head back slightly, grimacing at the concoction and its snake-like hiss. 'It's only aspirin. I'll make some coffee while you tidy yourself up.' The smirk on his unshaven, square-jawed face spoke of insolence, disrespect – but it was her own fault for letting herself get into this situation. She was the only female head of a murder squad in the whole country. She couldn't have people calling her a whore.

'Hadn't we better get straight there?' she shouted through to the kitchen. 'It sounded urgent.' The words reverberated in her head, each one a hammer blow.

'It is,' Tilsner shouted back. 'The body of a girl. In a cemetery. Near the Wall.'

Müller downed the aspirin and water in one long swallow, forcing herself not to retch it back.

'We'd better get going immediately, then,' she shouted, her voice echoing through the old apartment's high-ceilinged rooms.

'We've time for coffee,' Tilsner replied from the kitchen, clanging cups and pans about as though it was an unfamiliar environment. It probably was, except on International Women's Day. 'After all, I've told *Oberst* Reiniger I don't know where you are. And the Stasi people are already there.'

'The Stasi?' questioned Müller. She'd moved in a slow trudge to the bathroom, and now studied her reflection with horror. Yesterday's mascara smudged around bloodshot blue eyes. Rubbing her fingers across her cheeks, she tried to stretch away the puffiness, and then fiddled with her blonde, shoulder-length hair. The only female head of a murder squad in the whole Republic, and not yet in her thirtieth year. She didn't look so baby-faced today. She breathed in deeply, hoping the crisp morning air of the old apartment would quell her nausea.

Müller knew she had to clear her head. Take control of the situation. 'If the body's next to the anti-fascist barrier, isn't that the responsibility of the border guards?' Despite the reverberations through her skull, she was still bellowing out the words so Tilsner could hear down the corridor. 'Why are the Stasi involved? And why are we –' Her voice tailed off as she looked up in the mirror and saw his reflection. Tilsner was standing directly behind her, two mugs of steaming coffee in his hands. He shrugged and raised his eyebrows.

'Is this a quiz? All I know is that Reiniger wants us to report to the senior Stasi officer at the scene.'

She watched him studying her as she pulled Koletta's hairbrush through her tangled locks.

'You'd better let me clean that brush after you've used it,' he said. Müller met his eyes: blue like hers, although his seemed remarkably bright for someone who'd downed so much vodka the night before. He was smirking again. 'My wife's a brunette.'

'Piss off, Werner,' Müller spat at his reflection, as she started to remove the old mascara with one of Koletta's make-up pads. 'Nothing happened.'

'You're sure of that, are you? That's not quite how I recollect it.'

'Nothing happened. You know that and I know that. Let's keep it that way.'

His grin was almost a leer, and she forced herself to remember through the hangover muddle. Müller reddened, but tried to convince herself she was right. After all, she'd kept her clothes on, and her skirt was tight enough to deny unwanted access. She turned, snatched the coffee from his hand and took two long gulps as the steam rising from the beverage misted up the freezing bathroom mirror. Tilsner reached around her, grabbed the mascara-caked pad and hid it away in his pocket. Then he picked up the brush and started removing blonde hairs with a comb. Müller rolled her eyes. The bastard was clearly practised at this.

They avoided looking at each other as they descended the stairs, past the peeling paint of the lobby, and walked out of the apartment block into the winter morning. Müller spotted their unmarked Wartburg on the opposite side of the street. It brought back memories of the previous night, and his insistence that they return to his place for a sobering-up coffee – Tilsner seemingly unconcerned about his drink-driving. She rubbed her chin, remembering in a sudden flash his stubble grazing against it like sandpaper as their lips had locked. What exactly *had* happened after that?

They got into the car, with Tilsner in the driver's seat. He turned the ignition key, his expensive-looking watch shining in the weak daylight. She frowned, thinking back to the luxurious fittings in the apartment, and looked at Tilsner curiously. How had he afforded those on a junior lieutenant's salary?

The Wartburg spluttered into life. Müller's memory was slowly coming back to her. It had only been a kiss, hadn't it? She risked a quick look to her left as Tilsner crunched the car into gear, but he stared straight ahead, grim-faced. She'd need to think up a very good excuse to tell Gottfried. He was used to her working late, but an all-nighter without warning?

The car's wheels spun and skidded on the week-old snow that no one had bothered to clear. Overhead, leaden grey skies were the harbinger of more bad weather. Müller reached out of the car window and attached the flashing blue light to the Wartburg's roof, turning on the accompanying strangled-cat siren, as they headed the few kilometres between Prenzlauer Berg and the cemetery in Mitte.

AVAILABLE NOW IN PAPERBACK AND EBOOK

Want to read
NEW BOOKS
before anyone else?

Like getting
FREE BOOKS?

Enjoy sharing your
OPINIONS?

Discover

READERS FIRST

Read. Love. Share.

Get your first free book just by signing up at
readersfirst.co.uk